Throttle's Seduction

AN INSURGENTS MC ROMANCE

Chiah Wilder

I love hearing from my readers. You can email me at chiahwilder@gmail.com.

Make sure you sign up for my newsletter so you can keep up with my new releases, special sales, free short stories, and other treats only available to newsletter readers. When you sign up, you will receive a FREE hot and steamy short story. Sign up at: http://eepurl.com/bACCL1.

Visit me on facebook at www.facebook.com/Chiah-Wilder-1625397261063989

Description

Throttle, Road Captain of the Insurgents Motorcycle Club, likes his women willing, stacked, and no strings attached. His life and needs are simple: riding his Harley, bedding as many women as can fit in his bed, and scorching his throat with whiskey.

The tall, rugged outlaw is a magnet for women who love life on the wild and dangerous side. They know not to expect anything from the tattooed biker but sheer pleasure.

Life couldn't be better.

Until he meets Kimber. The black-haired mechanic at Hawk's bike shop. What the f@#k? In his world, the only thing a woman should do on a Harley is spread her pretty legs wide.

She is sassy-mouthed, aggravating, and not his type at all. And he doesn't need any woman—let alone a chick in mechanic coveralls—messing with his head.

It's a shame all he can think about is doing nasty things to her on his motorcycle.

Kimber Descourts has had to fight to be accepted in a man's world and she is not a quitter. Always attracted to the bad boy biker, she has had her share of unfaithful, jerk boyfriends. Swearing off all bikers since her last boyfriend made her his punching bag, she's content with working on Harleys, taking a few business classes, and being blissfully alone.

Then she meets Throttle.

He's a cocky, chauvinistic bastard. Oh yeah… he's also incredibly handsome, built, and sexy as all hell. He's *exactly* her type. She should run far away from him, but her body wants him in the worst way.

They say opposites attract, but when a hardened biker and a tough free-spirit ignite, their world combusts. Will their differences bring them together or pull them apart?

In the midst of Throttle and Kimber's tug of war, a Peeping Tom has been creeping around Pinewood Springs watching ladies behind the shadows of the night. He spots Kimber Descourts and is drawn to her. And he's beginning to grow bored of just watching….

Can Kimber put her pride aside and ask for Throttle's help? Is Throttle ready to let the feisty mechanic melt his icy heart?

The Insurgents MC series are standalone romance novels. This is Throttle and Kimber's love story. This book contains violence, sexual assault (not graphic), strong language, and steamy/graphic sexual scenes. It describes the life and actions of an outlaw motorcy-cle club. If any of these issues offend you or are triggers, please do not read the book. HEA. No cliffhangers! The book is intended for readers over the age of 18.

Previous Titles in the Series:

Hawk's Property: Insurgents Motorcycle Club Book 1
Jax's Dilemma: Insurgents Motorcycle Club Book 2
Chas's Fervor: Insurgents Motorcycle Club Book 3
Axe's Fall: Insurgents Motorcycle Club Book 4
Banger's Ride: Insurgents Motorcycle Club Book 5
Jerry's Passion: Insurgents Motorcycle Club Book 6

PROLOGUE

ANNIE LOFTIS AND her parents arrived home from spending an evening in Clermont Park listening to the free concert and watching the sky light up from the fireworks display. It was a perfect summer night: clear sky with thousands of twinkling stars; a light, cool breeze carrying a subtle whiff of jasmine; and crickets chirping in the trees and shrubbery.

When they entered their home, eighteen-year-old Annie rushed to her room to check out her e-mails and chat with her friends on Facebook. She'd graduated from high school a month before, and she'd decided to work for a year before heading out to college. Happy that her two best friends decided the same thing, she looked forward to a year of hanging out, no studying, and earning more money than she had at her after-school jobs while she'd been in high school.

Her parents, Julia and Kurt, had long gone to bed by the time Annie turned off her computer. Slipping off her cotton top, she unfastened her bra. The man, hidden by the shadows and bushes, sucked his breath in sharply. Although her curtains were pulled, her silhouette danced about like a shadow puppet on a rice paper screen. Her young, pert breasts were outlined perfectly, and the man's pants grew tighter as he watched her slip on her nightgown, then switch off the light.

He stood there for a long time, watching and waiting. Waiting until the cul-de-sac fell asleep, waiting for the pounding in his ears to stop, waiting for his chance to make his move. And when the moon lit a path to Annie's opened window, he crept like a lion on the prowl, his sneakers silent on the lush grass. The gleam of the blade from his pocketknife flashed briefly before he cut the window screen.

He'd been watching her for over a week, getting to know the habits of the household. He'd even sneaked inside the home a few days before when the family had gone to a cousin's house to celebrate a birthday. The man had wanted to familiarize himself with the layout of Annie's room. On that night, he'd taken one of her pretty lacey bikini panties— the white ones with the baby pink bows all around. They were so sexy, he couldn't help himself.

The intruder knew Annie had a large hand-painted trunk to the left of the window, so he had to be careful to avoid it lest he wake her up. With the screen cut, he pushed himself up. He was an athletic fellow, worked out in the gym a lot and watched what he ate. In a couple of movements, he was standing in Annie's room, hearing her soft breaths as she slept. He inched closer to her double bed, her coconut scent wafting up to his nostrils. A soft smile spread over his lips. Annie was so adorable and young; she had all the innocence and idealism of youth. He'd watch her come and go with her giggling girlfriends, and it almost made him wish he were eighteen again so he could date her.

She stirred in her sleep, a small whimper escaping through her slightly parted lips. He froze. He didn't want her to wake up, not yet; he wasn't ready for that. Like a statue he stood, not daring to move a muscle until the deep sounds of her breath assured him she was sleeping heavily. Then he moved next to her bed, looking down at her while he reached in the pocket of his hoodie and took out a roll of duct tape. The rip of the tape bounced off the walls in the quiet room, and Annie stirred again, that time her eyes fluttering open. Bleary sleepiness was soon replaced with bulging eyes fraught with terror, but before she could cry out, he'd secured the tape firmly across her mouth. She thrashed in her bed, her arms flailing, her legs kicking, but she was no match for him. In a matter of seconds, he'd subdued her, her hands taped together as well as her feet. Small whimpers attempted to break through, but the tape caught them and kept them on the surface of her lips. Wetness dampened her cheeks, and in a show of empathy, he brushed the tendrils of hair clinging to the side of her face and wiped away her tears.

"I'm not going to hurt you," he whispered as his eyes slowly ran down the length of her, lingering at her rounded hips before coming back to her frightened brown eyes. "You're beautiful," he murmured.

Annie tried to scoot away from him when he caressed her body with his hand. It felt cool to the touch as he slid his fingers over her cotton nightgown, the one with little unicorns and half rainbows. When he touched her bare thigh, she whimpered again and shook her head furiously.

"Shh, little one. You don't have to be afraid. I'm not going to hurt you. I just want to see your panties." He pushed up her nightgown and gasped loudly when his gaze fell on her white bikini undies with tiny purple polka dots. "How perfectly beautiful." Without hesitation, he reached out and touched them, loving the way the fabric felt on his fingertips. Pushing her nightgown up higher, he stopped just under her breasts. "Do you have a matching bra?"

She nodded, her gaze wide. The intruder glanced at her closed door. The urge to see her in her bra and panties was too great. He took out his pocketknife and a sting of sadness pricked his skin when he saw the fear in her eyes. "Look, I'm not going to hurt you. I want you to put your bra on. I won't touch you. I just want to see you. Okay?"

She nodded, a tear rolling down the side of her face toward her ear.

"If you try to scream or anything, I'll hurt your parents. If you do as I say, you and your parents will be all right. Do you understand?"

Again she nodded. He slowly helped her sit up, then carried her over to her dresser. Cutting the tape from her hands, he watched as she rummaged through the first drawer. He spotted a yellow checked panty and grabbed it, stuffing it in the pocket of his hoodie. He'd use it when he returned to his place, when he remembered how pretty Annie was with her perky breasts, soft hips, and in her purple polka-dotted undies.

Annie pulled the matching bra out. He told her to put it on, and she turned her back to do so. The man escorted her back to the bed, secured her hands again, that time above her head, and posed her while he took pictures of her in her underwear. After snapping about sixty pictures in so many provocative poses, he stopped and leaned against the bed. The tightness in his pants was too much. He was harder than he'd been in a long time. Stepping up his voyeurisms and visits into pretty women's homes when they were out had proven to be very effective.

Unzipping his pants he exposed himself to Annie, who promptly squeezed her eyes shut. The man didn't care. He didn't need an audience; he was perfectly content to make himself come into her yellow gingham panties. After several grunts, he spilled his sperm into her undies, making sure to keep it contained. With his head thrown back and eyes closed, his body slowly returned to normal. When he opened his brown eyes, his gaze fixed on hers. He smiled widely, then pushed his limp dick into his pants and zipped them up.

Taking out his pocketknife, he approached Annie, who tried to wiggle away from him. Leaning down, he kissed her gently on the forehead. "Thank you. I appreciate what you did for me tonight." He cut off the tape from her hands. "Wait until I go. Then you can get up and do what you have to do."

In two long strides, he was at the window, slipping out. By the time he reached his car around the corner of the cul-de-sac, he heard Annie screaming. He hummed under his breath, switched on the ignition, and disappeared into the darkness of the night.

CHAPTER ONE

THE STACKED REDHEAD slipped her lips around Throttle's stiff dick, and a jolt of pleasure zapped him. "Fuck," he murmured as he buried his fingers in her thick curly hair.

"You like that, baby? Mmm… I love the way you taste."

He chuckled and decided it was going to be a fun afternoon, what with this sexy redhead and her blonde girlfriend who was rubbing her big tits in his face, begging him to suck her hard nipples. Of course he'd have to oblige; after all, the two women had agreed to come to the clubhouse to have a bit of fun with him. He'd met them at the Rusty Nail, a biker bar where a good game of pool with a side of fucking was the norm. All the back rooms were taken, so he'd asked the two chicks to come to the club. They couldn't drive fast enough. They were definitely biker groupies—women who loved biker cock and wanted a taste of the dark and dangerous life for a night or two.

Throttle was fine with that. New pussy was always fun, and if they proved to be as adventurous as he thought they would be, he may even let them spend the night with him. He normally didn't do overnights, not even with the club whores or hoodrats, but sometimes he'd make an exception and let a woman or two share his bed.

Damn, the redhead gave good head. He placed his hands on each side of her face and thrust his hips forward, plunging harder and deeper into her throat while he sucked her friend's pink nipples. The blondie's rack was big and high, just like he loved it. She pulled away and gave him a deep kiss, her tongue plunging into his mouth, mimicking a dick in a pussy. He pushed her away. He didn't go in for that kind of shit, didn't like a woman who was too aggressive in taking control.

"What's the matter, honey? I'm just showing you what I want your dick to do to my pussy."

"I'll get there. Right now, I'm enjoying the way your friend's sucking my cock. Show me how you can eat her out, sweetheart. I'd fuckin' love to see that." Throttle pushed her away and she scooted down and went by the redhead, who parted her knees. The blonde slid between her friend's knees, flat on her back, then spread the redhead's wet lips apart and started lapping away. Seeing her pink tongue play with the redhead's slick sex made him blow hard, his cum shooting down the woman's throat. It was fucking awesome. He leaned back and watched the blonde play with her friend's clit as the redhead licked off all the cum from his shaft. Life was just too good sometimes.

The women's moans filled the room as they pleasured each other, and he grew hard again as he saw them sucking and finger-fucking each other. Throttle ripped open a condom package, slipped it over his throbbing dick, crawled over to the blonde and pulled her off her friend, pushing her on her back as she squealed in delight. Placing her ankles on his shoulders, he rammed his length into her wet slit and pumped it in and out while the redhead sucked on her friend's hardened nipples. Throttle pushed his finger into the redhead's pussy and finger-fucked her as he slammed in and out of her friend.

"That feels so good, Throttle," the blonde moaned as he rode her rough.

He wished he could remember their names, but all he'd been really interested in was the blonde's rack and the redhead's ass when they had made conversation at Rusty's. He'd known from the moment their eyes had landed on his that they'd wanted to fuck him, and he was more than willing to give the women a treat.

Women flocked to Throttle, and regardless that he was known as a cold-hearted bastard, they still wanted to spend time with him even if it was for only a quick screw. At six feet, with long dark brown hair, eyes as black as coal, a perpetual five o'clock shadow, and a sculpted physique, women usually drooled over him. The fact that he was a player and could be a cocky jerk didn't deter them. With a defined jaw, straight nose, a lopsided grin that melted a woman's panties, and colorful tats curling around ripped arms and shoulders, Throttle had no shortage of women. In all his thirty-five years, he'd never met a woman he couldn't bed. And it suited him perfectly, because he wasn't about to chase any chick. Hell, *they* chased *him*. If a woman started that princess bullshit, well, he was on to the next one without even a backward glance. That was the lifestyle he loved—easy pussy, and the more the merrier.

Just when he spread the redhead's ass cheeks, positioning his hardness to enter her puckered hole, someone banged loudly on his door. He let out a frustrated sigh. "I'm busy here. Come back." He pushed onward.

"Open up. Banger's got something he needs you to do," Rock's baritone voice cut through the door.

"Can't it wait for fifteen minutes or so? I got something I'm doing here."

"Make him go away," the blonde pouted as she kneeled behind him and played with his balls.

"I'm fuckin' tryin', sweetheart."

"So, you want me to tell Banger to wait?"

That one question proved to be the perfect cock-blocker. "Shit." He pushed back with his feet and stood, scooping up his jeans from the floor. "Sorry, ladies. My president is calling."

The two women, flushed with arousal, looked confused. "You're going? *Now?*" the redhead asked as she sat up and leaned against the headboard.

Sighing, a deep sense of regret coursing through him, he nodded. "Yep, and you both gotta get your asses outta here. Like now."

"Don't you want us to wait until you get back?" the blonde asked as she squeezed her tits.

He groaned. "I don't know what I have to do. I don't like people in my room when I'm not here."

"We're not just *any* people. Right? Can't you bend your rules?"

"Baby, you two are some hot chicks, but there's plenty of hot pussy around here. Now get going. Dress fast. I gotta go."

The women cursed under their breaths but put on their clothes while throwing Throttle dirty looks. "You said we could party with the brothers tonight."

"That's the way it goes. Go back to Rusty's. You won't have any problems finding another biker who's horny. Leave your numbers. I'll call you when we have a big party. Sound good?" He walked over and squeezed the blonde's tits and the redhead's ass. The women laughed, then wrote out their numbers and walked out with him.

Rock smiled broadly at Throttle, his hungry gaze checking out the two women. "Sorry to have disturbed you, but you know how it is when the president wants something."

"No worries. Hey, these two chicks still wanna party. You doing anything?"

Rock's black eyes lit up as he shook his head. Throttle leaned in. "The redhead has lips for sucking and an ass made for fucking, and the blonde's pussy is tight and her tits are damn big." He winked.

"What're you two guys whispering about?" the redhead asked, batting her eyelashes.

"My brother here, Rock, is the Sergeant-At-Arms of the club, and he was telling me how hot he thinks you two are."

"Are you telling us the truth? You're really the muscle of the club?"

"Yep."

Throttle shook his head, marveling at the way the biker groupies acted like the officers of an outlaw MC were like gods or something. "He *loves* pleasing women. You think you can take care of my brother while I'm away? If you're still here when I get back, we can have a foursome. Would you like that?"

The women's eyes shined as Throttle stood before Banger's door, ready to knock. Tucked snuggly under each of Rock's arms, they waved to him, telling him to hurry back as they disappeared in the stairway. Laughing, he knocked on the door.

"Come in," Banger's voice boomed.

Throttle walked in and stood in front of his president, who was seated behind his desk. "Rock said you wanted to see me?"

"Yeah. I need you to go over to Hawk's shop and see if he's done with my Harley. He's had the bike for over a week, and I'm getting fuckin' antsy to ride it."

Banger pulled me away from a luscious ass to check on his goddamned Harley? Is he fuckin' serious? "You can't get a hold of Hawk?"

Banger narrowed his eyes. "If I could, I wouldn't tell you to go over to his shop, would I? He's not at the shop, and he's not answering his phone. Probably in some damn country club tasting the food for his upcoming wedding. Fuck, he's turning into a real pansy-ass." Banger and Throttle chuckled. "Anyway, I want to go on the charity poker run next week, so I need my damn bike back. I've got a ton of shit to do here." Banger waved his hands over the papers scattered on top of his desk.

"Sure, I'll go. You want me to call when I'm there?"

"No. When you get back you can let me know what's goin' on with my Harley."

"That it?"

"Yeah."

"Cool. Later." Throttle ambled out of the office, stopping to have a quick beer before he jumped on his bike. Why he couldn't finish fucking that sexy piece of ass *before* he went on this errand was beyond him. Remembering that the two women would still be at the clubhouse when he returned, he revved his engine and blasted out of the parking lot, eager to finish quickly so he could have some fun with Rock and the sexy girls.

CHAPTER TWO

WHEN THROTTLE ENTERED Hawk's shop, a blast of cold air slapped him in the face and he sighed in relief. It was damn hot outside, and he looked forward to the cool nip in the air that autumn always brought to the high mountains.

A lanky teenager sat behind the cashier's counter, his head bent down as his fingers flew over the keyboard on his phone. Throttle recognized him as Banger's nephew; he'd seen the kid at a couple barbecues he'd gone to at Banger's sister's house.

"Hey, do you know anything about Banger's Harley?" Throttle looked through the closed door's glass window at the service garage.

The teenager raised his head and smiled. "Hey. Your name's Throttle, right?"

He nodded and drummed his fingers on the counter. He wanted to finish fast so he could get back to the horny chicks he'd left at the clubhouse. "So, do you know what's going on with your uncle's bike?"

"Not really. Hawk just asked me to watch the place and check customers out while he was gone. He said he'd be back in a couple hours."

"I got somewhere I need to be. I'll ask one of the mechanics."

"That's a good idea."

Throttle clenched his jaw in exasperation and headed to the bays. When he stepped into the repair area, oil and gas fumes curled around him. He loved the smell; it always made him think of the ride and the wind wrapping around him. Damn, being on his bike, going a hundred, was better than sex most of the time. It was total freedom, and when he was soaring, it was like an out-of-body experience. He'd never found anything in the world that compared to it.

"Hey, Throttle, what brings you here? You got problems with your 1250?" asked Dwayne. He was the manager of the shop, and he'd been working for Hawk for nearly ten years.

"Nah, my baby's good. Banger sent me here to see if his bike's almost ready. He's going crazy without it. Besides, he's got a poker run coming up soon."

Dwayne wiped his brow with a dingy cloth and jerked his head to the right. "I think it's almost done. Go ask the mechanic."

Throttle walked over to the third stall and saw a short, slight mechanic bent over Banger's Harley, turning a wrench. The mechanic's back was to him, and Throttle noticed a full sleeve of tats and slightly rounded hips. Hard rock blasted from the radio on the shelf next to the stall. Surprised someone so slight could handle a powerful bike like Banger's, he took a few steps forward and said in a loud voice, "You almost done with this bike?" as he turned the radio down.

The mechanic spun around, and Throttle's eyes widened when he realized that the dude was a chick. "Uh... sorry, I thought you were the mechanic. Get the guy who's fixing this bike to come here. I need to talk to him."

She looked confused. "What? I'm fixin' this bike. Is it yours?"

Fuck, I don't have time for someone playin' a joke on me. I bet Banger and Hawk are in on this. "Look, darlin', I got something I gotta do, so I don't have time to play this out. Be a nice little girl and bring the tech. Now."

Her blue eyes flashed and she placed her hands on her hips, her chin jutted out. "I'm the tech, so fuckin' deal with it. And I'm not 'darling' or 'little girl.' I'm Ms. Descourt. The bike will be ready tomorrow by five o'clock. I'm replacing the alternator. It took a while to get the part in." She smirked. "You can close your mouth now."

"You're the fuckin' mechanic who's been working on the president of the Insurgents MC's bike? I don't think so."

She laughed dryly. "I don't remember asking you what you thought. I'm busy, so move it outta here. Hawk will call Banger and let him know." She turned around and cranked up the radio, the hard rock beats reverberating off the walls.

Throttle narrowed his eyes, anger crawling over his skin. The bitch had a mouth on her, and she was pretending to be a mechanic. There was no fuckin' way Hawk hired a chick to do a man's job. No way the VP would have a chick with a wrench near any Harley. Throttle stormed over to Dwayne and motioned him to follow him back into the shop.

When the heavy metal door closed, Throttle said, "Who the hell is fuckin' around on Banger's bike? Man, aren't you watching what the shit's going on in the bays?"

Dwayne scrubbed his face with his fist. "Whoa, there. What the hell are you talkin' about? I have a damn good mechanic fixing his bike."

"You have a bitch fixin' his Harley. What the fuck?"

Dwayne burst out laughing. "Is that what this is all about? Kimber's a damn good mechanic. You know how picky Hawk is. He wouldn't have hired her if he didn't think she'd do a good job."

"Hawk hired her? There's no way I want her near my bike if it ever needs fixin'. What the hell do chicks know about fixin' bikes?"

"Kimber's better than some of the younger guys we have for the summer."

Before he could answer, the metal door banged open and Kimber walked in, throwing a smile at Dwayne and a grimace at Throttle. She slid between the two men and walked up to the counter. "You got some cold bottled water, Patrick?" She propped her elbows on the counter and rested her chin on her hand.

"Yep." The teenager bent down, then stood up and tossed a large plastic bottle at her.

She straightened up and caught it, then grinned at him, causing his cheeks to redden. "Thanks." She unscrewed the top and took a long, deep drink. Throttle watched the way her shoulder-length black hair spilled out from her baseball cap. The tips of her hair were colored a bright pink. He hadn't noticed how snug her blue coveralls were, especially around her small hips and firm ass. She glanced at him. "What the hell are you lookin' at?"

Hot sparks rose in him. "Not you, that's for fuckin' sure." He turned to Dwayne who had a goofy smile on his face, one Throttle wished he could smack off. "I'm outta here. I'll tell Banger that his bike will be ready tomorrow."

"It will." Kimber wiped her mouth with the back of her hand. Amid the grease on her fingers, a splash of neon purple filtered through. One of her arms was covered in colorful tats of flowers, butterflies, and crosses. It seemed the chicks always went for the frilly shit.

"I wasn't talkin' to you."

"You should've been, since I'm the one working on the bike." She tossed the empty bottle in the trashcan across the room, and, much to Throttle's chagrin, it made it in. Smiling smugly, she brushed past him and went back to work behind the metal door.

By the time Throttle arrived back at the clubhouse, he was fuming. Who the fuck did the little bitch think she was? He ought to teach her a lesson about disrespecting an Insurgent. And what the hell was Hawk smoking? Hiring a chick mechanic. Cara had definitely brainwashed him, and he was thinking with his cock instead of his brain. *Fuck it!* He slammed the club door behind him and went to Banger's office.

"When's my bike gonna be ready?" Banger asked as Throttle slumped into the chair in front of his desk.

"Tomorrow at closing. Did you know a bitch is working on your Harley? Can you fuckin' imagine that? What the hell was Hawk thinking?"

"You mean Kimber? She does damn good work. Bruce over in Silver Ridge recommended her. Seems she was workin' there for a couple years."

"You're cool with this?"

"Yeah. I don't give a shit if it's a baboon fixin' my bike, as long as it's done right."

They've all become fuckin' pussies now that they got old ladies. One more reason not to have an anchor around my cock.

"Does it bother you?" Banger asked, an amused smile playing on his lips.

"Yeah, it sure as shit does. You can let her get her nail-polished fingers all over your bike, but she's not ever gonna touch mine. I'm gonna make sure Hawk is clear 'bout that."

Banger shrugged. "Rock was lookin' for you a few minutes ago."

"Thanks." He pushed himself out of the chair and sauntered out. He was still pissed as hell when he bumped into Rock coming down the stairs.

"Good, you're back. Fuck, why didn't you tell me how hot those two bitches are? We've been having a good time, but the redhead is anxious to have your cock up her ass." He chuckled. "And it's a very sweet one."

"I don't know. I'm not really into it right now."

Rock stared at Throttle. "What's wrong?"

"I'm just pissed as hell. Did you know Hawk hired a chick as a mechanic?"

He shook his head. "When did he do that?"

"Fuck if I know. And she's got a real mouth on her."

"Is she hot in her little greaser outfit?"

Throttle glared. "She's a bitch. I mean, she looked okay, but she doesn't have any tits, at least not the big ones I like. What the hell am I sayin'? Even if she had humungous tits, I'd never be interested. She's a smartass, and she's got pink shit in her hair. No way is she ever touching my bike."

Rock laughed. "I gotta check out this chick who's got you all riled up."

Throttle crossed his arms across his muscular chest. "She hasn't got me riled up. I don't give a fuck."

"Really? You coulda fooled me. Let's go and have some fun with the horny bitches in my room."

What the hell was wrong with him? When he left, he'd been anxious to get back to the two women's pussies, but now he was too pissed to even get it up. It was all *her* fault. *What was her name? Something like timber. Oh yeah. Kimber. Well, fuck her!*

When he and Rock came up to the third floor, Throttle went to his room, shrugging off a surprised Rock. Since Throttle had been elected Road Captain for the club, he had been moved from his room in the basement to one of the officers' rooms on the third floor. He liked being closer to the club whores who had rooms in the attic; it made it easier when he was horny as hell. Since he'd patched in with the Insurgents fifteen years ago, he'd always lived at the club. He never saw any reason for moving away and getting a place of his own.

He slammed his door and peeled off his T-shirt, anxious to take a cool shower to wash off the sweat of the day. After an hour, he sat naked on his bed, a glass of Jack Daniels in one hand and a joint in the other, staring at the TV screen, watching the images of the world's disasters play out on the international news. The sound had been muted—he rarely listened to what the establishment said—and the image of Kimber leaning over the counter with her uniform tight across her ass floated front and center in his mind. Why the hell he was thinking of *her* pissed him off immensely. He'd have to put her in her place. *Tomorrow, I'll go to Hawk's shop and set her straight. Show her not to mess with me.* A faint tingle of anticipation pricked at him, but he crushed it with another large glass of whiskey. He didn't have time for that. She wasn't even his type. Hell, it looked like she had mosquito bites for tits. Besides, she was a chick who was a mechanic. In his world, that concept didn't make any sense.

Fuck her—cute ass, pink hair, smart mouth, and all.

CHAPTER THREE

Kimber Descourt laughed aloud when she heard Throttle's Harley peel out of the parking lot. *What a chauvinistic asshole. I bet I fix a Harley way better than he does. I probably ride better too.* She smiled and went back to fixing Banger's motorcycle. Since she'd decided to earn a living as a mechanic, she'd run into all types of guys, but the worst, by far, were the bikers, especially the old-school jerks like Throttle. She loved yanking on their chains, confident in her abilities as a class-A Harley tech. She had her dad to thank for that.

Kimber paused and took a deep gulp of air; oil, gas, and grease filled her lungs. Her dad had often told her that the smell of exhaust fumes and earth were the best scents in life because they symbolized freedom. A small ache pulled at her heart; she missed her dad. Even though he'd died seven years before, the pain was still raw, and she missed talking to him, riding with him, and working with him, side-by-side at his repair shop in Johnston, Iowa.

At twenty-three years old, she'd felt lost, even though she and Chewy had still been together. They had gone back about five years. They'd met at a motorcycle rally, and he'd tried really hard to impress and catch her. When she finally let him in, they were inseparable until she was hooked and hopelessly in love with the tall, tattooed biker. After that, club parties until four in the morning had been the norm for him, and when she'd threatened to move on, he'd calm down only to start it all up again when things had smoothed over.

She'd suspected that he'd been fucking the club whores at the parties, but she couldn't pin anything on him, and none of his brothers would ever have breathed a word. When she'd found the neon thong in his back jeans' pocket, she'd been livid and had been ready to shove it in his face when she'd received the call that'd changed her life: her father had been in a life-threatening motorcycle accident. Chewy's late-night partying with his brothers, his drug use, the scent of cheap perfume, and the neon thong paled in comparison to what she'd been told over the receiver.

After a month on life support, she'd made the toughest decision of her life—letting her father fly free to join her mother, who'd died when Kimber had been three years old. She'd had to admit that Chewy had stepped up to the plate and had been there for her, holding her close while she'd wept inconsolably, supporting her decision to set her dad free and holding her up at his funeral.

Chewy had told her he wanted them to get serious, so they'd rented a small house together, and he'd given her his patch. She'd been thrilled to wear it, and she'd even begun dreaming of having kids. She'd stopped her studies at the local college and threw herself into running her dad's repair shop, even though she'd have to lock the door to his office several times during the work day to hide her tears of sorrow. It'd seemed so incongruous.

A couple years later, Chewy had begun using again, staying out all night with his brothers, and reeking of cheap perfume. The fights between them had escalated until one cold winter night he'd slammed her head against the wall, causing bits of plaster to fall on the floor. Two black eyes, a couple broken ribs, and a bump the size of the state of Iowa later, she'd lain on the hospital bed realizing that she'd had enough. In all the times they'd fought, he'd never once laid a finger on her. Everything had changed. His bouquets of flowers, his apologies, his pleas for forgiveness, and his statements of undying love meant nothing; they'd all been crushed with that first punch.

By the time Chewy had staggered home from one of his club parties, she'd been on her way to Silver Ridge, Colorado, to work at her dad's old Army buddy's bike shop. She'd sold her dad's business to Buster, the manager, and left everything behind except for her photo albums, cards her dad had given to her over the years, and her clothes. She'd left her patched vest on the bed with a note that had simply said, "Don't come looking for me, asshole. We're through."

"Kimber, you got a phone call," Patrick's voice echoed in the bay.

She looked up from the floor and realized she'd been daydreaming. She headed out to the shop and picked up the phone.

"Hi, Kimber. This is Riley. We met the other night at the Neon Cowboy?"

She racked her brain for a few seconds, trying to recall someone named Riley. She'd had too many shots and had danced with so many cowboys. Since her disaster with Chewy, she'd decided bikers were out and she'd give cowboys a chance. And there were plenty of good-looking ones who treated her just fine. "Riley? I'm sorry but I was kinda wasted the other night." *Wasted? That's an understatement. I was fuckin' trashed. Thank God Sarah was the designated driver.*

"You don't remember me?" Disappointment crept into his voice. "I was the one with the black cowboy hat."

All the guys had either black or white cowboy hats, you idiot! "Oh yeah, now I remember. How're you doing?"

"Doing great. I'm glad you remembered because we sure danced good together."

"Uh-huh."

"I remembered the shop you told me you worked at. You didn't want to give me your number."

"Yeah, well, I don't usually give out my number until I get to know someone better."

"That's why I called. I want us to get to know each other better. You doing anything tonight?"

Who the fuck calls and asks for a date the day of? *No way.* "Yeah."

"Oh. What about tomorrow night?"

"Busy again." She yawned.

"How about Thursday night?"

Oh God, he's gonna go through all the days of the damn week, probably the whole month. "Thursday night could work. What do you have in mind?"

"Dinner and maybe a drink somewhere?"

I gotta eat, and he sounds nice enough. I haven't had a date in a while. What the hell? "That sounds good. It'll have to be around seven 'cause I don't get off work until five thirty or so."

"That's awesome. Yeah, seven is fine. What's your address?"

"I'll meet you." Kimber rarely let a man she didn't know pick her up at her home. She didn't like him knowing where she lived in case he gave out weird vibes or things didn't click. It made it safer and less complicated that way. So, she'd meet men in a public place on first dates. The fact that she'd obviously met him a few nights before didn't count since she'd been wasted. If he wanted to give her a hard time about it, she'd chalk him off. It didn't really matter to her since she had no intention of getting serious with any man. She'd done that before and it had been disastrous.

After a few seconds of hesitation, Riley said, "Can we meet at your work and go from there?"

Kimber thought about it for a few moments. "Let's meet at Jim's Service Station. Do you know it?" She was friendly with the old guy who owned the gas station and she knew he kept it open until ten o'clock.

"Yeah, I do. Can you give me your number in case I have to get a hold of you."

They exchanged phone numbers, and she placed the receiver back on its cradle. The front door swept open and a blast of hot air blew over her. Hawk walked in, taking his gloves off as he approached the counter.

"Hey, Kimber. How're you doin' with Banger's bike? He left me a bunch of messages wanting to know when the fuck it'll be ready."

"Tomorrow. He sent over one of your members. The guy seemed to have a real problem with me being the mechanic. You know, me being a woman and all?"

Hawk looked at Patrick. "Who was it?"

"Throttle."

Hawk laughed. "Yeah, he would have a problem with that. He's old-school. Did he give you a hard time?"

"Nothing I couldn't handle." She smiled. She liked working with Hawk, and he never treated her any differently from the other mechanics who worked at the shop. She'd been surprised he'd hired her on because, from the way he looked, she'd have thought he would've been old-school. But his fiancée was a lawyer, so maybe he was a biker who'd slipped through the caveman cracks. She headed back to Banger's bike.

A couple hours later, Kimber swung her leg over her metallic pink Harley and made her way to her small house on the outskirts of town. She wanted to live in the town, but the rents were too expensive and she didn't want to spend all her money on housing. Her house was a cute two-bedroom/one-bathroom in a semi-shady part of town. Her next-door neighbors were a couple in their late twenties, and they made her feel very welcome. They seemed to have a perpetual barbecue, and Chyna was always coming over and knocking on Kimber's door with an invite. She'd gone over a couple times, but mostly she wanted to just crash and veg in front of the TV, watching her favorite shows after a long day of work in the garage.

She didn't think either Chyna or her boyfriend, Delacoma, worked since they were always home, drinking on the front porch, the back patio, in lawn chairs—anywhere they could find a place to plop their butts down. Lenora from across the street told her they were on disability and supplemented their income with garage sales, but Kimber didn't want to be a part of the gossip group in the neighborhood. As long as people left her the hell alone, she didn't give a shit what they did.

She turned her swamp cooler on, and a damp smack of cool air covered her. She made her way to the bathroom for a quick cold shower. After thirty minutes, she was cooled down, lounging on the couch while munching on a large salad filled with nuts, feta cheese, pineapple, and sunflower seeds, and sipping a cold bottle of Coors. Grabbing the remote, she switched on the TV.

During her show, an ad for a motorcycle accident attorney came on, and her mind drifted to Throttle. When she'd first looked at him, she'd been surprised by how good-looking he was, with his long brown hair and big dark eyes that could make a woman lose her senses. He was tall, ripped, and the tats on his arms intrigued her; they were sexy, especially the ones curling around his sculpted biceps. And his strong jaw and straight nose made his rugged good looks seem more refined. The three earrings in his right ear and the dangling silver chain in his left made her stomach tighten. Too bad he'd opened his mouth. If he weren't so insufferable, she could imagine riding on the back of his Harley.

Wait! What the fuck are you thinking, Kimber? He's a nice-looking jerk. They're a dime a dozen. And he's an outlaw biker. No fuckin' way! She'd bet he had a woman in his bed all the time. She could definitely guarantee that he wouldn't be faithful to any woman. He was just like her ex. Chewy saw women as playthings, as commodities. She shook her head. *These fuckin' bikers are all alike.* The only reason she was even thinking of Throttle was because she'd been going through a dry spell for the last six months. She didn't want to do anything stupid because of her hormones. Then she remembered cowboy man. She'd give Riley a chance. She hoped he was tall and ripped with sexy tats on his arms. Long brown hair would be good too. *Stop it, Kimber! The biker's a douche.*

She placed her empty bowl on the table and drained her beer bottle. Settling back, she sighed and hoped Riley was at least tall and had one skull tattoo. Turning up the volume, she watched zombies stalk survivors on the screen.

CHAPTER FOUR

THE FOLLOWING MORNING, Throttle entered Hawk's shop and went straight to his buddy's office. Without knocking, he went inside and plopped into one of the leather chairs in front of the desk. Hawk waved to him as he continued his conversation on the phone, and Throttle glanced around his friend's workplace as he waited.

"Hey," Hawk said as he put his phone down.

"Did you hire a fuckin' chick to work on the bikes?"

Hawk chuckled. "Dwayne told me you were upset about Kimber working here."

"So you did? What the fuck, brother?"

"She's a damn good mechanic. Bruce called me and asked if I needed some help in the shop. You know summer's the high season for me. I told him I did, and he said that Kimber had been working for him for over two years and was a kickass mechanic. She learned all that shit from her dad when she was growing up. I said I'd give her a try, and she's one of my best."

"A fuckin' chick?"

Hawk laughed. "Yeah. Fuck, I'm just as surprised as you are."

"There's no way you woulda even thought about hiring a bitch to fix bikes a couple years ago. Cara's got you pussy-whipped." Throttle pushed back roughly in his chair.

Hawk's jaw clenched. "Cara's got nothing to do with this. I run the fuckin' shop and decide who I'm gonna hire. Why the fuck do you care, anyway? She's not working on your bike."

"And she better never get near it. If I bring my bike here, I don't want a goddamned woman fucking with it." He scowled, the heat rising to his temples.

"Noted. How's the planning going for Sturgis?"

"It's going," he mumbled. Being the Road Captain, Throttle was in charge of planning all the road trips and rallies. He'd recently taken over the position from Bruiser, who was much older than him and had to slow down according to his doctor's orders. Throttle loved the extra perk of having the patch "Road Captain" on his leather jacket. It made getting prime pussy even easier.

"You wanna inventory some items that came in? I could use the help."

Throttle nodded slowly. "I can do that." He stretched out his legs. "Is that chick around?"

"Kimber? She'll be in at one. She takes some business classes at the community college. That's the reason she moved here from Silver Ridge. She told me she wants to open her own shop someday."

Throttle snorted. "Who the fuck would go to a bike repair shop owned by a chick?"

"You never know." Hawk pointed to a stack of boxes piled against the wall. "You wanna get started? I'm so fuckin' busy right now."

"And she's got a real mouth on her. If she didn't work for you, I would've put her in her place yesterday. Doesn't she know who the Insurgents are?"

Hawk stared at him. "Has she tweaked your dick?"

Throttle leapt up, his eyes flashing. "Fuck no!"

Throwing his hands up, Hawk smirked. "Damn, you're overreacting, dude. You've been talking about Kimber since you came into my office."

"Bullshit. I'm not interested in a chick who wants to be like a fuckin' man. You've insulted me. You know my type—big tits, fleshy ass, and total air brain. This"—he waved his hand in the air—"whatever her name is, hardly has any tits. And her hair is pink and black like some fucked-up zebra. There's no way she's done anything to my cock except make it shrivel. She's so not my type." He crossed his arms, his chest heaving.

"You finished? I don't think I've ever seen you worked up over any woman like this before," Hawk teased.

"I don't like chicks who don't know their place. And you can act all high and mighty, but I know that before Cara grabbed your dick, you'd never consider hiring a fuckin' female mechanic."

Hawk stood up. "You're probably right on that. I guess since I've been with Cara, I've realized that it doesn't matter if a man or a woman does the job as long as it's done well. We hang out with her friends who are doctors, lawyers, and accountants. She has a good friend who's a welder. That shit doesn't bother me anymore."

"Like I said, pussy-whipped," he muttered under his breath.

"You wanna get started on the boxes or do you wanna keep ranting about my employee?"

"Give me a fuckin' box," he growled.

After two hours of unwrapping and categorizing motorcycle accessories, Throttle stretched his arms high above his head. "You wanna grab some lunch?" he asked Hawk.

"Patrick can get us some sandwiches. Let's put this inventory on the shelves."

The two of them each carried a few boxes into the shop and began placing the items on the stainless steel shelves. Hawk gave Patrick money to run over to Fleischmann's Deli to pick up a couple pastrami sandwiches.

"The hood ornaments Jerry makes are wicked. They just fly outta the shop."

Throttle grabbed a grinning skull with iridescent eyes and stuffed it in his pocket. "I've been trying to get one of these since I first saw them in Jerry's online store, but they're always sold out. I'll pay you when we're done stocking."

"It's yours for helping me out. It's a good thing you got it 'cause that's my number one seller."

A gush of hot air breathed over Throttle before he smelled the aroma of pastrami. Placing the last skull ornament on the shelf, he walked over to the mini fridge under the counter and took out a beer. "Want one?" he asked Hawk.

"Yeah. Toss me a Coors."

The two bikers spread out their sandwiches on the counter and munched away, talking about Harleys. As Throttle swallowed his last bite, a sultry, dark scent of rose-patchouli curled around him, and he imagined the wearer was a sexy, stacked brunette with lacquer-red lips. His dick twitched as the aroma wrapped tighter around him. He turned in its direction, his pulse racing from the anticipation of seeing the lovely creature who was inadvertently enticing him. His panty-melting smile dissolved into a scowl when Kimber came into view.

"You're back," she stated.

His eyes narrowed as she passed by him, a large tote bag slung over her shoulders. "Hiya, Hawk. Sorry I'm late. My class ran over."

"That's cool. How much longer you got on Banger's bike?"

"It'll be done in an hour." She jerked her head at Throttle. "Is he taking it to Banger?"

Hawk glanced at Throttle, who turned his back on both him and Kimber, busying himself with crinkling the wax paper the sandwiches came in.

"Guess not," Hawk said with a chuckle. "I'll call Banger and let him know."

"Sounds good. I'll just change and get on it right away." Kimber went behind the counter, her body brushing against Throttle. "Sorry," she quipped as she bent down and took out a bottled water and a Sprite.

Throttle grunted while casting sidelong glances at her. When she stood back up, her body pushed lightly against him, and he cursed as his jeans tightened. He had no idea why in the hell his dick was acting like that with *her*. With a quick turn of his head, her gaze caught his, and he sucked in his breath; he'd never seen such beautiful eyes before. They were blue like the sky right before the sun disappeared—a dark rich indigo with specks of dark blue and white shimmering in the main part of the iris. They were fringed by very long soot-black lashes, and arched over by exquisitely tweezed dark eyebrows. She shot him a half-smile and walked away, her firm ass encased in tight-as-hell jeans. The metal door clanged shut behind her.

He stared for a long moment at the closed door, pissed that his dick wanted some action with this female mechanic. Damn, he should've joined Rock the previous night with the two horny chicks; then his cock wouldn't spring up at the mere sight of a woman.

Shaking his head, he came out from behind the counter. "If you don't need any more help, I'm gonna take off." He had to get out of the shop; he hated the urge he had to seek her out.

"I'm good. Thanks for your help, dude. You working later?"

"Not today. I'm gonna find Rosie and have her wrap her full lips around my cock. After that, it's a cold beer and a few joints."

"Sounds fun." Hawk smiled.

"Fuckin' right. You gonna come by the club for a beer and a game of pool?"

"Yeah. If Banger wants me to ride his bike over, I'll be by in a couple hours."

"Cool. I can give you a lift back in my truck."

"Or I can call Cara."

"No reason for that. I can bring you back to the shop. You planning on coming back before closing?"

Hawk threw him a quizzical look. "Probably. Why?"

"Just wanted to know so I can plan my evening. I'm going by Jerry's later and didn't want to make two trips." From the way Hawk lifted his eyebrows, Throttle knew he wasn't buying that shit. He knew the biker wanted to come back to the shop to grab another glimpse of the black-haired woman.

Fuck. I'm never gonna pass on screwing two willing chicks again—it makes me want to do crazy shit with a woman I can't stand. I gotta get Rosie to cool my fire. Like now.

"On second thought, give Cara a call. I gotta check out the equipment for a job tomorrow." Throttle and Rags had owned Rain or Shine Landscaping for the past three years. They hired contract workers to help on bigger jobs, but mostly it was the two of them. Throttle loved being outdoors, loved the smell and feel of dirt, and after transforming an overgrown garden or a dry patch into something alive and luxurious, he'd get a real buzz from it. He and Rags worked real well together, and it supplemented the income they received from the club's numerous businesses and dispensaries.

"What kind of a job do you have to do?"

"We gotta clear out a bunch of dead trees and shit, then plant twenty-four trees at a mansion in Glenmore. It's gonna be a long, hot day."

"Are just you and Rags doing the job?"

"Nope. I hired some extras to help."

The metal door swung open and the smell of oil seeped into the shop, mixed with rose and patchouli. Throttle stiffened.

"Hawk, can you come and check something out for me? I'm pretty sure I got it right, but I want you to look it over."

The shop's phone rang and Hawk leaned over to pick it up. "Give me a minute."

Pretending to be engrossed in a motorcycle catalog on the counter, Throttle glanced at Kimber from the corner of his eye, and caught her checking him out. Turning his head to her, he chuckled when she darted her gaze away. "Baby, if you like what you're seeing, you don't have to look away."

Facing him, her arms crossed over her chest, her face scrunched and red, she tapped her booted foot on the vinyl floor. "Not only are you full of shit, but you're full of yourself too. Oh wait, that's the same thing." She tossed her hair over her shoulders and muttered under her breath, "You wish, jerk."

Throttle jumped in front of her, causing her to slam into his chest. Startled, she glanced up, straight into his eyes which were darkened by anger. "Watch your goddamned mouth. Someone needs to teach you respect, woman."

"And you're gonna be the one to do it? Hah!" She tried to get around him but he blocked her. "Let me pass." She jutted her chin out defiantly.

"Not until you apologize," he gritted through his teeth.

"For telling you the truth? I don't think so."

A low growl came from deep in his chest. He reached out to grab her arm when Hawk shoved himself between them. "Both of you cool the fuck down." He turned to Kimber. "I heard what you said, and I don't like you disrespecting one of the brothers in my shop." She started to protest but Hawk held up his hand, silencing her. Turning to a smug-looking Throttle, Hawk said softly, "Why don't you leave this alone, okay? I'll see you at the clubhouse when I bring Banger's bike."

Throttle breathed heavily for a few seconds, then clasped Hawk's shoulder. "See you." Without acknowledging Kimber, he stomped out of the shop, slamming the door behind him so hard the glass vibrated. His Harley roared to life, and he sped away from the shop and the infuriating woman with the loud, smartass mouth.

When he walked into the clubhouse, it took him a minute to adjust to the low light. Thin wisps of weed and cigarette smoke wound around him as he went straight to the bar, motioning Puck for a double shot of Jack. Before he reached the counter, a short glass full to the brim with a dark amber liquid greeted him. He threw it back, loving the way the smooth fire scorched his throat then warmed it as the whiskey made its way down to his stomach. Jerking his head at the prospect, another double appeared before him.

"Bad day?" Rock asked as he slid on the barstool next to Throttle.

"No." He threw back the double shot.

"You're hitting it pretty hard for a good day."

"Just enjoying my day off."

Rock eyed him, suspicion lacing his gaze, but Throttle ignored him and took out a joint. "Want one?" he asked the Sergeant-At-Arms. After handing him one, Throttle took out another, lit it, and inhaled deeply, letting the tension he'd felt ever since he'd entered Hawk's shop that morning slowly seep away. With each drag, his body relaxed, and he actually smiled when Rock recounted his escapades with the sexy twosome the previous night.

Hawk's new employee was a class-A bitch, and Throttle's plan was to ignore her and not let her get under his skin. She came across as a man-hater, and he didn't need any of that shit. There were plenty of delicious women who couldn't wait to spend a few hours fucking him. He wanted a woman who was soft, sexy, and compliant. He didn't need to put up with Kimber's shit.

Wheelie came up to the two brothers. "Hey, you got another joint on you?"

Throttle jerked his head and handed him one, lighting it for him.

"I heard Hawk's got a bitch working on the bikes at his shop." A cloud of smoke billowed around Wheelie as he breathed out.

Tension pushed into Throttle's body again. He nodded, gesturing to Puck for another double.

"You seen her?"

Throttle swung up on the barstool and leaned forward, his elbows resting on the bar. "Yeah. She's got tits that could fit on two of my fingers, and she's got pink tips in her hair."

"No shit." Rock whistled softly. "No tits?"

"Nope."

"Damn," Wheelie said. "Does she know her way around a Harley?"

Throttle shrugged. "Hawk seems to think so. I guess we'll find out once he brings Banger's bike to him. She worked on it. I can't believe how fuckin' pussy-whipped Hawk is. Hiring a chick to do a man's job. I know Cara was behind this. No way Hawk would've done it. That's the trouble with these career women—they want to butt their fuckin' noses in everything. Nothing's sacred anymore, you know?" The whiskey created a nice buzz in his head, and all he could picture in his mind's eye as he lamented the slow death of the good old boys club was Kimber's nicely rounded ass so snug in her jeans. And what the fuck was up with her seductive, dark perfume? She smelled like a hot vixen who needed a good fuck. *Damnit! I need to get laid. How can I even think about* her?

"You listening to me, man?" Rock's voice sliced through his whiskey fog, and Throttle stared at him bleary-eyed. "You're fuckin' wasted."

"She smells like patchouli and roses. Fuck, have you ever smelled that before? It's damn sexy. It hits you in your cock. Right. Smack. In. Your. Cock." He slammed his fist on the bar on each word.

"Fuck," Wheelie said after taking another drag.

Laughing, Rock helped his swaying brother to his room on the third floor. Before he left, he turned to Throttle, who sat at the edge of the bed with his head in his hands, and asked, "You want me to tell Rosie to come up here to get rid of your patchouli-induced hard-on?"

Throttle shook his head. "Another time."

"You sure? She was looking for you earlier."

"I'm fuckin' wasted. I just wanna crash."

With a chuckle, Rock closed the door behind him. Throttle lifted his head and stared at the closed door. What the hell was the matter with him? Rosie was ready to open her sweet mouth and wrap her lips tightly around his aching hardness, but he'd said no. *What the fuck?* The truth was the snarky chick mechanic pissed him off so bad that he wasn't in the mood for banging Rosie's mouth. *This is the second time the little bitch has made me too mad to fuck.* Groaning, he flopped onto his back and placed his arm over his hot eyelids. Incredible blue orbs filled his mind, and he felt drawn to them as he had at Hawk's shop when he and Kimber locked gazes. Her eyes were striking but soft, and they made his blood dance as he drifted further into them until darkness took over.

Then he passed out.

CHAPTER FIVE

L EAH MOORE'S HIGH heels clacked on the brick walkway as she sprinted to her car. Her dark hair caught the early morning sun's rays, and ribbons of light intertwined with her dark strands. With a muted jangle, her keys fell on the ground and she cursed under her breath. When she bent over to pick them up, her short turquoise skirt revealed a toned, upper thigh.

He held his breath as he took in the way her thigh muscles flexed under all that creamy skin. Hidden behind the cluster of evergreens, he watched her, thrilled to have caught a glimpse of her body that he hadn't seen before. He wondered if she had on panties or a thong.

Two weeks before, the man had spotted Leah at the grocery store when he'd stopped after work to pick up dinner at the full-service deli counter. She'd been waiting in line to place her order for the two pieces of baked chicken and two sides. Her long dark hair cascaded down her back, and it glistened under the bright store lights. She was his type: slender build, dark hair, and a nice rounded ass that would look sexy in any panty.

After she'd received her order, he'd skipped his, for fear of losing sight of her. He'd followed her home, and for the past week he'd watched her from the shadows of the trees. The previous night, she'd given him a bonus and undressed without closing the blinds. Her small, pert breasts looked beautiful in a sheer gold bra, and her matching panties made him salivate. He'd come back early that morning, hoping to have some time with her lingerie before she returned from work. For the last seven days, he'd learned everything about her routine.

The good-looking man loved the anticipation before he made his move. Sometimes he'd spend three weeks watching the women he targeted. He'd even slip into their rooms while they slept and watch them, careful not to wake them up, and always leaving with a few pairs of panties. Later, he'd use the undies to pleasure himself, the image of the sleeping woman whose breasts rose and fell as he watched her foremost on his mind before climaxing.

Leah Moore drove away and the brown-haired man stood frozen for quite a while, his gaze still transfixed on the road. Finally, he wiped his hands on his jeans and crossed the street, a notebook in his hand. Going directly to the meter, he pretended he was reading it as his glance darted over to the sliding glass door. He moved slowly to it and tried it with his gloved hand. It opened. A wide smile spread over his face. It never ceased to amaze him how many people left their windows and doors opened. Sliding it open, he slipped inside.

Leah lived alone, which made it easier for him to do what he needed to do. From stalking her, he knew she wouldn't be home for at least eight hours. He had time before he had to go to work that evening. Before going to her bedroom, he looked at the pictures of her and other people—family and friends, he'd guessed—in various phases of her life. Her sparkling blue eyes and heart-shaped face were beautiful. Leah looked to be about thirty years old, and if he were a different person, if he didn't have the craving, he'd ask her out. And she'd probably go out with him—several women found him attractive and a real catch. Sighing, he climbed the stairs to the second floor and went straight to her bedroom.

Without hesitation, he strode over to her long dresser and opened the top drawer. In his experience, women usually kept their lingerie in the first drawer of their dressers. And Leah did not disappoint him—various colors and shapes of panties and bras dazzled him. Picking them up, he caressed his cheek with their silkiness, marveling at how soft they felt against his skin. As he lost himself in the world of undergarments, his phone rang, startling him out of his euphoria. Looking up, he caught a glimpse of himself in the dresser mirror: bikini panties in his hands, lust glazing his eyes, stiffness punching against his jeans. Then disgust washed away the excitement, and self-loathing set in as he dropped the panties on the dresser. Tears poured down his tanned cheeks and he sat on the edge of her bed, his head in his hands, sobbing.

After a long time, he pulled himself together, picking out the gold panty he'd seen Leah wearing the previous night, and a periwinkle blue one. Shoving them in his pockets, he closed the dresser drawer—making sure not to look in the mirror—then slipped downstairs and out the sliding door.

By the time he returned home, he was horny as hell, and he bolted all the locks on his doors and sat on the couch in his darkened family room. He slowly took the panties out of his pocket, unzipped his jeans, and firmly grabbed his hardness. Placing the gold prize over his dick, he began rubbing it up and down. Leaning his head against the wall, he closed his eyes and let the image of Leah undressing in her room play out in his mind.

KIMBER SAT CROSS-LEGGED on her kitchen chair, munching on a piece of buttered toast with blueberry jam, reading the *Pinewood Springs Tribune*. Even though everyone she knew received their news via the Internet, she still liked browsing through the newspaper, loving the smell and feel of the ink under her fingertips.

As she scanned the local news section, a small article caught her eye: "Lingerie Bandit Strikes Again." Intrigued by the heading, she read the most bizarre story in the paper that day. Amazed at how weird people were, she wondered what compelled the perpetrator to risk breaking into a woman's house to steal a couple pairs of panties. Shaking her head, she pushed the paper away and poured herself another glass of orange juice.

She stared out the large window above her sink. The main reason she'd decided on renting this house was because of the windows; there were many and they let in a lot of light. Running a hand through her hair, she was happy that she didn't have to be to work until noon.

Kimber wondered if *he'd* be in the shop when she arrived. Why did she even care? It wasn't anything to her, but she found herself secretly hoping she'd bump into him. Not that she wanted anything with him, but he was good eye candy, and she enjoyed teasing him because it pissed him off so much. When she recalled how he'd checked her out the previous day, her stomach did that weird flip-flop thing and it made her mad. She couldn't let herself be involved with another biker. And even if she wanted to, it was obvious the guy hated her for daring to throw a wrench in his chauvinistic idea of what jobs women should have. For a man to have that attitude in the twenty-first century was unbelievable.

She wasn't shocked at his reaction to her being a mechanic. She'd hung with bikers for most of her life, and more than the majority of them felt that a woman shouldn't mess around in a man's world. Even though the guys she knew weren't in one-percenter clubs, they were still just as bad. A friend of hers became the old lady of an outlaw biker, and she couldn't even speak her mind lest his club brothers think he didn't have a respectful wife. For Kimber, that was bullshit and a very small step away from damn slavery. No way would she ever sign up for that crap.

Since she'd run away from her ex, she'd thrown herself into her work, and now school. She attended Pinewood Springs Community College part-time and her area of study was business. Ever since she could remember, she'd dreamed of owning her own motorcycle repair shop, and taking business classes was the first step in fulfilling her aspirations.

All work and no play wasn't the best way to meet people. Her only real friend was Sarah, who she met at a bike rally soon after she came to Pinewood Springs. She didn't know her very well, but so far they seemed to have some things in common. Sarah loved bikes and bikers, but she also loved cowboys. She was always game to go out on the weekends, and they usually had a good time. Sometimes she was too much when it came to men, though, and Kimber thought she threw caution to the wind when she'd leave with men she'd just met at the bars.

Maybe Riley, the cowboy man, would turn out to be someone Kimber would actually like to date. She hadn't dated very much in Silver Ridge, and since she'd come to Pinewood Springs, she'd only had a few dates, nothing serious. She couldn't remember the last time she'd screwed anyone worthwhile. Hell, she couldn't remember the last time she'd been with a man. She was so overdue. *Maybe that's why I keep thinking about that jerk friend of Hawk's. Damn, the way he looked at me with his deep black eyes made me want to melt at his feet. Fuck, Kimber, if Riley is halfway decent, you gotta get laid tonight.*

She couldn't risk even fantasizing about Throttle's mouth on hers— it was too dangerous. What was it with her and bikers? Shaking her head, she decided to go to work early—she could use the hours. As she pulled her sleek mane up in a high bun, a small shiver of excitement ran through her in anticipation of seeing Throttle. If he were at the shop, she'd make a real effort to be civil to him, maybe even a bit flirty, but if he said anything stupid—and the chance of that was extremely high— she'd cut him down to size. Biker or not, gorgeous or not, there was no way she was ever going to let a man get the best of her. *Been there, done that.*

Walking out into the heat of the day, she pushed up the kickstand and swung her leg over her bike. After she'd sold her dad's shop, her first purchase was a Harley Street Glide Special. She'd popped for the custom metallic pink body and loved the way it shimmered, its brightness bouncing off all the chrome. Her bike was her baby and her best purchase ever. Grasping the handlebars, she revved the engine and pulled away from the curb.

CHAPTER SIX

"YOU WANNA GRAB a beer?" Rags asked as he loaded one of the lawnmowers in the back of the truck.

"Love to, but I got a date in a few so I gotta get back and clean up," Throttle replied.

"A date? Who's the victim?"

Throttle chuckled as he pulled the chain through the wheels of the lawn equipment. "The new waitress at Ruthie's."

"The blonde with the big tits?"

"Yep, and I got all kinds of shit planned for those big tits." He pulled out a bottled water from the cooler and guzzled it. "She's been eye-fucking me for a while." He threw a water to Rags.

Catching it, he unscrewed the top. "What took you so long to hook up with her?"

"Wanted her to appreciate me more when I banged her."

Downing his cold water in one long gulp, Rags crushed the plastic bottle and threw it in the bed of the truck. "You lucky bastard. I've had my eye on her for a while, but she wouldn't give me the time of day. What're your plans?"

"Have some chow at Ruthie's—Big Tits loves to wait on me—then take her to Arrow Lake and fuck her like she's never been fucked."

"Aren't you worried 'bout her wanting more than tonight, or have you decided on taking seconds?"

"Hell no. With the citizen chicks, I'm always upfront with 'em. I tell them how it is with me. If they don't like it, they don't have to hook up with me. If I do seconds with the citizens, they always read way more into it. Not up for that shit. From the start, I tell the women it's a one-night stand only. I was honest with Big Tits."

"Sounds good, but it doesn't always work. Remember Tina? Fuck, how many times did she call and text you a day?"

Throttle pulled out another bottle of water. "Tina was a fuckin' psycho. She practically had us married. She'd call me all the time and text me nonstop, but I never responded. Not once. After a couple weeks, she caught on." He laughed and took his truck keys out of his pocket. "I sometimes bump into her at the liquor store and she always gives me the death stare. Fuck, you'd think she would've moved on by now."

"You better hope this one tonight is okay with your 'fuck 'em and forget 'em' rule."

Throttle shrugged then opened the pickup's door. "Well, I gotta get going. I wanna stop by and pick up some vodka coolers." He laughed when he saw Rags grimace. "Yeah, she likes that shit. Hell, I'd buy her flavored whiskey if it got my dick between her tits."

Rags cuffed him on the shoulder. "Have a good time. You can let me know if buying the horse piss for the chick was worth it or not."

"With the way she sways those hips, I'd say it's gonna be worth it. See ya."

Rags nodded then jumped on his Harley and rode away before Throttle settled in the driver's seat. He switched on the ignition, and as he threw the truck in gear, his phone buzzed.

"Hello?"

"Hiya, sexy. You still comin' to the diner after my shift?"

"Hey. Yeah, I'm comin'. I'll be by for dinner."

"I thought we had a date," Big Tits whined.

"We do, but I gotta eat. After dinner, we'll go for a ride and have a few drinks. What's your favorite flavor?"

"Blueberry." He heard her clucking her tongue. "So you're gonna take me for a ride on your Harley?" Excitement laced her voice.

"Nope. I'm bringing my truck." There was no way the waitress was getting her ass anywhere near his bike. Throttle never let chicks on the back of his bike. And if he ever did, it sure in hell wouldn't be a citizen who didn't know the difference between a Harley and a rice burner. No fucking way.

"Your pickup?" Her voice dripped with disappointment.

"Yeah." He actually felt bad for being such a bastard. "The Harley's in the shop," he lied.

"Oh," she said, her voice perking up. "I'll take a raincheck on that ride, then. When you get it back, let me know."

There isn't gonna be a next time. This is strictly a one-time deal. "Sounds good."

"So, what time you comin' by?"

"Around seven thirty."

"I'll plan my break about that time. I get off at nine o'clock."

"I better get going."

"Okay. I can't wait for when you come. This is gonna be fun."

Fuckin' right it is. I can't wait to bury my dick between your tits. "See you."

He tossed his phone on the passenger seat, cranked up the radio, and headed to the liquor store.

BIG TITS WAS at his side the minute he entered Ruthie's Diner. Her white uniform with the pink piping stretched across her ample breasts. She smiled widely at him and leaned in, saying in a low voice, "You look real good." She ran her long fingernail up his arm.

Damn, she's fuckin' ready. Those nails are gonna feel real good scratching my back while I fuck her hard. "You look good too," he replied, his eyes fixed on her chest.

She inhaled deeply and arched her back a bit, thrusting her breasts closer to him. "Thanks," she breathed.

"Smells good in here." He moved away from her and walked to a booth by the window.

"Meatloaf's the special tonight. It's really good. You want that, handsome?"

He nodded as he scoured the menu. "Bring me a salad to start—ranch dressing. You gonna join me?" He looked up and his gaze fell on her nametag—Peggy. *That's right. Her name's Peggy.*

"I can join you in twenty minutes. Crystal called off for swing shift." She tucked a strand of blonde hair behind her ear. "She's always pulling that shit."

"Fuckin' sucks, Peggy. Bring me some water with a ton of ice." Handing her two brown glass bottles, he said, "Put these in the fridge for me and bring them out when my dinner comes."

The waitress's eyes widened as she looked sideways to the kitchen. "Are you crazy? I can't do that. If Ruthie catches me, I'm toast, and I need this job. You know the place doesn't have a liquor license."

"Then you better make sure Ruthie doesn't catch you." He leaned back, his head cocked to the side. "Be a good girl and do what I said."

She shifted her weight from one foot to another, and then her eyes lit up. "I know. I'll put them in one of my grocery bags. Ruthie won't suspect anything."

"Sweetheart, I don't give a damn how you do it, just fuckin' do it." He placed the two bottles in her hands. She smiled and then sashayed to the kitchen.

Throttle looked out the window, watching the cars pass by. The heat shimmered off the asphalt, and the leaves on the trees remained motionless; the heat from the day had melted into the dusk. A cherry-red Dodge pickup caught his attention as it turned into the diner's parking lot and secured a space in front. A man in a black cowboy hat jumped down before he rushed over to the passenger door and opened it. Throttle whistled under his breath as he saw a pair of tanned, shapely legs. The truck door and the cowboy blocked the woman's face, but if the rest of the chick matched her legs, he'd have to figure out a way to get to know her. He could easily see those gams around his waist.

"Here you go." Peggy placed his dinner salad and cup of dressing on the table, diverting his attention back to her. "Did you work hard today?"

Shaking black pepper on his salad, he nodded. "It was fuckin' hot out there today. Hell, it still is and the sun's getting ready to set."

"I heard it was ninety-eight."

"Wouldn't be surprised."

She licked her lips and leaned her thigh against the table. "Do the people you do work for ever invite you in to cool off?"

He glanced at her then threw her a half-smile. "Sometimes. Why?"

"I heard that you and your partner get a lot of housewives hitting on you. That's all." She shrugged. "Is that true?"

He mixed the dressing in his salad and took a big bite. "Us, the postman, the milkman, and probably the pizza guy. All the fuckin' stereotypes, you know?" He winked.

The truth was many of the women would invite them in for a cold drink and make a play for them. If the women were attractive and they weren't too busy, they'd accommodate her, but they worked as a team. None of the women complained, and even though they didn't hook up with most of their female customers, the word leaked out that the two buff men sometimes gave a free bonus. He and Rags would always laugh when they'd arrive at a job during the day and find the husband home sick for the day. Damn, if they didn't know better, the two bikers would've thought that Pinewood Springs was one of the unhealthiest towns in Colorado.

"Are you being funny, or are the rumors true?"

"Hire us. Then you'll find out for sure." He lifted his eyebrows.

At first she just stared at him, but then a wide grin spread across her face as she swatted his arm. "Oh, you. You're such a kidder." A hot rush of heat fell over his back as the diner's door opened. She pushed away from the table. "I gotta get this." She walked away, and he heard her say, "Can I help you?"

A male voice said, "A booth for two."

Throttle finished his salad as the couple ambled past him. He recognized the woman's sexy legs as the ones coming out of the cherry-red pickup. Shifting his glance upward, he took in her firm, high ass, and her glossy black hair with neon pink tips—*What the fuck?* He sat up straighter. *It can't be. Those legs and that ass can't belong to* her. *Wait. She did have a cute ass in her fuckin' coveralls.*

When the sexy-legged woman swung around and sat in the booth facing him, there was no mistaking her striking blue eyes—the ones that did weird shit to him, like making his dick twitch and his stomach tighten. *Fuck. It is* her. *What the hell is Kimber doing with a goddamned cowboy?* He grunted and watched as Peggy wrote on her pad, taking the couple's order. When she finished, Throttle motioned her over.

"You want some more salad, honey?"

"No. Bring me one of the beers." He jerked his head to the couple. "What's up with them?"

Peggy glanced over her shoulder, confusion etched on her face. "Them? I don't know 'em. They're just customers."

"Are they holding hands?" he blurted out. *Why the fuck am I asking that? What the hell's the matter with me?*

"No. Why?"

Pissed at himself for asking such a wimpy-ass question, he clenched his jaw. "Get my beer." Looking away, he dismissed her.

"Okay." She shuffled to the kitchen.

Throttle pretended to be engrossed in the dessert menu, but his ears were pricked on Kimber and the cowboy's conversation. From the bits he could hear, he gathered they were on their first date. He watched her as she spoke, fascinated with the way her pink tongue skimmed over her front teeth before disappearing in her mouth. With the way her ebony hair framed her face, her flawless skin looked almost like porcelain. He wondered why he hadn't noticed that before. Her smoky makeup made her eyes more intense, and the gloss on her lips made them fuller and oh-so-tempting. For a split second, Throttle had the urge to go over to her table, yank her to him, and then suck and nip on her bottom lip before driving his tongue into her mouth.

What the fuck am I thinking? Damn, I need to get laid like now. Maybe I can take Big Tits out back for a quickie. I gotta get rid of this crazy fire.

Then her blue orbs locked on his dark ones. For a breathless second, they pulled each other in; it was like lightning tearing through his body. And from the surprise, then panic, reflected in her eyes, he knew she felt it too. Breaking contact, she looked down, but the intensity was still there, crackling in the air between them.

Cowboy turned around and ran his gaze over Throttle's taut face. *So he noticed something sparked within her. What in the hell was* that? He'd never felt such a sensation like that with any woman. Hell, he hadn't *felt* anything but lust with a woman for a very long time.

"Your beer." Peggy giggled as she placed a large plastic glass full of beer in front of him. "We going to Arrow Lake later?" She brushed the top of his hand with her fingers.

Forcing himself not to look at Kimber again, he grabbed his beer and chugged it. He wiped his mouth with his hand. "Maybe."

"I heard you like taking women there."

"You hear a lot of shit 'bout me, don't you?"

She smiled. "You're a popular guy. So if we go there, are we gonna skinny dip?"

He knew Kimber was watching him; he could feel her pull. "Not into swimming."

Peggy chuckled and squeezed his arm. "It doesn't matter. I got a feeling I'm gonna be real wet anyway. You get my meaning?" She ran her fingers through his thick hair.

Damn, the black-haired vixen is doin' a fuckin' number on me. And what the fuck is Big Tits jabbering about? Looking at Peggy, he nodded absentmindedly. Cowboy swiveled around and waved her over.

"I gotta get this, honey. Be back soon." She went over to Kimber's table, and Throttle watched with interest as she stood at the booth.

After she wrote something on a notepad and went to another table, he saw Kimber lean back and laugh at something Cowboy said, each note of her laughter hitting him in the groin. Saying something to Cowboy that Throttle couldn't hear, she slid out of the booth and walked to the hallway where the bathroom was. Without thinking, he jumped up and followed her, settling himself in a corner as he waited for her to come out of the ladies' room, hoping Peggy wouldn't come and look for him.

A few minutes later, Kimber exited the bathroom, adjusting her short black skirt. "Hey there," he said in a deep, hushed voice. From the way she jumped and whirled around, he knew he'd startled her.

Locking on his face, she took a step back. "Oh... Hi."

Not wanting Peggy to come up to him, he grasped a startled Kimber by her wrist and tugged her behind him as he pushed open the door which led to the alley. Outside, the heat surrounded them, and the smell of rotting food invaded his nostrils. With her wrist still in his hand, he moved them away from the diner's dumpsters.

"What are you doing?" she snapped as she jerked out of his grip.

Good question. What the shit am *I doing?* "I want to talk to you."

Taking a couple steps back, she stared at him. "About what?"

He shrugged. He hadn't been thinking clearly. All he knew was that for some illogical reason, he wanted to be close to her. His gaze traveled up her body then landed on her face. "You look pretty when you're all fixed up."

A smirk danced on her glossy lips. "That's a half-assed compliment."

He held his hands up. "No, I didn't mean it that way. I just meant you look good without the coveralls and grease."

"You dragged me out in the stinking heat to tell me that?" He gave her a half-smile. "Unbelievable," she said as she rolled her eyes.

He felt stupid all of a sudden, like a teenage boy talking to his crush for the first time. This wasn't him at all. He didn't act like some bumbling teenager who couldn't control his damn dick. This whole thing was fucked. His muscles tensed and he frowned. "You work in a bike shop and you're out with a fuckin' cowboy? How the hell does that work?"

She lifted a defiant chin. "Tell me how who I'm out with is any of your damn business."

"I don't give a shit who you're with. I just pegged you as a biker chick, not a rodeo one. That's all."

"Well, I'm neither. I'm an individual who can't be fit into a mold." She crossed her arms over her chest.

"He your boyfriend or something?"

Fixing her eyes on him, she said, "Something."

In one long stride, he stood in front of her, his hands itching to dig into her skin and pull her to him. His gaze lingered on her mouth, her bottom lip shiny and tempting. He so wanted to taste it. *Whoa. What the fuck is wrong with me?*

Kimber leaned in closer to him and he lowered his head, her warm, minty breath fanning over his face.

"Kimber?" a deep voice said from behind Throttle. She jumped back as though she'd been stung by a bee.

He spun around and saw the cowboy standing right outside the doorway, a befuddled look on his face. Throttle glanced at Kimber and saw her fidgeting with the snaps on her tight-as-hell top. He chuckled under his breath, every bit of him enjoying her discomfort.

"Hey, Riley," she muttered.

"What's going on here?"

"Uh… I was just going over some stuff from work." She jerked her chin at Throttle. "He's a member of the club I was telling you about, remember?" She sidled over to him and then laced her fingers through his. Riley threw her a boyish grin, and Throttle wanted to slam his face into the brick wall.

"Okay. So you know him from work?"

She bobbed her head up and down too many times, saying, "Right. That's right" over and over.

Her date extended his hand to Throttle. "I'm Riley."

He looked at it, then the guy's goofy, grinning face. He snorted and bumped Riley as he walked past him and entered the diner. From behind him, Riley said, "What's up with him? Did I offend him or something?"

"No," Kimber replied. "He's just a jerk."

Throttle stopped, his blood boiling, but before he could go back outside and punch Riley in the face and kiss Kimber hard, the scent of citrus curled around him. A soft arm encircled his trim waist. "What were you doing outside, handsome? Your meatloaf's ready."

Wrapping his arm around Peggy, he pulled her close. She was the woman he should want to kiss. Without answering, he walked back to his table, squeezed her shoulder, and slid into the booth. He placed a forkful of meatloaf in his mouth.

"Is it too cold? You want me to nuke it for a few seconds?"

He shook his head.

"Let me give my customers their dinner, and then I'll come join you." Peggy rushed off.

He kept his eyes down on his plate as he shoveled in his food, but he sensed her when she walked into the room. He didn't look up, his mind still reeling from the fact that if the cowboy hadn't come out, he would've kissed Kimber. And she'd acted more than willing to be kissed by him. He gulped down his beer, pissed that he was stoked Kimber wanted to kiss him.

"You must've been hungry. You're all done. Want some more?" Peggy asked as she slid into the booth, sitting across from him.

He shook his head. The only thing he wanted was to get out of Ruthie's as fast as he could. He was furious with himself for giving a shit who Kimber was with, for wanting to kiss and be with her. He glanced up and caught her staring at him before she darted her eyes away. Satisfaction weaved through him, and he breathed out.

He placed his hand on top of Peggy's. "I'm sorry I have to do this, but I'm not feeling so good. It kinda just hit me. We're gonna have to go to Arrow Lake another time."

Peggy's face fell. "Really? Maybe you ate too fast. Why don't you relax and wait a bit. I bet you'll feel better."

"Don't think so. Sorry." He squeezed her hand.

"Do you wanna come over to my place and lie down? I'll take care of you. I can ask to leave now."

He smiled ruefully. "I'm sure you'd take real good care of me. I don't know what the fuck is wrong with me, and that's the absolute truth, sweetheart, but I'm just gonna head home. How much do I owe for the dinner?"

She handed him the bill. "You sure you don't want to come to my place? I was really looking forward to spending some time with you tonight."

"Me too." *I couldn't wait to play with your tits. I fuckin' can't believe I'm walking away from this sexy sure thing.* "Another time, okay?"

Her eyes lit up. "What about tomorrow?"

"That won't work." He handed her a twenty-dollar bill. "Keep the change." He scooted out of the booth.

"You'll call me, right?"

He nodded as he pushed open the glass doors.

"Now don't forget," she said at his retreating back.

He waved his hand up in the air as he walked to his truck. When he started it, he looked at Kimber and her gaze caught his. He put on his sunglasses, backed out, and turned out of the parking lot. He couldn't even begin to figure out why he blew off Big Tits. She should've been in the truck with him right then, and they should've been driving to Arrow Lake for some real fun. But he was headed back to the clubhouse, and instead of a busty blonde on his mind, a flat-chested brunette invaded it.

What. The. Fuck?

CHAPTER SEVEN

KIMBER WATCHED AS Riley's red taillights disappeared into the darkness. He'd wanted to go dancing after dinner, but she wasn't in the mood, and she had that asshole Throttle to thank for ruining her date. She'd be surprised if she ever heard from Riley again. Who would've thought she'd have bumped into *him* at the diner. The timing totally sucked. And the way he acted, telling her that she was a biker chick and all that crap? He had nerve, that was for sure.

She switched on her Harley and it roared to life, then she exited Jim's station and headed to her house. Fifteen minutes later she turned off the engine, shut the garage doors, and stepped into her kitchen. She opened her fridge and pulled out a can of beer, popped it open, and took a long pull. The biker looked damn gorgeous in his tight black jeans and muscle shirt, his tats moving whenever he flexed his muscular arms. *Fuckin' stop it, Kimber. Right now!* It didn't look like Riley had any tats on him, but then she'd stopped paying much attention to him from the moment she'd spotted Throttle. She groaned. She couldn't start something with the dude. The only thing he had going for him was that he was gorgeous. And, yeah... he had a kickass Harley.

She turned on the TV and channel surfed, images of new cars, puppies, buildings, and people flickering by quickly. She'd almost *kissed* him. She covered her mouth with her hand as tingling swept up the back of her neck. And she'd wanted to. With Riley sitting at the booth, she was ready to play kissy-face with a guy who irritated the hell out of her. How ridiculous was that?

If Riley called her again—and it was a huge *if*—she'd make it up to him. She had to forget about Throttle and concentrate on her studies, her work, and exploring something with Riley. There was no way she'd let a hot man in leather deter her, even though she'd always been a sucker for leather and Harleys. All she had to remember was what a jerk he was and all would be cool. She took another gulp of beer. She had a handle on it.

No problem.

THROTTLE OPENED THE shop door, welcoming the gust of icy air that shrouded him. He waved at Hawk as he came up to the counter. "How's business?"

"Good. Didn't expect to see you. You're not working?"

"Rags is on it this morning. We hired a few guys to help out on that landscape job over in Fernwood."

"How come you're not working it?"

Throttle's skin pricked. "What the fuck? You're not my employer. I had shit to do earlier." He pushed his boot against the corner of the counter. "You got a problem with me being here?"

"Not at all. I'm just surprised. Fuck, you've come to the shop more in the past couple weeks than you have all year. Just find it curious."

He rubbed the back of his neck. "I thought I'd come by to help you out with all the fuckin' boxes you had in your office. You told me you needed the help, but I'll just fuckin' leave." He spun around and stomped to the door.

"Dude, calm the fuck down. I could use your help. I've an errand I gotta do, so you can man the phones and plug all this shit"—he waved the papers in his hand—"into the computer."

Throttle turned back and followed his buddy into the office. "Take a seat." Hawk gestured at the desk chair. "I'll show you how to put in the inventory on a program I came up with. It kicks ass and makes keeping track of products a whole lot easier."

As Hawk showed and explained the software, Throttle wondered if Kimber was at work. He was going to ask, but Hawk had made such a big fucking deal about him coming to the shop to help out that he kept silent. He shook his head. Hawk knew exactly the reason he'd come by, and he was right—Kimber. Throttle wanted to see her again, be close enough to breath in her scent. The things she did to him were incomprehensible, and it pissed him off and excited him at the same time.

"So it's pretty easy. You got a handle on it?" Hawk picked up his keys on the desk.

Throttle nodded, pointing at the stack of boxes on the file cabinet. "You want me to unpack and categorize those for you?"

"Those are from Jerry. Damn, I can't keep his ornaments in the shop. I'll take care of it when I get back. I just need you to plug in the items and codes. I should be back in a couple hours."

Throttle swung the desk chair to face the computer. "See you when you get back." He typed in the first item. He knew he should've been working on the big job he and Rags had landed, but instead he'd hired an extra person to take his place while he sat hunched over typing a bunch of numbers, hoping to maybe get a glimpse of Kimber. *Fuckin' pitiful.*

After forty-five minutes of tapping numbers into the computer, he regretted his decision to come to the shop. *Knock. Knock.* He looked up. "Come in."

The door opened and Kimber walked in, her hand flying to her throat. "Uh… Is Hawk here?" She moved her head around searching for him in the small office.

Enjoying her discomfort, he swiveled to face her. "No. I'm manning the store. What do you need?"

She stood silent, her gaze fixed on his face.

"So you wanna just admire my good looks, babe? I'm down with that." He sniggered.

Her face flushed. "Hawk told me he'd leave a part I need to finish up a bike I'm working on. When will he be back?"

He shrugged. "What part do you need? I can help you with that." He winked at her.

She pressed her lips together. He slid his gaze up her body, admiring the way her blue coveralls encased her hips. Desire teased at his stomach. Looking up at her, he gave her a lopsided, cocky smile.

She fidgeted with the snap on her side pocket, looking everywhere but at him. "I need the iridescent skull. The hood ornament the dude in your club makes."

"Jerry's skull is fuckin' popular."

"No shit. There was a shelf of them yesterday, and today they're all gone. I should've grabbed one when I had the chance."

"Hawk got some more in." He jerked his head to the boxes on top of the filing cabinet. "I think the skulls are in the top box. I'll help you get it down." He stood from the desk.

She waved him away. "No worries. I can handle it." She rose up on her tiptoes.

"You sure, 'cause you're not that tall. Why don't you be a good little girl and let me get the box down for you."

"I said I'm good." Irritation crept into her voice as she reached up and grabbed the box. Throttle came behind her just when she pulled hard at the box; it dislodged and came tumbling down. Jumping back, she lost her balance and fell into Throttle's arms. "Oh!"

He wrapped his arms around her small waist, leaned down, and breathed in deeply her scent of rose and patchouli. "You smell incredible, and your ass wiggling against my cock feels fuckin' awesome." She twisted around, trying to get out of his arms. "Fuck. Will you settle down?" Kimber tilted her head back and he drank in her magnetic blue orbs and plump lips, just begging to be kissed. He roughly pulled her closer to him. "Give me your mouth," he ordered.

Under his firm grip, she relaxed, and then her lips parted and she closed her eyes. He lowered his head and took fiery possession of her mouth, tasting, sucking, and nipping her lips with urgency, his tongue plundering her dark recesses. A soft moan escaped from her throat, and he felt his cock swell in his jeans. Running his hands down her back, he cupped her firm ass, the one he'd been dreaming about since he first saw it. Against him, he felt her tremble as he continued to devour her mouth.

She tangled her arms around his strong neck as she pressed closer against him, the contact of her body heat melding with his. He pulled away slightly, his lips working their way down her jawline to her neck. "You feel good in my arms. I want my cock inside you, babe." His teeth grazed across her earlobe and he gently pulled it in between his lips, sucking it as she moaned and held him tighter. Squeezing her ass, he whispered, "I want this too." She didn't respond, merely gasped, then arched toward his broad chest before she moved back to his lips, kissing him feverishly, making sexy noises in the back of her throat that drove him wild.

I'm hard as a fuckin' board. There was something about her that made his dick stir. He wanted to tear off her uniform and give her a hard fucking on Hawk's desk, shove his length into her dripping pussy. She ignited a fire in him so intense he thought he'd explode. He couldn't remember ever wanting a woman as much as he did Kimber at that moment.

As he plunged his tongue in and out of her luscious mouth, a loud knock broke through their daze of lust. Kimber pulled away. Panting, she rested her head on his shoulder. "I'm busy here. Come back." Throttle placed his hand behind her head, securing her against him.

"Need your help in front. Patrick's gone on break, and I'm up to my balls in work that's gotta get finished today," Dwayne said gruffly.

"Fuck," Throttle muttered under his breath before calling out, "I'll be there in a couple minutes."

"Just hurry it up." His retreating footsteps oozed in through the crack under the office door.

Kimber broke away from Throttle and smoothed her hair down, mumbling, "It was a mistake. Sorry."

"A mistake? There's no way that was a fuckin' mistake, sweetheart. We both been wanting that for a while."

"Speak for yourself," she said as she finger-combed her hair.

He gripped her wrists and turned her to face him. "You gonna look me in the eye and tell me you didn't want me to kiss you?"

With a downward glance, she shrugged one shoulder.

"Damn, you're a piece of work. You can't even admit you wanted and enjoyed our kiss? Shit, babe. You been eye-fucking me for the past several days, and you know it."

She raised her eyes, anger flashing in them. "So what? You're a good-looking guy and I was curious. You don't have to act like it's anything more."

"You can act like it was no big deal, but I know chicks, and sweetheart, you loved it. You'll be back for seconds. I can guarantee it."

She narrowed her eyes. "It's too bad I'm not the betting type. I could use the money." She pushed past him, flung open the door, and stormed off.

Throttle guffawed, wanting her to hear how he didn't give a shit if she wanted more or not. He didn't waste time chasing chicks. The only reason he'd even consider a second round with the smart-assed mechanic was because he wanted to nail her. He didn't like giving chicks the upper hand. He'd show Miss Know-It-All that he couldn't care less about her. He gave her a week max before she came crawling back, begging for him in her pussy.

"You comin' out?" Dwayne said.

"Yeah!" Throttle picked up the iridescent skull that Kimber had forgotten to take and slipped it in his pocket. She'd need him sooner than he thought. He shoved his hands in his pockets and walked to the front of the store.

The rest of the morning, Throttle waited on customers and finished inputting the numbers into the inventory software. Kimber stayed in the service garage, sending Jorge, one of the technicians, to retrieve the hood ornament from Throttle. He didn't want to admit he was disappointed that she was hiding out from him. He knew she felt the charge between them. She was the most stubborn and infuriating woman he'd ever met. Why couldn't she give in to the feelings that were coursing through her body? The way she kissed and pressed herself against him showed she was hot for him, and he was cool with that because he was hot for her. So what was her fucking problem? He knew later on, in the quiet of the night as he lay on his bed watching the clouds skate across the moon, he'd remember the feel and taste of her. *Fuck! This woman is screwing with my head. Damn!*

His phone rang and he answered it, grateful for taking his thoughts off her. It was Rags telling him that one of the guys became ill in the heat and had to leave. Throttle told him he'd be there shortly, as soon as Hawk returned.

As soon as he hung up, Hawk walked in. "Hey, man. How much headway did you make with recording the inventory?"

"Finished it. Rags just called, said one of our guys went home sick. I gotta go. I'll catch you later."

"Thanks, man."

Throttle swung his leg over his Harley and turned the switch, making his favorite lady come to life. He adjusted his sunglasses and made a U-turn in the parking lot. When he drove past the shop, he spotted Kimber standing by the window, peeking out at him. Satisfaction radiated throughout his body, and his lips curled into a cocky smile. He revved his engine and blended into the traffic, confident that he'd be between the sexy mechanic's legs in less than a week.

CHAPTER EIGHT

DETECTIVE MCCUE GLANCED over at the petite, dark brunette who stared at the ground, her nose dripping. He exhaled. At times like that, he hated his job, despised the broken pieces the bad guy left, expecting the justice system to put them back together. The investigator glanced down at his notepad. The woman's name was Sela Ramirez and she was twenty-five years old. The one-bedroom house was the first place she'd ever lived alone. She had a good job at an accounting firm, made a nice salary, was pretty, and should've been having the time of her life, not sitting on her chintz sofa staring at the ground as a team of law officers swarmed around.

McCue trudged over. "Miss Ramirez? I'm Detective McCue, and I have a few questions I need to ask you. May I sit down?" No reaction. He slumped down in a straight-back chair near the sofa. He pushed a couple tissues into her hand, and the touch of his hand against hers appeared to have startled her. She whimpered, her brown eyes searching his face. He smiled faintly, flipped open his notebook, and uncapped his pen.

After a tearful, stammering rendition of the chain of events that brought McCue to the victim's home, he stood, thanked her, and went over to the crime scene investigator. "Did you get anything?"

The lanky man smiled, pushed his glasses up the bridge of his nose, and nodded. "A few drops of semen near her bed. I can't be sure it's the intruder's, but we finally have something concrete."

McCue's eyes lit up for the first time since he'd arrived. He thumbed through his notes. "I'm damn certain it's the perp's semen. The victim said he jerked off into her yellow lace panties while she lay tied up and duct taped on the bed. According to her, she hasn't been intimate with any man in her house since she moved in eight months ago." Elation spread through the room, and a thread of hope that the perpetrator's DNA would be in the database weaved its way around the crime team. "Do your magic," McCue said to the CSI, "and let me know the minute the tests are done."

As he left the house, he glanced over at the victim; she rested her head against her hand as a victim advocate spoke softly to her. He walked out into the bright sunshine and pervasive heat. The perp was a cruel, depraved sonofabitch who had to be stopped before he did more than take pictures, jerk off, and steal the women's bras and panties. A funny feeling twisted around his gut; the intruder left evidence, which meant he was becoming sloppy. Sloppiness usually indicated tension and frustration on the part of the criminal. The twisting inside him told the seasoned detective that his perp was growing bored with his usual antics. That concept turned his blood to ice. They had to find the sociopath before his actions escalated to the next level. So far, the women had been degraded, mentally and emotionally traumatized, but he hadn't exhibited any violence toward them.

McCue tightened his grip on the steering wheel as he pulled away from the curb, his gaze sweeping over the small group of people who gathered on the sidewalk. He wondered if one of them was the intruder. Another twist in his gut.

The man had to be caught… and soon.

"HAVE YOU MADE the trip arrangements for the motorcycle expo at the coliseum in Denver?" Banger asked.

"Yeah. I secured all the tickets, hotels, and contacted our charter to see if they could put up some of the single men. We're good to go." Throttle leaned back in his chair. The motorcycle expo was one of the biggest in the Rocky Mountains, and it attracted biker aficionados as well as clubs, both mainstream and one-percenters. Each year, several

Insurgents would ride down to Denver to attend the event. The collection of bikes, the gear, the custom jobs, and the newest models was something most of the members didn't want to miss, even though the Sturgis rally was coming up fast. In the past thirty years, there had been major tension between the Insurgents and the Deadly Demons, but now that there was a truce, the expo and Sturgis were a lot calmer, at least for the Rocky Mountain clubs. Most of the time, the rival clubs exchanged glares and scowls, but everyone pretty much stayed away from one another.

"That's good. It'll be a kick-ass time. This year most of the old ladies will be comin', and some of the brothers are bringing their girlfriends, so we gotta be on high alert. We don't want anything happening to the women." Banger took a gulp of beer and pointed to his vice president. "Hawk's gonna take it from here."

"I got a call from Steel, and he's have a fuckin' bad time with that goddamned brat club, the Skull Crushers. You remember the three punks who tried to deal meth on our turf a while back?"

Several grumblings and curse words filtered among the membership. "They must be causing all kinds of hell, 'cause Steel isn't the type to ask for our help," Jerry said.

Steel was the president of the Night Rebels, an Insurgents affiliate in southern Colorado. He, Hawk, and Throttle went way back from the time they all joined. Steel had started out as an Insurgent but had to head back to his hometown, Alina, in southwestern Colorado to take care of his sick mom. Missing the camaraderie of the brotherhood, he contacted Banger and Hawk, and the Night Rebels sprung up as a support club to the Insurgents. The two clubs had a clandestine relationship, and the Night Rebels operated under the control of the Insurgents, although, to the public and law enforcement, they appeared to be a separate club.

"We need to help 'em out. What does Steel want?"

"He wants to know if we're down to kick some Skull Crushers' asses if they don't heed his warning and quit selling smack and crystal on

Night Rebels turf. Since we get a percentage of all monies collected at the club's dispensary, the fuckers are also selling on Insurgents' turf. Again."

"Don't these fuckers ever learn? You'd think that, after we eliminated some of their members last summer, they'd fuckin' get that we mean business. These punks are dumber than shit," Chas said.

"Agreed. We just need to take a vote on whether we're gonna haul our asses down to help our affiliate brothers."

The consensus was unanimous—help the Night Rebels stamp out the new club in town who didn't give a shit about respect or rules. After church was over, the brothers shuffled into the great room to down a few drinks, play pool, and enjoy the club whores. Throttle sat at one of the tables, a bottle of beer in front of him, as he surveyed the room. Rags was practically buried in Wendy's pussy and Rock sat on a chair, his knees spread wide to give Rosie the access he wanted while his fingers played with her swaying tits.

Throttle leaned back, his hands laced together on top of his head, and realized he hadn't fucked a woman in nearly three weeks. That was a record for him. The closest he'd come to fucking was when he'd kissed that smart-ass witch at Hawk's shop. He hadn't been to the VP's shop in over a week, and he was surprised he hadn't heard from Miss Know-It-All. Maybe she was getting it from the cowboy; that thought made him madder than hell. Not too sure why, because he'd decided he didn't need to put up with her shit. He'd only wanted to try her out, but he had no interest in her other than another fuck to add to his overflowing list. Hell, he could fuck the club girls anytime he wanted—and he usually did—although he hadn't wanted to for the last few weeks.

Throttle grabbed his beer and guzzled it. He and Rags had been killing themselves working in the hot sun for ten hours a day. When he got back to the club, he was beat. *Anyone would be.* He stared at Rags as he pounded into Wendy's heat. *Rags is younger than I am. He's twenty-nine to my thirty-five. Each year makes a big difference.* It was funny that a month before he'd been able to fuck three club whores and still be up for a foursome romp with Rock. But then it wasn't as hot outside a month before. That was it. He was sure of it.

"Why aren't you getting in on some fun?" Jerry asked as he sat down next to Throttle. "Isn't this your scene?"

"I'm beat. Working in the heat is a bitch."

"Never seemed to bother you before."

"Well, today it is. Are you taking notes on who's fuckin' since you can't do it with anyone but Kylie now?" He was sick of Jerry's stupid questions. Couldn't he be tired? *Shit, I need to get my own place.*

Jerry laughed. "I don't give a damn who's banging who. I'm so happy with Kylie. I still can't believe she's all mine."

"Glad your fuckin' Pollyanna dreams came true." He finished his beer and saw Hawk coming over to him. He wanted to ask about Kimber, but he wouldn't dare. Since the day they'd shared the searing kiss, he'd wanted to drive by the shop to see if he could catch a glimpse of her. Pissed for even thinking of doing a pansy-assed stunt like that, he forced himself not to go near Hawk's shop. But at night, when he drifted to sleep, his dreams were filled with her softness, her scent, and the taste of her mouth.

"I haven't seen you at the shop this past week. Have you already lost interest in Kimber?" Hawk chuckled then downed his shot of Jack.

Throttle stiffened. "We've had a lot of gigs, and I've never been fuckin' interested in her."

"Could've fooled me." Hawk's blue eyes twinkled, mocking Throttle. A slow burn rode up his spine.

"Who's Kimber? I thought a chick was behind your sulking," Jerry said.

"She works at the shop. She's one of my best mechanics."

"Isn't she the one you were spastic about?" Jerry looked at Throttle, who stared straight ahead, his jaw taut. "Can't say I blame you. I can't wrap my head around a chick fixing my Harley."

"Don't let Kylie hear you say that or she'll rip your ass." Hawk threw back another shot. "Come to think of it, Cara would too. You do know my woman is Kylie's mentor, right?"

Jerry groaned. "Just fuckin' great."

Throttle pushed his chair back and stood up. "I gotta go."

"Didn't mean to drive you out," Hawk said.

"You didn't." He stomped out, slamming the door behind him. As he sat on his bike, breathing heavily, his phone beeped. He looked down and saw it was his sister, Dawn.

Dawn: *Whatcha doing?*

Throttle: *Not much. Y?*

Dawn: *A big spider in the basement.*

He laughed aloud, glad his sister's paranoia cut through his anger.

Throttle: *Where's Pedro?*

Dawn: *Out on his ass.*

Throttle: *Already?*

Dawn: *Shoulda done it sooner. Olivia says hi.*

His sister played the Olivia card whenever she wanted him over right away. She knew Throttle adored his eight-year-old niece. He was like a surrogate father to her since her own dad disappeared once Dawn had told him she was pregnant. The douche was a tourist staying at the Hot Springs Hotel the summer Dawn had worked there. They'd had a two-week affair, and then he'd gone back to Phoenix, promising to call her, only he never did. When she'd found out she was carrying his child, she'd reached out to him but he'd shut her out—changed his phone number, moved from his old address, and shut down all social media. So Throttle had stepped in, and he'd tried to be there for her whenever he could.

Throttle: *Leaving the clubhouse now. See u in a few.*

The Harley jumped forward and headed out the parking lot. He took a shortcut to his sister's house and came up the alley, parking his bike in her backyard. The neighborhood was an up and coming one, but there were still enough worn houses with overgrown weeds to classify the area as shabby. He'd told Dawn many times that he wanted to buy her and Olivia a nicer house in a better neighborhood, but she told him she didn't want his handouts. Throttle was determined to move them out and place Olivia in a private school. The girl was very smart, and he sensed she was bored with her current classes.

Before he could get off his bike, a girl with long brown braids, dark almond-shaped eyes, and a wide grin came barreling to him. "Uncle Throttle," she said. She flung herself at his open arms and he easily picked her up, her small arms clinging around his neck. "Why haven't you been over to see me? Do you know it's been over ten days since you came over here?"

"You sound just like your mom. And I'm sorry. I've been so busy that I lost track of time."

"Don't do that again, okay?"

He laughed. "Okay. I hear you got a badass spider hanging out in the basement."

She nodded. "You gonna catch it?"

He shook his head. "Nope."

"Mom's gonna be mad at you if you don't. She's been real scared and won't let me go downstairs."

"I'm gonna kill the fucker. You wanna help me?"

She shook her head. "I'll wait upstairs for you."

He kissed her cheek before he planted her on her feet. "Let's go."

Twenty minutes and one less spider later, Throttle sat on his sister's couch drinking a beer and watching Olivia play a video game with rainbows, ponies, and a shimmering princess. She was damn good at finding the princess's jewels and hiding them from the ogre who was always trying to steal them. Her small fingers worked the control like a pro, and whenever she secured a jewel she'd turn to him and smile.

Dawn came in and sat on the other side of the couch. She lit a cigarette, inhaling deeply. "Guess who I bumped into yesterday at the Stop and Shop Market."

He shrugged, his eyes glued on the princess in the tower.

"Mariah."

He turned his head sharply. "Mariah?"

"Yep. She's back in town. She came up to me. I didn't even see her. I was looking for a bag of Cheetos, and she called my name. At first it didn't register that it was her, and then I recognized her."

Throttle took a gulp of beer. What the fuck was Mariah doing back in town after all this time?

"The first thing she did was ask about you. Wanted to know if you were married or had a girlfriend."

He snorted and leaned back as an image from deep in his past surfaced: a pretty brunette with hazel eyes smiling at him.

"I told her you were having too much fun. She seemed happy that you didn't have anyone special in your life."

Kimber's blue piercing eyes and jet-black hair dipped in pink replaced the image from his past. Every time he thought of a woman, Kimber would wiggle into his brain; it was like her image was burned on it, branding him.

He felt a small yank on his jeans and he looked down to see Olivia's small hand pulling on them. "Did you see me get the tiara? That's the best of the princess's jewels."

He leaned down and gently tugged one of her braids. "I did. You kicked that green dude's ass."

She giggled. "He's called an ogre." He smiled at her.

"Anyway, she told me to tell you hi and that she'll be in town for some time," Dawn said, refocusing him back to her.

"So?"

"I think she wants to see you."

He narrowed his eyes. "I don't have any interest in seeing her. That was all in the past."

"But it couldn't—"

"Leave it alone, Dawn. This conversation is over."

She closed her mouth and shook her head. "You can be so stubborn."

He shrugged. "Whatever."

After Olivia made it through ten levels, the princess was finally free and the green ogre was banished from the kingdom. She set down her control and crawled up next to Throttle. As she curled up beside him, the front doorbell rang, and Dawn went to answer it. Olivia looked up at Throttle. "I'm sure it's Ella. She's my friend and she's sleeping over."

"That sounds like fun."

"Olivia," a small voice called from behind them.

Olivia leapt up from the couch and rushed over to her friend. Throttle rose and saw a blonde girl about Olivia's age with freckles and cornflower-blue eyes standing by a woman who wore shorts and a scooped neck T-shirt that showed off her nice cleavage. Throttle's gaze lingered on her chest and Dawn cleared her throat. "Throttle, this is Ella's mom, Clarisse. This is my brother, Throttle."

Throttle jerked his head back. "Hey."

The woman boldly ran her eyes over his toned body, her gaze eventually landing on his. "Hey," she breathed.

"I gotta go, sis. I'll call you about the three of us going out to dinner next week." He pulled his niece to him and hugged her. "Can you fit your uncle into your busy social schedule?"

"Oh, Uncle Throttle." She laughed and hugged him back.

"I take it that's a yes?"

She bobbed her head up and down.

"Do you have to leave so soon?" Clarisse asked.

He scanned her curvy body, loving the way her big tits strained across her top. He could have her legs spread and his cock inside her, pounding away, in a matter of minutes, but he wasn't interested. He didn't want a complication like her; he was better off with the club girls. But for right then, he didn't want any of them. He *did* want a small-titted smart aleck who had a great pair of legs and an ass he needed to fuck. *Go figure.*

He saw the hopeful gleam in Clarisse's eyes. "Yeah, I gotta go. I'll call you," he said to his sister. Olivia had already disappeared to her room with Ella. He jumped down the concrete steps and settled on his bike. He shifted on the seat. He was horny as hell and this bullshit of not getting laid in three weeks was driving him crazy. Maybe he should make it with the sex-starved housewife. He needed something... *someone*. Pressing his lips together, he decided to go back to the clubhouse and see who struck his dick. He had to exorcize the sassy-mouthed woman who'd cast some crazy-ass spell over him. Never had he cared about any woman since Mariah, and now this kooky woman who worked as a mechanic and had pink streaks in her hair invaded his mind and body. He exhaled. *Damn. I gotta fuck Rosie and Lola.*

He accelerated sharply, smirking when he spotted Clarisse standing on the porch, disappointment carved on her face. He turned the corner and never looked back.

CHAPTER NINE

A S HE CAME to the stop sign on Adams Street, he saw a woman in jean shorts who looked mighty damn fine. Glancing to the left, he saw a pink metallic Harley parked in the driveway of the woman's small bungalow. His gaze darted back to the woman watering flowers in front of her porch then he noticed pink tips brushing against the curve of her neck as they fell from her messy bun. Without hesitation, he made a U-turn into her driveway. Crossing his arms, he sat on the idling bike, knowing the hum of the motor would draw her attention.

She turned slightly, then placed her fingers over her mouth when recognition set in. They stared at each other for several seconds, and then she walked over to the side of her porch and turned off the hose. He killed the engine. Standing by her porch, her hand shielding the western sun from her eyes, she quirked her lips. "You stalking me?"

He climbed off his bike and leaned against it, his ankles crossed, his tanned arms made darker by the sunlight, and slowly took off his sunglasses. "A guy's got to be interested in a chick to stalk her."

"How do you know where I live?"

"I didn't. My sister lives a couple blocks away on Madison. Spotting you in your sexy shorts was just luck." He threw his best panty-melting smile—lopsided and smug.

She came closer, her hands pulling down her shorts. He had to laugh at the way she seemed so self-conscious. Her usual confidence seemed to have taken a backseat at that moment, and he loved that he was having an effect on her. It seemed fair since she'd been having an effect on him since the day he'd met her.

"I don't think you pulling your shorts down is gonna make them longer. Seems like the only thing you're gonna accomplish is pulling them down and giving me a glimpse of your sweet heat."

She gasped, but she didn't stomp away or wag her finger at him. *Yeah, she likes my dirty mouth. And my mouth can't wait to taste her all over.* "You got something cold to drink inside?"

"Yeah, but maybe I don't want you inside my house."

His gaze was riveted on her face, then moved over her body slowly and seductively. "You want me inside."

"Do I?" she asked playfully, glancing at him.

He slowly nodded, chuckling inwardly when color stained her cheeks under the heat of his gaze. He pushed away from his Harley, came up to her, and brushed away the tendrils from her face. Under his touch, he felt her shudder.

She looked away hastily, then cleared her throat. "I got some beer." Kimber moved away from him and sprinted to her porch.

Throttle glanced around the small living and dining room, liking the way she'd decorated it with punches of bold pinks, blues, and purples. The in-your-face color scheme and acrylic paintings adorning the walls reflected her personality, and he liked how she'd pulled it all together. "You did a nice job with your place."

"Thanks," she said over her shoulder as she rifled through the refrigerator.

"You like living in the neighborhood?"

"It wouldn't be my first choice if I had any money, but since I'm on a shoestring, it'll do. Some of the neighbors are sketchy, but I keep to myself most of the time. Where do you live?"

"At the club."

"Really? How long have you been doing that?" She set down a bottle of Coors and a bowl of pretzels on the coffee table.

"I've been living there since I patched in when I was twenty. So 'bout fifteen years."

"Wow. Don't you get tired of living in one room and having all those people around you all the time?"

He crunched on a few pretzels, then washed them down with a gulp of beer. "Not really. There are advantages to having some of the people around all the time."

"I bet. I know all about the free sex you guys have."

"Do you? Did you learn about it through TV shows or the one-sided documentaries the fuckin' FBI puts out?"

"Neither. I dated a biker. I was his ol' lady." She leaned back on the couch and stared at him.

His eyes bulged; he was caught off guard by her sudden revelation. "Fuck. I didn't know you were a biker's bitch."

"If I didn't know better, I'd be offended by your choice of words." She smiled and it melted over him. "That was a while ago. Me and leather dudes don't mix so well."

"I don't know about that." He reached out and placed his hand on hers. "We seemed to have mixed pretty well that day at the shop."

She exhaled and shook her head. "See, that's what I'm talking about. You bikers are all alike. None of you can see a woman as just a person. It's always about sex. It drives me crazy."

"Don't think it's only bikers, babe. It's all men. We're just wired differently. We see a hot babe and we want in. If she's cool with it, then what's the problem?"

"It just seems like you guys magnify the battle of the sexes by a million percent. Anyway, I've had my fill of the brotherhood."

"Have you?" He gently stroked the back of her hand with his finger.

Looking down and back up, she boldly met his gaze. "Yes."

He pulled his hand away. "Which club did your old man ride with?"

"The Demon Riders."

His face grew taut. "Which chapter?"

"Iowa."

His face darkened. It was the chapter Dustin and Shack—the Insurgents renegades—had joined up with after Banger ordered their charter club in Nebraska closed for not following the Insurgents MC's bylaws. "Do you have any contact with him?"

"Nah. I ran away from him when he wasn't around. He doesn't know where I am. Probably doesn't give a shit anyway."

"A man having his old lady leave him always gives a shit. He loses face with the brothers. Why'd you split?"

"The cheating, the stealing, the all-night partying, the lack of employment, the fists to my face—take your pick." She stood up. "You want another beer?"

"Yeah. The fucker hit you? What a fuckin' pussy."

"My sentiments exactly," she said as she took two beers from the refrigerator. "It's in the past now. I'm so over it." She gave him the beer and sat back down.

"You not wanting to go out with another biker means you're not as over it as you think. Fuck, baby. I pegged you as a biker chick when I saw you. You going out with a damn cowboy is crazy. You got the leather and denim in your blood. I see it in your eyes when you look at me."

She laughed. "You are persuasive, I'll give you that. Let's cut through the bullshit, okay? You know you're damn good-looking, and I'm sure I'm not the first woman to tell you that. I'd think you're good-looking with or without the leather. Being a biker is the turn-off. I'm done with that way of life."

"You letting one fuckin' asshole turn you off of all of us?"

"Try several fuckin' assholes." She grimaced. "You were right—I *was* a biker chick."

Silence spread between them, and all he could think about was how beautiful she looked with the early evening's glow washing over her. He wanted to take her in his arms and kiss her hard, fuck her harder, and dispel all hurts and memories of the goddamned Demon Rider. If he ever ran into him, he'd beat the shit out of him. Maybe even kill him for striking her. He reached over and grabbed her hand, bringing it to his lips and kissing it. When his gaze met hers, the arousal in them lit him on fire. In one smooth movement, he had her pressed to him, his mouth ravaging hers as he held her tight.

She pulled away, and the fire in him burned fiercely as he took in her swollen lips and smoldering eyes. "I need you bad, babe," he said.

Without a word, she grasped his hand and stood, taking him with her. She shuffled to a room in the back of the house. When they entered, his gaze landed on the bed, and the current they had between them exploded. He swung her to him and she jumped up, hooking her legs around his waist before he rushed forward, slamming her against the wall as his mouth assaulted her neck with hard, biting kisses—the kind that left deep red marks for days. She clawed his back through his thin T-shirt, and Throttle was sure she was shredding it with each rake of her nails. His cock was granite—harder than it'd been for quite a while—and he needed to shove it inside her before he exploded.

Running his hands through her hair, he gripped it firmly with his fingers and pulled her head back. "I'm gonna fuck your pussy rough and hard, and you're gonna fuckin' love it," he murmured against her mouth before he took her bottom lip and sucked it. Each moan that came from her, he swallowed, his fingers digging into her smooth, toned thighs. Her hot skin quivered beneath his touch, and he had to have it right at that moment before his cock erupted.

He carried her to the bed and pushed her down, then yanked his T-shirt over his head. When he'd kicked his boots off and threw off his jeans and boxers, he stared down at her, loving the way her body rose and fell with her panting. "Take your fuckin' top off."

Kimber complied and she lay back down, her black hair spreading around her head like spilled ink. He whistled under his breath and cupped her breasts in his hands. They fit with some room to spare and he squeezed and pinched them, pulling at her rosy nipples until they were hard. Fuck, he loved the sight of hard nipples on tits, and hers were the perkiest he'd ever seen. He sucked one hard bud into his mouth while his hands shoved down her shorts and panties. Normally, he'd admire her nakedness but for a small bit of fabric covering her pussy, but he didn't have time for that right then; he wanted her naked so he could feel their skin fused together.

As he bent over, sucking her tits and squeezing her inner thighs, a sting of pain then pleasure coursed through him. He looked down at her and she smiled wickedly at him as she bit his shoulder again. "You love rough fuckin'. I knew you were a hot one."

"Yeah. The rougher the better."

"Fuck, baby. I'm gonna blow before I even get into your wet pussy."

"Then you better hurry the hell up."

"Don't you like me sucking your tits?"

She nodded. "But I also like this...." She ran her hands along his broad shoulders. "And this...." She squeezed his taut biceps, then traced the tattoos with her fingernail. "And I love this." She circled her hand tightly around his pulsing cock.

Fuck! "Get on all fours. Now." He had to see her sweet ass as he plunged into her.

Kimber kneeled and he pushed her down to the mattress, making her luscious ass rise up. And she did have a tempting one, just like he'd imagined: round, creamy globes begging to be smacked, a small puckered opening inviting a good fucking. Rubbing his hands all over her ass cheeks, he lowered his head and bit them hard. She yelped and he rubbed the red area, peppering it with light kisses. "You like that?" he said against her skin. Her moan was her only answer.

He placed his finger against her opening and ran his other hand down her ass to her slick pussy. Slipping between her folds, he played with her clit while she whimpered and writhed against the mattress. "Feels so damn good," her muffled voice said.

"You're so wet for me, babe. I can't stand it. Before I push my cock in you, I need a taste." He pulled back and spread her knees wider apart, her dripping heat splayed open before him. With a long sweep, his tongue stroked her from the tip of her clit to her rounded cheeks. In response, she lifted her hips and pushed back against him.

"Fuck me. I'm on the pill. You clean?"

"Yeah. I always use a condom. You sure you want it raw?"

"You don't?" she panted.

"Fuck yeah." He hadn't done it unprotected since he'd walked away from a bad relationship many years ago.

"What the hell are you waiting for?" she nagged.

He chuckled. "Damn, you want it bad" He couldn't wait a second longer. Covering his dick in her arousal, he shoved it in, her cry of pleasure the best fucking music to his ears. Then he rode her, faster and faster. The harder he pummeled her heated core, the louder she screamed, "More!" until she stiffened then let out a yell which bounced off the walls and filled his ears, his dick, his body. With a grunt, he shot his hot seed in her tight heat as she panted into the pillow, the sheet crumpled in her fists. He kissed the back of her neck and crashed on the mattress, taking her with him. She fit perfectly under the crook of his arm, and he loved the way her damp arm felt on his sweaty chest.

"Fuck. That was hot." He kissed the top of her head.

"I fuckin' needed that." She brushed a kiss on his chest.

They held each other as the setting sun dyed the sky pomegranate pink. After a long while, he asked, "You up for round two?"

She tilted her head back and with a devilish smile plastered on her face, said, "Bring it on."

CHAPTER TEN

THROUGH THE WHITE blinds, lemony bars of sun slanted across the hardwood floor as Kimber cracked open her sleep-blurred eyes. At first she was disoriented, her eyes scanning the room, but then she heard him breathe and panic set in. Flung across her stomach, his arm pinned her to the bed, and she tried to slide out from under it without any luck. She turned and watched him, and he was gorgeous as he slept, his face peaceful with wisps of hair across his cheeks. His strong jaw was somewhat softened by his slumber, and his lips—oh, those wicked lips— were slightly parted, as though they waited for her tongue to enter. She wanted to sweep away the tendrils of hair and feel his rough stubble against her fingertips. He was an incredible lover, and she couldn't believe she'd let him fuck her brains out for the better part of the night.

She turned away and focused on the dust particles in the sunlight as they flitted about. A knot formed in the pit of her stomach as the enormity of what she'd done weighed down on her. *Really, Kimber? Another biker? Fuck. Why didn't you resist him?* But how could she have ever resisted him? He was all man—raw and powerful—and she'd been screwed the first day she'd met him at Hawk's shop. She'd been drawn to him, fluttering right to the center of his flame even though she'd pretended nonchalance. And ever since they'd kissed for the first time, a deep, slow burn had started inside her, making her yearn for him on the long summer nights until she'd almost relented and sought him out.

Then he was in her driveway, looking way too sexy in his tight jeans and sleeveless tee, his tattoos beckoning her to touch and lick them. When he'd pulled her to him on the couch, a blind passion like a fire swept over her, and she knew there was no way in hell she could stop.

The previous night, he'd awakened a desire in her she never knew existed. Their fucking was better than she'd imagined. She sighed. Continuing with Throttle wasn't an option; she'd be a goddamned fool if she did, knowing the biker lifestyle. And she was pretty damn sure Throttle was very popular with the club women and hang-arounds who were voracious for biker cock. Kimber didn't want to fall for the dangerous man who slept so peacefully beside her. She'd run away from the craziness of the brotherhood, and she had no intention of jumping back into the boiling water.

She carefully lifted his arm and shimmied out from under it, then tiptoed to the bathroom to wash up. After she slipped on a gauze sundress, she closed her bedroom door and went to the kitchen to have a glass of orange juice. In the bright light of the morning, she realized she'd made a mistake that she would never repeat, even though she didn't regret her night with Throttle.

She placed two pieces of buttered bread in her toaster oven and pushed down the lever, thinking maybe she should wake him up; she definitely didn't want him to hang around. She wasn't in the mood for chit chats, and knowing his sexual appetite, he'd probably want seconds. *That* was something she didn't want to give.

Leaning on her white tile counter, her elbows propped on it with her chin on her hand, she watched as the neighborhood woke up: kids riding their bicycles, mothers pushing strollers, vehicles backing out of garages, and service trucks searching for addresses. His familiar scent of soap, leather, and expensive whiskey caressed her before he encircled her waist and placed a kiss on the back of her neck. "Morning." His voice was like molten lava, scorching her.

Don't even think *it, Kimber.* "Morning," she answered, pushing away from the counter and him. "You want some orange juice?" She scooted over to the refrigerator to create some distance from him.

He swept his eyes over her face, a scowl threatening to form. "Sure." She filled a glass and plunked it on the table, then leaned against the stove, her arms crossed over her chest. "What the fuck's going on with you?" he asked.

Exhaling, she uncrossed her arms and fixed her gaze on his. "Last night was an awesome mistake. Awesome because you totally know how to fuck a woman, but a mistake 'cause I'm not looking for anything right now. I know we've had this lust thing going on between us, and we took care of that last night real good...." She laughed nervously.

Throttle's expression tightened and his flinty stare unnerved her. She picked at a mosquito bite on her arm. "I'm trying to finish school, save money, and start my own business. I don't have time for—"

"I never do seconds with citizens. I'm glad you're not the clinging type. A one-night fuck suits me just fine." His curt voice lashed at her.

She swallowed the small lump forming in her throat and placed two pieces of bread on a stoneware plate. "I made you some toast." She handed it to him.

"I don't eat toast." His icy voice chilled her. "I'm outta here." Without a good-bye, he marched out of her house and slammed her screen door. She rushed over and watched him through the mesh as he sped away on his Harley. The prickly heat filtered in through the screen door and she closed it.

Don't you dare cry. This is what you wanted. They'd shared an incredible night together, satisfying the lust they'd harbored since they met. It was finished, and it was time to get back on track. Everything turned out the way she wanted it to, but why was she so miserable right then? Her phone alarm rang and she realized she was going to be late for class. Rushing to the kitchen, she poured his untouched orange juice down the sink and threw away the toast. She wiped down the counters, grabbed her books and keys, and made her way to her afternoon classes.

As fast as she rode, she still ended up being ten minutes late to her business class. Professor Redman stopped mid-sentence and pressed his lips into a white slash when she came in. Red stained her cheeks, and she shuffled over to a seat in the back of the classroom. Opening her laptop, she hid her face behind the screen. After a few seconds, the professor continued where he left off.

Kimber was lucky to have been able to be in Professor Redman's course. He was head of the business department at the college and was an esteemed academic. He'd written numerous books on a gamut of business-related subjects, and he was an in-demand national lecturer. The prof was by far the best teacher she'd ever had, and his class was one of her favorites.

While she typed copious notes, her phone vibrated. She glanced at it and saw she'd received a text message. For one brief second, she held her breath, hoping it was Throttle; then she remembered he didn't ask for her phone number, and disappointment set in. She looked at the sender—Riley. There was no way she was going to open it with Professor Redman already annoyed at her for being late. Slipping her phone in her backpack, she focused on the rest of the lecture.

After class, she sat at a table in the student center and opened Riley's text.

Riley: *It's been too long. U wanna go for dinner?*

Ever since she and Throttle had kissed at the shop, she'd pushed Riley away. It wasn't like they had anything going between them. He seemed nice enough, but he wasn't her type. She didn't feel anything even remotely like the electric charge that sizzled between her and Throttle whenever they saw each other. She supposed she was hopeless, destined to be mistreated by the bad boys instead of cherished by the good ones.

Kimber: *Been busy. Tonight won't work. Don't want to lead u on, but too busy for anything other than studying and working right now.*

Riley: *U gotta eat. Right?*

Kimber: *Too busy for that too. Frozen or takeout while I study.*

Riley: *So u don't want to go out with me?*

Kimber: *Not looking for anything with a man right now. U're nice. U can find another girl.*

Riley: *I want u. I always get what I want.*

Kimber reread the text a couple times. *Wow, he's starting to sound kind of creepy. Time to sign off.*

Kimber: *Gotta go to class.*

Maybe Riley wasn't such a nice guy. The guy did give off weird vibes. When they'd gone on their second and last date, he kept asking her what she was wearing under her clothes. It was like he wanted her to engage in some kinky talk by describing her underwear, and they were only on their second date. Although, she'd fucked herself to exhaustion the previous night with Throttle and they hadn't even gone out on a date. She groaned. *That's it. I'm done with* all *men until I'm out of school and have my own business.* But damn, she couldn't deny the pull that connected her and Throttle; it was something she'd never felt with any man before.

Later that night, she closed her laptop, rubbing her sore eyes. She'd studied too much and her mind was foggy; it was time to call it quits. Grabbing an ice-cold root beer, she popped the top and took a long, refreshing drink. The TV blinked on and she channel surfed for a while as she tried to quell the restlessness growing inside her. Even though she hated to admit it, she wished Throttle were with her, but he was probably fucking some slut at the club. She knew bikers, and *everything* for them was for the moment: the booze, the ride, and the women. Throttle was no different than any of the others. Maybe he wouldn't smack her around like her old man had done, but she knew he'd carouse and cherish his brothers more than he would any woman. It wasn't for her. Not at all. When she decided to get involved with a man, she'd want someone she could trust and respect. Having her old man cheat on her and seeing the brothers fool around with the club women behind their old ladies' backs had disgusted her. She wasn't a glutton for punishment.

Kimber finished her root beer and stared at the TV screen, not really seeing it. A big grin danced across her face when snippets of the previous night flashed in her mind. *Damn, the man could fuck!* Content to relive the best banging she'd ever had in her mind, she propped her legs up on the coffee table, leaned her head back on the cushion, and closed her eyes. She could survive on the memories of his touch, his kisses, his thrusting dick and forget him if he would just stay the hell out of the shop. And if she didn't make excuses to see him.

Yeah. Fat chance.

CHAPTER ELEVEN

THE STENCH OF the weed killer permeated Throttle's nose as it soaked through his shirt. Flinging the stainless steel tank off his back, he whipped off his shirt, his back glistening from the chemicals. "Fuck!" He kicked the tank with his boot, grabbed the sledgehammer lying on the grass, and struck the leaking tank over and over, his face red and contorted.

"What the fuck, bro?" Rags said as he came over to his partner. "You're gonna destroy the tank, and they're fucking expensive to replace."

Through his panting, Throttle said, "I don't give a shit. We just got this fucker fixed a week ago and it's leaking again. It got all over my shirt and jeans. I'm bathing in weed killer. Fuck!" The tank had dents all over it as Throttle continued to assault it.

When he was finished, he wiped his sweaty face and neck with his bandana, went over to the cooler in the bed of the truck, took out a gallon jug of water, and poured it over his head. Grabbing another jug, he chugged some of it down and poured the rest on him.

"You cooled off now?" Rags asked.

"Not really, but it felt good to beat the shit outta the metal fucker."

Squinting, Rags leaned against the truck. "We gotta buy a new one since we're down to one and we have the big job at the Landley Estate next week."

"Then we'll get another one. Quit acting like a whiny pussy about it." He grabbed a bottle of iced tea from the cooler. "You want one?"

Rags shook his head. "You gonna tell me what the fuck's going on with you?"

"I don't like taking chemical baths. Nothing more." His jaw hardened.

"You been ripping everyone's head off for the last few days. You even got in a customer's face yesterday when he told us we planted the tree in the wrong place." Rags held up his hand as if to silence Throttle. "I know, he told us one place and he changed his mind, but the point is you've never flipped out on a customer like you did yesterday. Again, what the fuck's with you?"

"It's just been damn hot, and all these people are getting on my nerves big time. It's nothing more."

"Really, 'cause I've never seen you like this. I've seen you pissed, but it's usually been warranted. You've been a royal pain in the ass to be around."

Throttle gave Rags a hard, cold stare. "Enough. I said nothing's wrong, so leave it alone."

Rags held his hands up in front of him. "All right, but if you don't snap out of it, we're gonna lose a couple of our good guys."

Throttle grunted, then picked up the electric trimmer and turned it on. He wanted to drown out Rags because he was afraid he'd lose it and beat the shit out of his brother if he didn't shut the hell up. Throttle knew he was starting fights with the brothers over nothing; Banger and Hawk had already talked to him about it, but he didn't give a shit. Now his anger had spilled over to the workplace, and he was beyond pissed at himself for letting Kimber get to him. How dare she tell him she didn't want seconds. That was *his* line. And why the hell didn't she? Further, why the fuck did he *want* it again? The woman made him feel and want things that he'd sworn a long time ago he'd never go for again.

Kimber messed with his world and turned it upside down. Her pushing him away was supposed to be his part, and he was acting just like a fucking chick, moping about, wanting to see her again, and flying off the handle at anyone who looked at him. *Damn. I don't know why I even want to go near her pussy, but I do.* It was probably nothing more than male pride. After all, she loved to argue with him, threw the women's lib shit in his face all the time, and acted like she didn't need a man to take care of her. *But the sexy noises she made when I kissed and touched her turn me way the hell on.* So she didn't want anything with a man at the moment. So fine. *If I find out she's even looked at that cowboy, he's getting my fist in his face.*

All of a sudden it was quiet, and it confused him. Looking at the trimmer in his hands, he noticed the blades weren't moving. *Now this piece of shit is acting up too?* Ready to throw it on the ground, he stopped when Rags pulled it from his hands. "You've trimmed the bush too much. It looks like shit, man."

Throttle looked at the shrub whose fullness was cut away, making it look like a deflated balloon. *Now I gotta buy another shrub to replace this. Shit, this woman is in my head too fuckin' much.*

"Why don't you call it a day? Roy and I can finish up the work. Chill for a while. Tomorrow we got a busy day."

He blew out a long breath as he nodded. He pulled off his gloves and stuffed them in his back pocket. "You gonna need the truck?"

"Nah. Roy has his."

He turned around and walked to the truck, swinging into the driver's seat and taking off. Rags was right; he *did* need to chill. He decided to go back to the club and get his bike. He needed a good, hard ride. Riding was the only thing that chased away the bitterness, the regret, and the recriminations.

HEAT PRICKED AT his skin like coiled barbed wire; it bounced off the road and caused an illusion of wavering images. On the side of the road, the trees stood mute in the summer air. Throttle had ridden over the small roads, climbing up to Jasper Peak to admire the endless wave of craggy mountaintops for miles. This was his favorite place, and he loved the way the sheer strength and beauty of the rock walls made everything seem small. When he looked out over the overlapping mountains, the limitless evergreens, and the quilt of summer colors on the grassy canyon below, he felt as though he were the only person on the planet. It was like *this* was the real world and nothing else mattered. For him, the mountain was where time stopped.

He'd thought for one bright, shining moment that he'd share his oasis with Kimber, but she'd quashed any chance of that. It was just as well. He hadn't been thinking straight anyway, imagining bringing a woman with him. He didn't really want *that* type of connection with her. It would mean something serious, and he had no intention in getting serious with any woman ever again.

He took one last look and made his way down the peak, heading into Pinewood Springs. Without thinking, he rode to his sister's house, making sure he didn't take the shortcut. He wanted to go past Kimber's house just to see if a cherry-red pickup was in her driveway. As he came down the road before turning onto her street, he saw her living room lights on. He pictured her sitting on her couch, her lovely legs on the coffee table, her dark hair pulled up in a makeshift bun. He bet she was wearing shorts and a crop top, and her luscious lips would be shiny and so fucking kissable. He slowed down as he passed her bungalow; his desire to stop was intense, but his pride kept him away. A quarter of a mile down the street, he turned left and parked in front of Dawn's house.

He rapped on the screen door. "Sis, the screen's locked. Come open up."

Dawn, a cigarette dangling from her mouth, unlatched the door. "I didn't expect to see you. We're still going to dinner next week, right?"

"Yeah. I was in the neighborhood. Is Olivia here?"

"No. She's at camp, remember? You paid for it."

"That's right. I talked to her last night on the phone. I hope she has a good time."

"She will. Ella and some of her other friends are there. It's good for her 'cause it gets boring around here."

"I know. When she gets back, I'll take her to Arrow Lake for the day. And the carnival is coming in town next month. We'll all go to that.

You got a beer?"

"Sure." She walked over to the refrigerator. "Mariah called me this morning," she said as she handed him a can.

He took a long pull. "So?"

She sat cross-legged on the other end of the couch. "So… she wants to get together with you and set things right. She feels awful about how things ended between the two of you."

He grunted. "Yeah, I bet she does."

"I think she's found religion or something." She giggled when Throttle gave her an incredulous look. "No, I'm serious. It's like she needs your forgiveness. Like she wants to make amends."

Throttle stared at the dark TV screen. Picking up the remote, he turned it on, flipping through the channels until he settled on a wrestling match.

"I think she's sincere. So, what do you say? It could be good for you. I think you've been hanging on to all that bitterness for a long time."

He took another gulp, his gaze fixed on the two men trying to pull each other down on the mats. "I'm not interested in seeing Mariah. I already told you that a few days ago, and I haven't changed my mind. Nothing needs to be set right. I've moved on. All that shit was a long time ago." He placed his foot on top of the coffee table. "If she wants forgiveness, she should see a priest. He'll absolve her. You got another beer?"

"Why are you so hard? I know she was a bitch to you at the end, but you were both young. She's changed. I always thought you two were good together."

"You getting me that beer?" His body tensed and he rubbed his thigh with his fist.

"Don't go getting pissed at me. I'm just trying to help," she said as she rose to bring him another can.

"I don't remember asking you for any fuckin' help. Leave this alone." His voice had a steely edge.

"Okay, but you need a permanent woman in your life. Damnit,

Throttle, you're too old to still be living your lifestyle. Aren't you tired of mindless sex with women who spread on command? Don't you want a woman who loves only you and not all your club members? You're going to want someone when you get old."

"Stay the fuck out of my life. And since you're so great at giving advice, what about you? Why don't you find a nice man to take care of you? You only seem to fuck losers, and bringing in different men in front of Olivia pisses me off. It makes her think it's okay to be a slut." He finished his beer then crushed the can in his hand.

Dawn narrowed her eyes. "Don't you talk to me that way. I'm a damn good mother, and I don't bring a bunch of men over here. Pedro and I were together for over six months and I didn't let him move in. You can be a real sonofabitch. You asshole!" She sniffled.

He stood up and threw the crushed can in the bin. "I didn't come over for this shit. I'm outta here." He marched out the door and went to his Harley, then stopped and looked back at the house. Why the hell did he have to go and say all that shit to Dawn? She didn't deserve it; he thought she was an awesome mother and sister. *I gotta fuck the pink-haired bitch outta my system.*

He rubbed his chin, then trudged up the walk to the house. Looking through the screen door, he saw Dawn on the couch, blowing her nose. He opened the door slowly, his gaze catching hers when she looked up. "Forget the shit I said. I'm just having a real shitty day."

She smiled. "Thanks for coming back and telling me that. I shouldn't have prodded."

"Yeah, so… We good here?"

"Yes." She bobbed her head up and down as she wiped the corner of her eyes. "We're just great." She started to get up from the couch, but he stopped her with a wave of his hand. He didn't go in for the hugging and sobbing shit women loved to do. "You still have to go?"

"Yeah. I got stuff to do. Just wanted to come by and see how you and Olivia were doing. I'll call you about dinner next week. If you need something, let me know." Then he walked down the porch stairs and climbed on his Harley.

Instead of going straight, he made a U-turn and went back the way he came, hoping Kimber would be outside watering her flowers. When she'd done that before, it led to the best fucking he'd ever had with a woman. She wasn't outside when he passed her house; she was inside and he wished he were with her, snuggling her in his arms. He continued on his way to the club. He passed by Ruthie's Diner and spotted Big Tits through the window, thinking maybe he should stop in and ask her to Arrow Lake. He knew she'd jump at the chance, but he drove by knowing that he didn't want Big Tits or any other woman near his dick, except for Kimber.

Fuck. She's taken hold of my cock.

She's in my blood.

Aw, hell.

CHAPTER TWELVE

H<small>E WALKED STRAIGHT</small> to the bar and slid on the barstool. Puck placed a shot of whiskey and a bottle of Coors in front of him. The club was busier than usual for a weeknight. Most of the brothers were there, and a large number of hoodrats cozied up to them. Against the back wall, he saw a long table set up with sandwiches, corn on the cob, potato salad, and ribs. Normally, food was set up when there was a big party on the weekend, a special occasion like one of the brother's birthday or a bachelor party, or a family gathering. Maybe something was up that he forgot about. The smoky smell of barbecue made his stomach growl, and he pushed off his seat and moseyed over to the food. As he scooped a large helping of potato salad on his plate, Rock clapped him on the shoulder. "How's it goin'?"

"Good. Why all the food and brothers?"

"It's Rags's birthday."

"It is? Did we talk about this at church or something?"

"Yeah. It was a few days ago, when all you wanted to do was beat the shit outta anyone who looked at you." He chuckled.

"I didn't hear shit about it. I worked with him today, and he never mentioned it."

"He's only here for the pussy like most of the guys. He chose Brandi to do his lap dance. I was happy 'bout that one. She's fuckin' hot." Rock placed three sandwiches and a pile of ribs on his plate.

"She's got big tits, that's for sure."

"And they're fuckin' real. I'd love to bury my face between them. Damn."

"Are you ready to have an old lady?"

Rock looked at him in horror. "Watch your fuckin' mouth," he growled.

Throttle laughed. "Didn't think so."

"There're plenty of chicks with big racks around here. There's no way I'll ever take an old lady. Fuck all these brothers settling down with one pussy. Not for me. I know you're on the same page." He took a bite out of his roast beef and cheddar sandwich.

"You're damn right. There's no way in hell I'm aiming to have any woman wear my patch."

As was customary, whenever a brother had a birthday, the club threw a party and the recipient could pick any of the strippers from Dream House to give him a lap dance. The dancers at the Insurgents' strip club were not treated the same way as the club girls or the hoodrats; they danced and nothing else. The Insurgents were strict about it, didn't want the women to be public wells for the raunchy and wild parties at the clubhouse. Mixing business with pleasure never worked out. When big weekend parties were thrown, sometimes the dancers would be asked to entertain the local and out-of-state brothers. They'd perform and then be escorted out of the club right after. Every once in a while, a brother fell for a dancer, like Jax did for Cherri, and she'd become his old lady, but it wasn't common.

"Did you ever fuck the big-titted waitress at Ruthie's? Rags said you had a date with her a while back."

"Nah. I was planning to, but something came up." *Like Kimber.*

"You gonna try again?"

He shrugged. "Not too sure. You want some of her? She's hot for biker cock. I can give you her number."

"Rags said he'd been sniffing around her for some time, but she didn't pay any attention to him. I don't like working for a woman. If she's not easy, I move to the next."

"I'm with you." *Then why don't I forget about Kimber and move on? She's more than difficult.* "I don't think you'll have any problems with her. Rags is too skinny. She likes broad, muscular bikers. You'll do fine."

"Yeah?" Rock shoved a forkful of potato salad in his mouth as he and Throttle walked back to the bar. "Text me her number. I want some new pussy."

Throttle chuckled and began shoveling in his food. For the next hour, members came up to him and Rock, joking and talking with them. Soon a pretty, stacked blonde approached Rock. She curled her fingers around his bulging bicep. "Wow, my two hands can barely wrap around your strong muscles," she cooed.

Throttle smirked as he watched Rock's eyes light up when he caught sight of her generous cleavage. Like him, Rock was a tit man—the bigger, the better—so it still surprised the hell out of him that he was crazy for Kimber. With her it was more than her tit size; it was the whole damn thing.

"My friend and I were talking about something real important," Rock said, winking at Throttle.

The blonde turned and looked at Throttle for the first time, a smile spreading over her lips. "Wow, you're good-looking. Maybe you want to have some fun with me too?" Her hopeful eyes fixed on his crotch.

"Sounds like fun, doesn't it?" Rock said as he scooped the woman up and planted her on his lap.

"Could be, but I'm not feelin' it. Sorry, sweetheart." He swiveled around on his stool and scanned the crowd. There were a lot of hot-looking women, and he knew he could fuck any one of them. Somehow knowing that made it less appealing. He wanted a challenge, and Kimber was that and more. The only woman he wanted to be inside was the one who said no. How fucked up was that?

He wrapped his fingers around the amber beer bottle and took a drink. From the corner of the room, he sensed someone watching him. He glanced over and his eyes locked with a woman who had dark eyes and hair. For a split second, he thought it was Mariah, but she only looked like her when she'd been young. When she and Throttle had been together.

As he stared, the image of Mariah, her long, dark hair flowing around her, clouded his vision, and he was twenty-two again and in love with her. He'd met her at one of the parties the club had when he'd been prospecting, almost ready to be patched in. She had large hazel eyes, and a smattering of freckles on her nose. She'd hated her freckles but he'd loved them, kissing them whenever they'd been together.

From the moment they'd met, he'd let her into his heart. She'd seemed to have been what he was missing since his mom had died a few years earlier from a brain aneurysm. She'd just stopped talking, her face had contorted, and she'd dropped dead, right in front of him and his sister. It'd been the biggest shock he'd ever had, and he'd been lost. He and his mom had been real close; she'd always been there for him, so when she'd left him, his universe was off-kilter. It'd stayed that way until he'd met Mariah.

They'd fallen in love too fast and too completely, and a year later, he'd asked her to be his old lady. He'd received his full colors a few months before, so he'd been ready to make her his forever. It'd been a snowy day; they sat by the fire, kissing and touching each other until he thought he'd burst. Then he'd asked her, and she'd cried while nodding enthusiastically.

That had been a great time for Throttle, and six months later, he'd sneaked away early from the bike rally in Kansas to go home. He'd missed her too much, and wanted to surprise her. When he arrived at their house, he spotted Pony's—another brother—motorcycle in the driveway. He rushed in to the sounds his old lady and a fellow brother made while they fucked, filling the small house. Throttle's homecoming had morphed into a goddamned cliché. Seeing red, he'd charged into the room and saw the love of his life bent over, her ass in the air, taking Pony's cock. He'd nearly killed Pony that night. Mariah, in a panic, had phoned the club. If Banger and Hawk hadn't pulled him off, Throttle would've had his ass in prison for a long stint. After the brothers had taken Pony's beaten body away, Throttle told Mariah he never wanted to see her again. A block of ice had encased his heart that night, and he walked away from her without even a backward look.

At church the next day, the consensus had been that Pony didn't deserve to wear the Insurgents' colors. Fucking someone's old lady was grounds for banishment, and that had been what the club had done; they stripped Pony of his colors and threw his ass out. He'd walked out, his head held down in shame. He and Mariah had married and left Pinewood Springs since he was no longer safe.

Throttle had moved to the clubhouse, where he still lived. He'd sworn he'd *never* let another woman near his heart. He decided love was overrated, and he'd lost himself in easy pussy and a hedonistic lifestyle for years. And it suited him perfectly until *she* crashed into his life. It'd taken him by surprise because she was unlike any woman he'd ever dated, fucked, or known. How was it that Kimber was the only woman he could think of?

"I figured we should stop eye-fucking each other and just get to it." The woman from across the room leaned in close, her breath hot against his neck.

"I didn't mean to stare. You reminded me of someone from my past." He turned away.

"A good memory?" She scratched the back of his neck.

He craned his neck and fixed a hard look on her. "No. Believe me, sweetheart, you don't want to go there. Find yourself another brother." He stared ahead, seeing her surprised look reflected in the mirror behind the bar. There must have been something in his gaze that told her not to fuck with him, because she moved away and got lost in the crowd.

He finished his beer, slapped Rock on the back, who had his tongue halfway down the blonde's throat, and left the great room. Taking the stairs two at a time, he reached his room, shut the door on all the noise, pulled out a bottle of Jack from his dresser, and lit a joint. That night, he planned to chase away the past and the present with booze.

Oblivion was his goal.

He poured a shot, letting the smooth fire slide down his throat.

The night was just beginning.

CHAPTER THIRTEEN

DEPUTY SHARON MANZIK pulled into the station after her night shift. She and her partner, Bryan Wessels, had had a busy night of drunken brawls, domestic disturbances, DUIs, and a call from a freaked-out woman who told them someone had stolen her underwear from her dresser drawers. The dark-haired victim swore that the culprit stood outside her window watching as she'd made her discovery. When Deputy Wessels asked her to describe the man, the woman admitted that she hadn't actually *seen* him, but she'd *felt* him staring at her, enjoying the fear that shrouded her upon discovering someone had invaded her safe space. The cop glanced at his partner, rolling his eyes before putting away his notepad.

Deputy Manzik knew Bryan was skeptical and probably thought the woman's fear made her imagine a stranger in the shadows, but she believed the victim. As a police officer, she often went by what her instincts told her, even though her partner and the other male deputies would tease her about it. She also could relate to what the victim was saying. When she was relaying the series of events, a deep shiver had run through the deputy's body. A few weeks before, Sharon had felt the same way as the victim, even though nothing had been missing or even overturned; she'd just known someone had been inside, in her bedroom. As hard as she tried, she hadn't been able to shake the feeling.

"I think we're done here," Bryan said.

Sharon went over and handed the victim a card with the name of the victim advocate. "If you feel that you need some help, please call Julie. She's very nice, and she's helped a lot of people get through the distress of being a victim. If you need anything, call me. Detective McCue is handling these cases, but you can call me anytime." She smiled warmly at the shivering thirty-five-year-old woman. Trauma was written all over her face: white pallor, quivering lips, and vacant stare.

Sharon walked out into the bright sunlight. "McCue will want to see our report. I'm convinced this woman's case is connected to the whack job who's stealing underwear around this vicinity. What a fuckin' pervert."

After they both climbed in, Bryan pulled the police car away from the curb.

Detective McCue had been assigned to the Peeping Tom burglary cases. The *Pinewood Springs Tribune* had coined the pervert the "Lingerie Bandit," a name that caught the public's attention. She hated the way the media came up with titles for criminals. In her opinion, the names minimized the seriousness of the crime, and they probably boosted the ego of the criminal.

Sharon turned to Bryan. "The perp's been at it for eight months, and we're no closer to catching him than we were when he first started. He has to slip up sometime. The whole thing is degrading and humiliating. As a woman, knowing a man broke in your home and took your bra or panties, it would be awful. He violates the women each time he does it."

"Yeah. This time, the victim was damn lucky she wasn't home when he broke in. The perp's a nut job. You going to the office picnic next weekend?"

"Maybe. I wish I had a guy to bring. I'm so damn busy I never have time to meet anyone."

"What about Tyler? I've seen him checking you out when you weren't looking." Bryan laughed and pulled up at Ruthie's Dinner. "Let's get some lunch before we head back to finish up our reports."

"Okay. By the way, women *always* know when a man is giving her the once-over, even if it looks like we're unaware." She slammed the car door. "Tyler, like some of the other guys, resents me being in the department."

"I don't."

"You did at first. Remember how pissed you were when the sergeant assigned me to work with you? I thought you were going to burst a blood vessel."

He chuckled. "I was an idiot. I didn't know you, and all the asshole guys were razing me about it." Bryan smiled. "I wouldn't trade you for any of the guys."

"Thanks, but you know me. No one else has wanted to really get to know me in the five years I've been on the force. Don't think I care because I don't. It's just the way it is. I've accepted it." She walked into the diner.

Deputy Manzik was the only female police officer on the small force in Pinewood Springs. Being a cop was something she had wanted to be ever since she could remember. Her parents had been against it even though her father had retired from the force, but she was determined and she held steadfast.

For the most part, her colleagues accepted her with quiet indifference, but there were a few who made it clear that they were not happy to have a female officer among them. There was one man in particular who didn't think women belonged on the force and hated like hell that she was under his command—Sergeant Jay Stichler. She grimaced when she thought of him. The sergeant always made sure to give Sharon a hard time, and he'd made it very clear that he didn't want to have to depend on her if he was in a jam. He'd sneer at her and say crude comments to her under his breath. When her locker had pictures of naked women in vulgar positions, and her picture was taped on their heads, she'd been positive that Stichler was the instigator. Her friends told her to go to the captain and report the incident, but she didn't want the assholes to think she couldn't take it. So she ignored it like she did all the snide remarks, the looks, and the occasional vulgar gestures. Sharon just let them roll over her. She figured in time the frat-like mentality would wane, the guys would grow bored of the game, and drop it. After time, the antics seemed to let up, and only Stichler and a couple other hardcore chauvinists bothered her.

They slid into the booth and Sharon ordered a large iced coffee; she was beat and needed the jolt of caffeine. Bryan took out his phone and called McCue to give him the heads-up on the victim. Sharon could hardly wait until she returned to the station, turned in her report, and went home. Her sixteen-hour shift was starting to get the best of her.

A few hours later, the dark-haired deputy unlocked her front door, anxious to hit her comfy bed and sleep. The minute she stepped into her air-conditioned house, she knew someone had been inside. Her body tensed; she could sense he'd been there *again.* She drew her gun and checked her three-bedroom home thoroughly. No one was there.

After making sure all her windows and doors were secured, she took a quick shower, then went to her dresser to take out a nightshirt. And that's when she noticed it—the top drawer wasn't closed all the way. She grabbed a tissue and opened the drawer slowly, noticing her bras and panties had been rifled through. She sucked in a deep breath, picked up her cell phone, and placed a call to Detective McCue. She was positive the Lingerie Bandit had been in her house. The hairs on the back of her neck rose as a small tremor vibrated through her. Not wanting to touch anything, she glanced quickly over the contents of the drawer, realizing her fuchsia, laced boyshorts appeared to be missing.

Sitting at the edge of the bed, she sighed, knowing that her much-needed sleep would have to be delayed for a few hours more. She crossed her legs and waited for the detective and his team to arrive.

HE BREATHED HEAVILY as he looked at the pictures he'd taken of several of his victims. Taking out all the underwear he'd stolen over the course of eight months, he masturbated as he relived the moments of seeing the women for the first time, touching their soft panties, and taking pictures of some of them. The thrill he'd received when he broke into his first house had begun to wane, and his fetish and urges had required that he take it up a notch. So he made the women wear the soft French cuts, thongs, and bikinis while he posed them and took their pictures. Just thinking of pressing his erection against the lovely panties while they were still on the women made him come hard.

He'd been peeping in women's windows since he was thirteen years old and caught Mrs. Donner's silhouette against the white shade one breezy summer night. He'd been fascinated by how high her breasts were and how slim her waist was. She was nothing like his mother, aunts, and grandmother. From that moment on, he'd been hooked. He hadn't done it all the time but in the past eight months, his urges were no longer satisfied by merely looking. He wanted to feel the silky panties between his hands. The peeping in the shadows no longer filled his craving, so he'd taken a bold step one autumn day and broken into the home of a beautiful young woman he'd been watching for a few weeks. That day and many weeks after, he'd slipped into the ladies' houses and played with their sweet underthings, deeply breathing in their scent. He'd always take souvenirs for when his wife and children would be tucked snuggly in their beds upstairs, and he'd be alone in the basement in a locked room.

For months he'd been on a perpetual high; then he'd grown restless again, and his depravity required more stimulation. And he'd broken into his first house when his target was home. The first time he'd done it and ran his fingers down the soft skin of a luscious woman, he'd climaxed harder than he had in a very long time. He was hooked.

Right then, as he carefully folded and placed his silky treasures in a large trunk, he realized he needed more from his lovely victims. His craving dictated it. After he locked the trunk and then the door, he slowly climbed the stairs, his mind made up: when he went back out to hunt, he'd push his fulfillment to a new level. He had to.

"You all done?" his wife asked as she bustled about in the kitchen. "Dinner's almost ready."

"It smells good. What're we having?"

"Roast chicken and mashed potatoes. Your favorite." She smiled wide at him.

He came beside her and kissed her on the lips quickly. "You spoil me."

"I know. Tell Aiden and Callie to wash up and come down. Dinner's going on the table now."

He shuffled out of the kitchen and climbed the stairs to round up the children for supper.

CHAPTER FOURTEEN

"KIMBER, CAN YOU drop over to the clubhouse to pick up the work orders? I fuckin' forgot 'em when I left last night and I need them. I'd go, but one of my good customers is coming by to bring his grandfather's old Harley. I'm fuckin' excited to see it."

"What year is it?" she asked.

"He thinks it's a 1936 Knucklehead. He's had it for a few years and wants me to restore it."

"Wow. I've seen photos of the old bikes but never one up close and personal. I'd like to check it out when I get back from the clubhouse. If you need some help restoring it, I'd love to be a part of the team." Kimber flushed when Hawk looked at her. Sometimes she wasn't sure if she was overstepping the line between employer and employee. She wasn't sure how Hawk really felt about a woman in his shop. She heard some of the brothers giving him a hard time when they came in to shoot the shit with him. Kimber suspected Hawk's old lady had a lot to do with her getting the tech job, but she could be wrong. She just couldn't read her boss; he usually had a scowl on his face, except when his old lady was around. "Maybe I spoke out of turn," she mumbled. "I'll go get the work papers. Be back soon."

"I was gonna ask you if you wanted to help me restore the Harley. You're a top-notch mechanic. I could use your help."

A rush of adrenaline rushed through her body, and she bounced from foot to foot. "Cool. Awesome. Like over-the-top awesome." She beamed.

He nodded. "You better get going. I need the work orders. The directions to the clubhouse are up at the front counter." He dismissed her by turning his attention to the computer. She slipped out of his office.

Rereading the directions one more time, she started her bike and drove to the Insurgents' club. When she arrived, the prospect who stood by the tall chain-linked and barbed wire fence waved her in. Surmising that Hawk must have called ahead, she rode through the checkpoint and parked in the shade under an aspen tree. She opened the heavy door and entered a large room, pausing until her eyes adjusted to the dim light. The smell of weed, whiskey, and pussy enveloped her and took her back to the days when she'd meet up with her ex at the Demon Riders clubhouse. Looking around, she spotted several men smoking joints, their beers in front of them, as they watched the car races on TV. A few men and women were banging noisily on the couches that lined the back walls. *Yep, just like I remembered it. Glad it's behind me.*

Normally, every guy in the place would check out the new chick, but since she wore her coveralls, the men didn't pay much attention to her. With her hair wrapped up under a skull bandana, they probably thought she was a dude. Happy not to be accosted by a bunch of bikers, she walked over to the bar and tapped on it. A large tatted man ambled over.

"Where's Hawk's office? I have to pick up some work orders to take to him at the shop."

The burly man frowned at her. "You a chick? He said a chick was coming."

She squinted and whipped off her bandana, her black hair cascading down her back. "Now where's the fuckin' office?"

The bartender balked, then pointed to a hallway. "It's the third door on the left."

She lifted her chin, aware that a few of the guys stirred, seeing she was a woman after all. Normally, she would've ignored the glowering biker's comment, but she was so sick and tired of all the attitude. Working in a man's field was damn exhausting. The work itself was hard, and fending off the comments, insults, and resentment sometimes proved to be too much.

From behind her, someone said, "Fuck, that's a good shot." Throttle's smooth-as-whiskey voice slid over her and caught her attention. Slowly she pivoted, her gaze drawn to the back of the room. And there he was, bent down with a pool cue in his hand, a joint dangling out of the corner of his mouth. A busty, pretty blonde ran her fingernails down his back as he sank a ball into the far right pocket. A few of the guys watching yelled, "Way to go," or "Fuckin' good shot."

Even though Kimber knew she had to get the work orders and get back to the shop stat, she couldn't take her eyes off Throttle. The way his biceps bulged against his tanned arms when he slid the cue stick made her feel funny between her legs. His sleeveless T-shirt showed off his toned arms perfectly, and she had a strong urge to curl her hands around them and trace his hot tattoos with the tip of her tongue. As he lowered his head, his dark hair gleamed under the light from the fixture over the pool table. Dangling silver earrings moved fluidly as he tilted his head. The muscles rippling under his tank top quickened her pulse. He was gorgeous, and her body ached for his touch.

Just before his shot, he glanced up, as if sensing her; his dark orbs met her blue ones, his burning intensity holding her still. As they held each other in a smoldering gaze, it was as if no one else in the room existed. The ever-present tension and longing between them pulled them together in that one stare. With a smirk playing around the corners of his mouth, he struck the ball and it slammed into two more, pocketing all of them. The blonde beside him squealed and rubbed her big breasts against his outstretched arm before she bent down and planted a kiss on his cheek. Tucking her fingers under his chin, she tried to turn his face toward her. He shook her off, laid down the pool cue, stubbed out his joint, and headed toward Kimber, his gaze never leaving hers.

Her heart beat wildly against her rib cage as the indiscernible voices from the people around her rushed in her ears. In vain she tried to swallow, but her throat and mouth were filled with cotton. She knew she should walk away, but she couldn't; their connection grounded her, and she couldn't move even if she wanted to. Without a word, he yanked her to him, and she offered no resistance. He tilted her head back, then took her mouth with a savage intensity. Instead of backing out of his embrace, her trembling limbs clung to him as he rammed his tongue into her mouth, its writhing and pushing motions sending a burst of passion through her from the tips of her breasts to her aching sex.

After what seemed like forever, Throttle pulled back, winked, and sauntered back to the pool table. Picking up his cue amid whistles and hoots, he prepared for the next shot.

Kimber, wild-eyed and panting, watched him as the blonde sized her up. With all her strength, she forced herself to move, taking a few shaky steps to Hawk's office. Once she left the great room, she was safe from his magnetic pull; she gathered up the work orders, held her chin high, and reentered the main room. She glanced furtively at the pool table, but Throttle was gone. Scanning the room, she didn't spot him. Disappointment crawled through her. *Quit being such a fool. It's a good thing he's gone. He's such an arrogant SOB.* She left the clubhouse, happy to be out in the sunshine and away from Throttle's presence.

After she placed the files in the saddlebags, she swung her leg over her Harley. Gathering her hair up, she coiled it on top of her head and covered it with her bandana once more.

"Figures you have a pink Harley." Throttle's voice startled her.

"You've seen it before," she said curtly.

"I was gonna mention it then, but we got kinda… sidetracked." He slowly ran his finger from her earlobe down to her collarbone. She sucked in her breath.

"I gotta go. Hawk's waiting for me to give him some papers." She put on her sunglasses, relieved that he couldn't see the arousal in her eyes.

"What's up with all the pink shit?"

She shrugged. "It's my favorite color."

"Guess what mine is."

"I don't know. Black?"

"Nah." He leaned in close and ran his tongue down her neck. "Pussy pink has become my favorite. Yours in particular."

Red stained her cheeks, and she pulled back. "I gotta go."

"Really?" He flashed her a boyish, lopsided smile, the kind that women went mad for, and her stomach fluttered. He brushed his lips against her ear and she shivered despite the ninety-seven-degree temperature. "My cock wants back in your pussy. Don't tell me you don't want that too."

She pushed him back and switched on her bike. Kimber had to get far away from him before she lost herself forever. She had plans; a relationship with Throttle wasn't possible. Sex with him wasn't either because if she let him back in, she'd be forever hooked on him, and she couldn't allow that to happen. "I told you that night was a mistake."

"Babe, a woman doesn't kiss a man like you just did if our fucking was a mistake."

"I have to go."

"All right, ride your pretty little ass outta here on your pink Harley. I'll wait until you come to me. There's no way in hell you'll ever be satisfied with any other man."

"You're pretty sure of yourself, you cocky bastard."

He laughed. "Damn straight."

"Well, if you wait for me to contact you, you'll be old, wrinkled, and bald."

He put his arm around her and pressed her against him, then lowered his head and kissed her hard and rough. Just the way she liked it. A small moan escaped through her parted lips, and she hated her body for betraying her like that.

He released her and chuckled. "Like I said, babe. I'll be waiting when you want a good fucking."

Anger curled around her nerves as she watched him swagger back inside, leaving her aching for his touch. She revved the engine and peeled out of the parking lot, wanting to create as much distance as she could between them.

He's dangerous because he knows the effect he has on me.

Damnit!

THE MINUTE THROTTLE came back in, his brothers were on him for kissing the chick in coveralls. Rock laid down his pool stick, went up to him, and punched him in the arm. "Is that the woman mechanic at Hawk's shop?"

Throttle braced himself and nodded.

"You sure in hell got over your contempt. Now I know why you haven't been fuckin' any of the club whores—you've got new pussy for now. She must be a pretty good fuck for you to pass on Big Tits for No Tits."

The brothers standing around Throttle and Rock howled. "Damn, man, how in the hell could you find her tits? Her pussy must be extra special to make her worth fuckin'," Wheelie joked as the other brothers threw in their jabs.

Throttle's jaw tightened. The brothers knew he loved big tits, and a few weeks ago, he'd have agreed with them. But now that he'd tasted Kimber, sucked her perky, soft breasts and pink nipples, he couldn't imagine wanting her to be anything more than what she was—perfect. Even her sassy attitude appealed to him. She was a challenge that set off high voltage shocks in him. He fucking loved it.

"You planning on sharing your little secret?" Rock asked.

Before Rock could pick up his beer, Throttle had him by the throat, hissing, "Don't you ever fuckin' ask me that again. You show her respect or I'll beat your ass."

Rock shoved Throttle back, his nostrils flaring. "You wanna beat my ass? Come on, let's go." He stood in a fighter's stance, his fists clenched.

Throttle stepped toward him and raised his arms, but then Rags, Wheelie, Chas, and Bear intervened. "What the fuck you gonna fight about? Pussy? Shit, that ain't worth it." Wheelie grabbed Lola and pulled her to Throttle. "We got good pussy whenever we want, so why let a chick get between you?"

Rock breathed out, his face relaxing. "He's right, brother. Pussy is just pussy." He picked up his beer and guzzled it.

Throttle, still tense and pissed as hell, leaned back against the bar. Lola wrapped her arm around his waist and whispered in his ear, "Rock's right. I'm always here for you, baby. Rosie, Wendy, and I have been dying to do a stint with you, but lately, you never have time for us. We miss you. You don't need a woman who has grease between her nails 'cause she's doing a man's job. You need women who are soft and sweet-smelling and know how to get your dick up and sucked good. Real good." She licked his earlobe.

Throttle unwrapped her arm from him and gently pushed her away. "There're other brothers to pleasure, and you know a lot of them love spending time with you, Rosie, and Wendy. Hit on Rock. He's always ready."

"You used to be too."

He ran his hand through his hair. "I know." What the hell was he doing? He was passing up a sure thing with Lola and the other club girls for a maybe with Kimber? "I got something in my blood that needs some time to work out. After I have my fill, I'll be back in business." *I just need to get Kimber out of my system.* His cocky demeanor pleased Lola, but deep down he suspected it wouldn't be that easy to walk away from the woman who'd gotten into his head and dick.

He watched Lola walk away, the curve of her ass cheeks shaking in her Daisy Dukes. She stood by Rock, her talons running down his back, as he and Axe played pool, her gaze fixed on Throttle. Turning away, he motioned for another beer.

Kimber's scent lingered on his T-shirt, and the taste of her was still on his lips.

CHAPTER FIFTEEN

KIMBER SCREECHED HER bike to a halt and jumped off, storming into the shop. Without a word, she handed Hawk the file and made her way to the service garage.

"Don't you wanna check out the 1936 Harley? It's a beauty," Hawk said.

"I got work to finish. Maybe later," she grumbled as she closed the door behind her. *Who the fuck does Throttle think he is? Like I'm gonna come looking for him. Arrogant sonofabitch! If I want to screw I don't need him.* Kimber went to her area and picked up the torque wrench. She was madder than hell about losing her head at the club. How could she have let him kiss her like that in front of all the other bikers? She bent down and secured the bike jack. What the hell was she thinking? And who was the blonde bitch who couldn't keep her hands off him? *He's probably banging her right now. What's it gonna take for me to learn that bikers, especially one-percenters, are bad news?* Just because he was good-looking didn't mean squat.

She went over to the radio and turned the volume to the maximum level, blasting the music loud so she could extricate him from her mind. She didn't want to think about him, the kiss, or the ache between her legs. None of that would do.

Throwing herself into her work, she'd successfully avoided thinking about Throttle for the past three hours. During her break, she sat at the table in the employees' room, sipping on an iced tea. Her beeping phone made her jump, and she held her breath before she noticed the text was from Riley. She groaned aloud.

Riley: Hi. What're u doing?

Kimber: *Working.*

Riley: *Right now?*

Kimber shook her head and drummed her fingers on the table. She was finished with this dumbass. She'd told him to get lost politely, and he obviously hadn't caught on.

Kimber: *Ya. Don't text anymore.*

She placed the phone in her uniform pocket and ignored the incessant pinging. It seemed like the day would never end. She rose from the table and went back to fixing the Harley.

After work, she'd gone for a long, fast ride around the dirt roads that crisscrossed the mountains and valleys. By the time she pulled into her driveway, the heat of the day had receded as the sun sank to the horizon, the sherbet orange and pink hues giving way to a dusty purple sprinkled with the occasional sparkle of a distant star. By habit, she glanced around, hoping to see Throttle on his powerful machine, his corded legs hugging it so perfectly, but the street was quiet. The only sounds were the sporadic din of dinner dishes and the garbled voices from random television sets. She pulled her bike into the garage and entered her home.

Deep down, she knew Throttle would never have been waiting for her on his iron horse. She was being silly; the summer sometimes made her yearn for romance. The long carefree days and breezy nights made her crave something out of the ordinary, but by the end of the season, her life was just the same as it was before summer began. Maybe if she went to him she could at least have a helluva summer fling, but she had no intention of running after him. He was cocky enough, and if she sought him out, he'd be downright impossible. Let the macho prick come to her.

But she knew, since he was a biker, he'd never chase her.

Sweaty from her ride, she took a cool shower. With a towel wrapped around her, she went over to her window to close her blinds, glancing out. She gasped and clutched her towel tighter around her. Straining, she fixed her stare on the cluster of pine trees across from her, her heart thumping. She swore she saw someone watching her from behind the trees. Quickly, she switched off her light and moved to the side, pinning herself against her wall, then peeked out the corner of the blinds.

She stayed like that for a very long time, and just when she was ready to abandon her post, deciding the light had been playing tricks on her, a shadowy figure emerged from behind the group of trees. Goose bumps carpeted her arms, and the hair on the back of her neck stood on end. From her view, he looked as if he were going to cross the street and come over to her house. Her stomach lurched as she tried to remember whether she'd closed her front door. She knew she'd latched her screen, but a hard jerk could open it in a second. Her thumping heart filled her ears, but then she switched her bedroom light on and off in rapid succession. The figure stopped, then bolted away. Leaning her head against the cool wall, she struggled to regain her normal breathing.

After she shut her blinds, she slipped on a nightshirt and went to the living room, checking that her front door was closed and locked. She debated about calling the police, but what could she tell them? That a figure of what appeared to be a man crossed the street, then jumped away after she turned the lights on and off? She couldn't describe him nor could she even tell them that he was coming to her house, even though she had a strong feeling he was. *He was fuckin' watching me.* She shivered.

For a long while, she sat on her couch trying to piece together what had happened, finally deciding that it was probably a neighborhood teenager who'd wanted to catch a glimpse of her taking her towel off. If he'd meant something harmful, he wouldn't have run off so quickly. She made a mental note to make sure all her drapes and blinds were closed the minute darkness hit.

She padded into the kitchen, grabbed a bottle of sweet tea and a leftover burrito, then settled on her couch and flipped on the TV. After she finished eating, her eyelids kept drooping so she stretched out. Within minutes, she fell fast asleep.

THE HEADLINE IN the morning paper read "Woman Photographed and Raped. Is this the work of the Lingerie Bandit?" Detective McCue threw the paper across the desk, his jaw clenched. "Fuck!"

"What's up, Earl?" Carlos, one of the other detectives, asked.

"The newspaper is having a field day with this 'Lingerie Bandit' shit. The goddamned reporter didn't spend most of the night with a traumatized victim who'd been humiliated, degraded, then raped for hours by this sick bastard."

"They don't give a shit. Only interested in what'll sell more copies."

"The poor woman," McCue muttered under his breath. In his gut, he'd known it was only a matter of time before masturbating, stealing underwear, and taking lewd pictures of women wouldn't be enough for the perverted bastard. The perpetrator's urges had now risen to a whole new despicable level. He sighed.

The victim was a nice, twenty-three-year-old clerk for the county court. The rapist had broken into her house a little bit after midnight. The woman had woken up when she felt something crushing her, and fear had spread through her when she'd looked into his cold, flat eyes. Before she could scream, he'd secured duct tape over her mouth and tied her hands behind her back. He'd cut off her pajama top, then removed her panties. After he'd raped her for several hours, he'd forced her to put on different bras and panties before he took photographs of her in various poses. After he'd finished, he'd helped her put on her pajamas, tucked her into bed, removed the duct tape from her mouth, and told her he was sorry. He'd thanked her and left.

The victim told the detective he'd used a condom, but McCue hoped the CSI was able to get something that they could test for DNA. He wanted to compare it with what they had picked up at one of the earlier crime scenes; if there was DNA found in the present case, he was pretty sure it'd match the one from before. Not having any strong leads was frustrating as hell, because there weren't any solid suspects. The usual registered sex offenders and newly released criminals who'd committed sex crimes were brought in for questioning, but after checking out their alibis, they were all cleared. Another dead end. Whoever this bad guy was, he definitely was staying under the radar.

"You know this doesn't bode too well," Earl said as he went over his report from the previous night again.

"What?" Carlos asked.

"Escalating to physically hurting women. It's just a matter of time before he wants a bigger thrill, and the only thing left is murder." He reclined in his swivel chair, his face taut. "We fucking have to stop him before that happens."

He tossed the paper aside and pushed his large frame into his jacket. "I'm going back to see if I can't find a neighbor who saw or heard anything last night."

"Do you want me to help you canvas the area?" Carlos asked.

"No. You're working on the stolen cars case. I can handle it."

"Okay. Just let me know if you need anything. Unless an emergency comes up, I'll be at my desk for the next few hours."

"Noted." With slumped shoulders, Detective McCue headed out.

CHAPTER SIXTEEN

A WEEK HAD passed since Throttle had kissed Kimber at the clubhouse, and he was damn surprised she hadn't come looking for him. What the hell was up with that? From the way she'd responded to him, he knew she'd felt the connection between them, so why was she staying away? *She probably wants me to come after her. Like that's gonna fuckin' happen.* She had a real "I don't give a damn" attitude, but she didn't fool him for one bit. She wanted him just as bad as he wanted her, but she was acting like a fucking princess in a tower. *Screw that. If she wants it, she better take her own ass out of the tower and come and get it. I'll be ready.* He chuckled as he drove the lawn mower around a large yard.

Business had been very good for the past month, and he and Rags were hustling their asses most days. Working under the sun's piercing rays had colored his skin a rich golden brown. Most days he and Rags worked shirtless, much to the delight of the housewives whose husbands paid for their landscaping services.

When he finished the lawn, he killed the motor and jumped off, then grabbed a bottled water from the cooler and walked over to the shade of an oak tree. He sat on the ground, his back against the trunk, and took a long drink. A light breeze rustled through the tree, and wisps of sunlight filtered through the branches thick with green leaves. He pulled out his phone to see if anyone had tried to call him. It was a habit of all the Insurgents—checking their phones often. Being in an outlaw club, a member never knew when they'd be needed to take care of something that threatened the brotherhood, or if another brother needed a helping hand. He noticed a missed call from his sister and dialed her number.

"Hey, what's up? Olivia okay?" he asked.

"She's great. Ella's having a birthday pool party at the community center. Olivia's been excited for days over it." He heard her inhale deeply.

"Are there enough adults to watch her and the other kids? You should've gone with her."

"She's fine. They have three lifeguards and several mothers are there. I had to do an early morning shift so I couldn't have gone. You fuss too much over her." She laughed.

"Maybe, but I'd feel better if you were with her."

"She's good. Relax. Anyway, I need you to come over and fix one of my sprinkler heads on the lawn. It's broken and it's near the basement window. I'm afraid it's gonna flood. I've called the landlord several times, but he's not returning my calls. Can you come over?"

"I don't know. We gotta finish this job. Turn the fuckin' water off from inside the house."

"I don't have a clue how to do that."

He exhaled loudly. "I've shown you at least ten times how to do it."

"I keep forgetting. Sorry."

"How long's it been running?"

"Like a couple hours. I called you but you didn't pick up."

"I was on the lawn mower and didn't hear the call. Let me see if Rags and the other two guys are good without me for a while. I'll let you know. If it doesn't work, I'll come after we call it a day."

"I'm afraid the basement will be flooded if you don't come soon."

"Hang on." Throttle called Rags over. "Rags, do you think you can go without me for a couple hours? Dawn has a broken sprinkler and is afraid it's gonna flood her basement."

"Sure, we can handle it. We're almost done here, and the next job is a small one."

Throttle nodded. "Dawn? Yeah, I can come over now."

"Great. Oh, and I want you to look at a tree in the front yard. I think it's dying. I water it and it just gets browner. I don't know if I'm overwatering it."

"I'll check it out when I get there."

Twenty minutes later, Throttle pulled his pickup in front of Dawn's house. He immediately saw the tree his sister had told him about, and he spotted the sprinkler shooting water straight up in the air. When he was halfway up the walk, Dawn came out on the porch. "That was fast," she said, holding a cigarette between her fingers.

He looked at her hand. "You smoke too fuckin' much."

"Tell me something I don't know."

"Just sayin'. You gotta think of Olivia." He pushed past her and dashed down the stairs, turning the water off before he began fixing the problem.

An hour later, the sprinkler was fixed. As he stood in front of the ash tree, he said, "This one's dead. I'll come by on the weekend with Rags and take it out. I don't have the equipment with me."

"You can't save it? I love this tree."

"Nope. It's got emerald ash borers."

"What the hell is that?"

He pointed to hundreds of holes. "See these? This is the sign that you have these insects all over the tree. They nosh on the leaves and lay their eggs and basically devour the shit outta the tree. I gotta get rid of it." Throttle wiped his forehead with a rag from his back pocket.

"Wow. I don't know a damn thing about trees, but I'm sad to see this one go. You look hotter than hell."

"That's 'cause I am. It must be a hundred degrees or more."

"Come in and I'll get you a beer. Why don't you take a cold shower to cool off? I washed the laundry you gave me last week, so you have some clean clothes to put on."

"I gotta get back and help Rags out."

"It'll just take ten minutes. Your T-shirt is soaked with sweat. Come on." They walked in the house, and Dawn handed him a towel and lightly pushed him to the bathroom.

When he came back into the family room, showered and changed, he felt a hell of a lot better. Dawn was on the couch, an unopened bottle of beer on the table. "Is that for me?" he asked.

"Yep. I thought you'd like one."

"I can't stay too much longer. I told Rags I'd be back after a couple hours to help out."

"It only takes a few minutes to have a beer, especially the way you guzzle it." She smiled. "You look nice and fresh. Feel better?"

He nodded. "This is one fuckin' hot summer. It's way hotter than last year."

The doorbell rang and Dawn padded over to answer it. "Oh. What are you doing here?" Throttle heard surprise laced in her voice.

"I was just in the neighborhood and thought I'd stop over for a quick visit." The woman's voice sounded familiar, and Throttle's muscles tensed. *Fuck, she sounds just like—*

"Throttle, look who's here," Dawn said.

Mariah. His eyes narrowed as they fell on his ex-lover. *She looks damn good. A bit worn out, but her curves are still there.* When his eyes shifted to Dawn's guilty ones, he knew she'd set the whole fucking thing up. She'd known all along where the valve was to shut off the water, but she'd pretended ignorance as a ruse to lure him over there to "bump" into his ex. The shower, fresh clothes, all of it had been a damn trap. *I wish Dawn would stay the fuck outta my life.* "I gotta go." He turned to leave.

"Don't go yet, Throttle. How've you been?" Mariah's fingers brushed against his forearm.

He jerked away. "Been fine."

"I'd like to talk to you in private," she said softly.

"I have some laundry in the wash that I have to hang up. Be back in a few." Before Throttle could say anything, Dawn scurried out of the room.

"It's good seeing you," Mariah said.

"You got ten minutes to talk. Then I leave." He crossed his arms over his chest and bristled when she raked her eyes over him, lingering on his powerful arms before shifting to his mouth.

"You look real good." She smiled seductively.

"You've just used up thirty seconds."

"You're still a hard man, aren't you? I've thought about you a lot over the last thirteen years." She pushed her hair over her shoulders and took a step forward. He just stared at her stone-faced. "I was a fool to hurt you like I did. I was a fucking idiot to have cheated on you and to have thrown what we had away. I'm so very sorry... I really am. Pony turned out to be a mean, drunken sonofabitch. He was nothing like you." She placed her slender fingers on her throat. "I was young and stupid when you and I were together. I didn't realize what a wonderful man you were."

"What the fuck do you want from me, Mariah?"

"I want your forgiveness." Her big eyes scanned his face.

He breathed out. "All the shit between us is in the past. Yeah, I was fuckin' pissed for a long time, but I got over it. I've forgotten it. What's done is done."

"So, you forgive me?"

A dark expression crossed his face and he pressed his lips together as he shook his head. "I'm not the forgiving type, but I'm over it."

She looked up at him from under hooded lids. "I hope you're not over *me*." She laughed softly, then skimmed her tongue over her upper lip.

He stared at her impassively.

"Do you think I look good?" She ran her hands over her curves.

He tilted his head in a nod.

She smiled widely.

"What the fuck do you *really* want?" His jaw tightened and twitched.

She stepped closer to him but halted when he held out his hand, stopping her from coming any closer to him. "I wanted you to know that I never stopped loving you. You've always been on my mind... I want you back. I still love you."

His laugh had a hard edge to it. "Pony threw your fuckin' ass out, didn't he?"

She shook her head and looked at him, her eyes shining. "I threw *him* out. I've been wanting to call you for the last ten years, but my stupid pride held me back. Finally I decided to come back home and see you. I want for us to get back together. I'll be real good to you, baby. Remember how much fun we used to have? How we'd fuck for hours under the stars at Arrow Lake?"

"That was a long time ago."

"Standing here with you, it feels like it was just a week ago. I still get the tingles when I look at you, baby. You're the only man who's ever had that effect on me."

"You fuckin' trashed what we had, and you come back here and think we'll just pick up where we left off? Fuck, you're crazier than I remember. I'm not interested. All the feelings I had for you died a long time ago."

"I don't believe you. I saw the way you looked at me, and I know the spark is still there. You still like these, don't you?" She cupped her big breasts and pushed them together.

Shaking his head, he snorted. "Any man's gonna look at a woman's tits. It doesn't mean shit. I fuck plenty of women. I don't need you."

Mariah's shoulders sagged a little and she wringed her hands. "We do need each other."

"I don't need any woman." He uncrossed his arms; he was growing weary of her.

"Can I hug you? I'd really like to touch you, and if you don't feel anything after we hug, I'll go away. I just want to hold you again."

"Your ten minutes are way over." He spun around and walked out of the house, the screen door slamming behind him.

"Throttle!" Mariah said, but he kept walking toward his Harley. She yelled out his name again and he revved his cams loud to drown her out. Then he sped off, never looking back.

NIGHTFALL ERASED ALL remnants of muted color as glimmering stars punctured the darkening sky. Sitting at a table nursing a beer, Throttle stared out into the night, the trees surrounding the clubhouse swallowed by the encroaching blackness. He'd ignored Dawn's phone calls that started ten minutes after he'd left her place. He didn't trust what he'd say to her, so he'd decided to wait until the following day to speak with her. She never should've had Mariah come over when he was there. Did Mariah seriously think he'd let her jump back into his life and bed just because she looked good? The truth was the only woman on his mind was Kimber. Not Mariah, not Lola and Rosie who kept trying to get back in his bed, and not Big Tits who kept asking the brothers about him when they'd eat at Ruthie's.

He picked up his phone and dialed Hawk's number. "Hey. I called for Kimber's number."

A pause ensued on the other end. "Sorry, dude, but I can't give it out."

"Fuck, man. I'm not gonna stalk her or anything. I just have to ask her a question."

"I was gonna say that if you happened to go into my office at the clubhouse and look under my duplicate employee files, I couldn't stop you."

Throttle grinned. "I owe you."

"Just hurry the fuck up and claim her. She's been in a pissed-off mood for over a week, and some of the other guys are fearing for their lives. She's pretty mean with a wrench." He chuckled.

Throttle stiffened. "No, dude, you got it all wrong. I just had a question I had to ask her. That's it. I'm not planning to claim any chick. You know me. I love my freedom and easy pussy too much. No way do I want a woman telling me what I can do and where I can go. Damn, that's not my style." He motioned the prospect, Johnnie, for a shot of whiskey.

"Are you trying to convince me or yourself that you're not interested in her?"

"You're starting to piss me off. I didn't call to hear all this shit about making a woman mine. No fuckin' way. I'm not interested. It's that plain and simple."

"Yeah, right. I gotcha. Have a good talk with the woman you're not interested in. Later."

Throttle heard Hawk laughing when he clicked off his phone and felt his body temperature rising. Couldn't he just call and talk with a woman without all this talk about *claiming* her? Hell, he'd screwed so many women, and he hadn't *claimed* any of them. Why was Hawk making a big deal about this? *I should just forget about calling her and take up with one of the club girls.* Frowning, he threw back the shot, jerked to his feet, and made his way to Hawk's office.

In his room, resting against the headboard, he dialed Kimber's phone number. The comments Hawk made still sizzled inside him. The rush of the Colorado River that ran behind the clubhouse sifted through his open window. She picked up on the fourth ring, and the mellow tone of her voice covered him like warm honey.

"How are you?" he asked. The way she sucked in her breath made him smile.

"How'd you get my number?"

"Nothing's secret anymore with the Internet. What've you been up to?"

"Not much. Work and school."

"Sounds dull."

"Not really."

A strained pause spread between them.

"You want to go out to dinner tomorrow night?"

She exhaled loudly. "Not really. I know where it'll lead, and I don't want it."

"Fuck, baby. You must think I'm a horny dog who can't control myself. Or are you afraid you can't control *yourself?*" He poured a shot of whiskey in his glass while he waited for her to answer.

After a long pause, she said, "You flatter yourself too much, but then all men with big egos do. Believe me, I can control myself just fine. Even if you were the last man standing, I'd be able to control myself."

"Then going out to dinner with me should be no problem."

"I'm not sure you'll behave."

He chuckled. "I'll behave just fine. No worries. It'll give us a chance to talk and find out some stuff, like how in the hell you ended up in a bike repair shop. I really want to know. I've been wondering about it since I first saw you working on Banger's bike."

"You could have fooled me. You were so pissed that day, I didn't figure you'd ever want to talk to me, let alone know anything about me."

"It just took me by surprise. I never ran into a chick who fixed bikes. You intrigued me, and you still do." He heard her breathing over the phone and he pictured her sitting on the couch, the TV on mute, debating with herself. "It's just fuckin' dinner. We both gotta eat. We'll be in a public place."

"All right," she said hesitantly. "I'll go, but if you try anything I'm going to smack you hard, and I won't care if we're in public. Got it?"

"Sure."

"I mean nothing. Nada. Not grabbing my hand. Not rubbing against me. Not even a kiss on the cheek. Nothing. Okay?"

"Yeah, I get it." A half-smile danced on his lips. "I'll pick you up at seven."

"I'll meet you at the restaurant."

"Meet me? No fuckin' way."

"Then it's off. That's the deal."

"Babe, do you think you'll ever agree with me on anything?"

"Probably not. So I'll meet you and if you don't like it, we don't have to go to dinner. No big deal." She yawned.

He forced a laugh. "Let's meet at Big Rocky's Barbecue at seven tomorrow night. Do you know where it is?"

"I'll find it. See you tomorrow night."

When he ended the call, he placed his head against the wall; a wave of anticipation washed over him, and he felt better than he had in days.

Replaying their conversation, he had to smile. She was by far the most stubborn, aggravating, and aggressive woman he'd ever known, and he was fuckin' crazy about her. How in the hell was he going to be able to keep his hands to himself all night? He'd have to be extra good, but if she wore her rose-patchouli perfume, there was no way he could keep away from her.

He smiled devilishly, finished his whiskey, stretched out on the bed, and switched off the lamp. Throttle would sleep well tonight—he was back in with his spirited woman.

THROUGHOUT DINNER, THEY talked about losing their parents, living in small towns, and of course, about Harleys. He was impressed on how much she knew about motorcycles; if it weren't for her seductive scent and hip-hugging dress, he'd have sworn he was talking with one of his brothers.

As they laughed and talked, occasionally her knee would casually bump against his, or her hand would briefly brush his, and her touch would magnetize him. It took every ounce of self-control he possessed to act like being out with her was no big deal.

"Have you seen Cowboy lately?" His muscles tensed in anticipation of her response.

"You mean Riley? No." He relaxed, a slow smile forming on his lips. "I just went out with him a couple times. There was nothing there."

"He didn't seem like your type."

She looked at him, and the smoldering flame he saw in her eyes made his dick twitch. "He didn't stand a chance. All I did was compare him to you."

"And, of course, there wasn't any comparison, was there, babe?" He held her gaze, an unspoken connection forging between them.

She shook her head, and her blue eyes looked as wild as the ocean during a storm. "None at all." Then she leaned over and kissed him hard.

"Fuck, baby," he groaned as he pulled her closer to him, his tongue pushing against the seam of her lips, demanding to delve into her mouth. Then she pulled back and took a sip of wine. He tugged her back to him, but she resisted. "What's up, baby? You teasing me?"

"Maybe." She licked her lips.

"Watch it. You're playing a dangerous game that's gonna get you fucked."

She laughed and he wanted to cover her mouth and swallow all sound from her. Everything about her that evening sent him into overdrive; she was driving him crazy with her scent, her eyes, her laugh, and her damn lips on his. She knew the effect she had on him, and she loved seeing him pant and stare just like a fucking novice. And he fucking *loved* it.

"Would you like anything else?" the waiter asked, breaking the crackling sexual tension between them.

Sitting back in his chair, Throttle took out his wallet. "No." He handed a hundred-dollar bill to the server. When the young man left, Throttle finished his beer and turned to Kimber. "Let's go listen to some music." He wanted to have her in his arms, her firm body pressed so close to him it'd be like they were fused together.

"I have to be at work early."

"I'll tell Hawk to excuse your tardiness." He slid his finger lightly up her arm, loving the way her skin pebbled under his touch.

"I really can't, but I'd love to go to Red Spot Creamery for ice cream. Have you ever been there?" He shook his head. "Oh man, it's the best ice cream ever." Her sparkling eyes made him laugh. "No, really, I'm not joking. Hands down, the best I've ever tasted."

"Then we better go so I can try it out. What's your favorite flavor?"

"They have so many and they're all homemade. I love their toffee ice cream, but for the summertime they have this awesome orange ice cream with fudge ripples. It's to die for. But then I love their pistachio with chocolate chunks. They're all so good."

Squeezing her close to him, he kissed the top of her head. "Fuck, you keep acting so goddamned cute, and I'm gonna have to fuck you in the back room."

She drew away after giving him a quick embrace. "Let's go."

He followed her to the ice cream shop, a line of people spilling out onto the sidewalk when they arrived. After twenty minutes, they placed their order—orange with fudge ripples for her and strawberry for him—and sat on the white parlor chairs outside.

"Isn't this the best?" She held her cone close to her mouth, licking away at the melting ice cream.

"It's good." *I want you licking my cock instead of your fucking cone.*

"I'm glad you like it. The strawberries in yours are fresh when they're in season."

"Do you have stock in this place?" he joked. Her laugh sounded like tinkling bells and it hit him in the groin. He couldn't believe he was fighting a hard-on in an ice cream place packed with families and awkward teens on dates. *She fuckin' pulls me in every time I'm near her. How the hell does she do that?*

"Maybe you could tell the guys about it. I bet they'd love to try some of the flavors, especially since it's been such a hot-as-hell summer."

"I don't think so." Like he could really see Banger, Rock, Rags, and the other brothers sitting their asses on the uncomfortable iron chairs licking a cone. Hell, if any of the brothers saw him with *his* ass there, they'd have a fucking field day with all the teasing. They'd think he was pussy-whipped for sure, but he didn't give a shit what they'd think. To his surprise, he was having a damn good time with Kimber, and he hadn't squeezed her tits or ass once. He was enjoying talking with her and hanging out with her, and even though he wanted back into her sweet pussy, he wasn't thinking about it the whole time. It'd been a long time since he'd enjoyed talking with a woman. The chicks he banged were just there for pleasure—his and theirs—and nothing more. Kimber was different from any other girl he'd ever been out with; she was confident, made him laugh, had a brain, and she captivated the hell out of him.

When they finished their cones, she rose from the chair. "I've got to shove off. I have a long-ass day tomorrow with work and school. I had a good time. Thanks." She smiled warmly as they walked to their bikes.

"Yeah, I got a long day tomorrow too. I'll follow you. I wanna make sure you get home safely."

She shook her head. "No, you don't have to do that."

"Don't bother arguing with me because I'm doing it. I don't give a shit what you say. There's no fuckin' way I'm not making sure you get in safely."

She stared wide-eyed. "Are you serious? How do you think I manage to live when you're not around? I've done perfectly fine without your guard service."

He leaned against his bike. "If you wanna keep arguing, I got all night, babe. It doesn't matter to me, but in the end, I'm still following your stubborn ass home."

Grumbling, she swung her leg over her Harley and started it up, and he followed suit. Soon he was behind her, their bikes rumbling through the neighborhood, and he was enjoying the way her cute ass hugged the seat. *Fuck, I got plans for that ass.* He also admired the way she handled her bike. In all the years he'd been riding, he'd never met a chick who could ride a bike that was worth anything. Watching her maneuver the chrome machine with such adeptness turned him way the hell on, and by the time he swung into her driveway, his jeans were damn tight.

She came over to him. "Thanks. I did have a nice time."

"I'm walking you to your front door." He got off his motorcycle.

"That really isn't necessary."

"It's very necessary," he breathed as he pulled her in his arms and kissed her hard, swallowing all her protests. She twisted in his arms, but he held her firmly to him, his kiss deepening. Soon she stopped pushing at him and began pulling him closer to her, tangling her arms around his corded neck.

"What the fuck are you doing to me, baby?" he rasped as he ran his hands down her back, resting them under her deliciously rounded, high ass. "Let's go inside. I know you want it as bad as I do."

Breathing heavily, she pushed back. "The agreement was just dinner, remember? Now we're kissing. I don't want it to go any further."

He pushed her hair away from her neck and trailed small kisses and nips on it. "Then you shouldn't be so damn sexy." He licked and bit the top of her shoulder, making her groan. "And you shouldn't wear perfume that fuckin' drives me wild." She tilted her head back, and he softly dragged his tongue across her throat, then kissed the pulsing hollow between her collarbones. The vibrations of her moans against his lips and tongue burned through him. He led her to her porch. "Open the door, babe."

She opened her eyes and blinked rapidly, then smiled. "Not tonight."

"You aren't feeling it?"

She put her key in the lock. "Of course I am, but I don't have time for a man right now. I told you that."

He nodded. "I got time to wait."

"I'm sure you've got other women to take the edge off," she said in a tight voice.

"I do, but right now I want you."

She sighed. "I know firsthand how bikers are, and I've learned to steer clear of them." She opened her door.

"I'm not your ex. Don't condemn all of us because you had a fuckin' asshole."

She smiled. "You're right." He started to come into the house, but she pushed him back. "The answer is still no. You can't always get everything you want."

He placed his hands on each side of her face and kissed her hard. "I always get what I want. Don't forget it, babe."

Laughing, she closed the door and switched off the porch light. Throttle stood on the dark porch for several minutes, waiting for his dick to calm down so he could ride more comfortably. He spun around and started walking to his bike when, out of the corner of his eye, he saw something move in the trees across the street. From habit, his senses heightened as his body went on the defensive. Not sure if it was a raccoon or possum, he walked to the driveway, his ears pricked up.

Bending down, he pretended to check something on his bike; his head was lowered, but his eyes glanced upward. Then he spotted a figure moving behind the cluster of trees. In a flash, Throttle sprinted, and the man took off. The watcher had a head start, but Throttle gained speed and could almost hear the fucker breathing when he tripped on a speedbump that he couldn't see in the darkness. The asshole avoided it, which told Throttle he knew the area well. Regaining his momentum, he pursued the man, who turned the corner. When Throttle reached the corner, he saw the man jump into an SUV, switch on the engine, and take off just as Throttle slammed his fist on the back window, trying to jump up on the bumper. But he couldn't. The vehicle disappeared into the night.

"Fuck!" His voice pierced the stillness. Bent over, he breathed heavily, cussing because he could only make out two letters in the dark; the fucker hadn't turned on his lights. *The sonofabitch was staring at Kimber's house.* A bad feeling rose inside him, and he wondered if the fucker was the one he'd read about who'd been breaking into women's houses and doing shit with them and their underwear. A knot formed in the pit of his stomach: What if he hadn't insisted on following Kimber home? If this fucker *was* the pervert, he'd just raped a woman not too far from the neighborhood the previous week.

Whether Kimber liked it or not, he was going to put in a security system first thing the following morning. There was no fucking way he was letting anyone hurt or get anywhere near his woman. And she *was* his woman, whether she liked it or not. He walked back to her house, plopped down on the lawn chair on her porch, and began his watch. He texted one of the prospects and told him to come relieve him at four in the morning. He'd make sure she was covered until the security system could be installed; he'd talk to Hawk about it in the morning.

Folding his arms across his chest, he stared out into the darkness.

CHAPTER SEVENTEEN

THE MORNING NEWSPAPER hit the mat, and Kimber opened the door to retrieve it. The paper and a large glass of orange juice were her morning ritual, and she cherished the pocket of time she had before her hectic day began. Beams of sunlight flooded over the landscape, lighting every blade of grass, and she breathed in the cool air. As the morning progressed, the coolness would melt into the dry heat of summer. To her left she heard a movement and whirled around, yelling out when she spotted a large man crammed into her lawn chair. The man, dressed in jeans, a T-shirt, and a leather cut, pushed up to his feet. She dashed inside her house and latched the screen door.

"Get off my porch or I'm going to call the police."

The man stood in front of her, his large frame shading the sun from her eyes. "Throttle had me watch out for you. I'm a prospect for the Insurgents. See…." He turned around and showed her his prospect patch on the back of his cut.

Her face tightened and she threw him a hard smile. "I don't need a fucking babysitter. You can tell Throttle that when you see him. I want you off my porch. Now."

The prospect shifted in place and cleared his throat. "I can't do that. Throttle's the only one who can tell me to leave. He said you know the biker ways, so you'd understand." He glanced away.

She squinted. "I see. I have to make a phone call." She went to the kitchen and called Throttle.

"It's good to hear your voice, babe. Fuckin' great way to start my day."

"What the hell were you thinking having a watchdog sit on my

122

porch? Do you ever ask? I want him off my porch and far away from me. I mean it. And don't try and sweet talk me because it won't fucking work!"

"You finished? Last night, after you went inside, I saw someone checking out your house. He was behind the trees across the street. I ran after him and almost got him, but he got away, the sonofabitch. I wanted to make sure he didn't come back so I hung out on your porch 'til about four in the morning, and then I had a prospect relieve me."

A flush crept across her cheeks as she grimaced. He was making sure she was safe, and she'd expected the worst from him so she flew off the handle. She'd thought he was exerting his cavemen attributes, but he was just looking out for her. "Sorry, I jumped to conclusions."

"You've got a knack for that."

"Thanks for watching out for me. I had a similar incident last week. It was a guy hiding behind the same trees across the street. He was watching me. It creeped me out big time."

"Damn! I'm sure it was the same bastard. Fuck, babe, this guy's up to bad shit. I'm installing a security system, and I don't want any fuckin' arguments over it. I already talked to Hawk about it and he's gonna get his guy. He's the best."

"I don't think the landlord will agree to it."

"I don't give a shit if a citizen agrees to it or not. It's going up. Discussion is fuckin' over."

Kimber smiled and wished he were there so she could give him a big kiss. She welcomed the extra sense of security the system would bring. Ever since she'd spotted the guy watching her, she'd felt vulnerable and jumpy. What if Throttle hadn't followed her home? Shivers ran up her spine when she thought of someone lurking in the shadows, watching her while she was inside her house, believing she was safe.

"I'll definitely feel better once it's installed. Thanks. I can't miss class, so can you arrange for them to come tomorrow? I don't have any classes, and I know Hawk will let me take the day off."

"It's gotta go in today. I don't trust that motherfucker. I'll take care of it."

"But you don't have the key to the house. I could give a spare to the prospect. What's his name, anyway?"

"Blade. You can, but I can get in without the key."

She shook her head while smiling. "Let's do this the easy way. I'll give it to Blade."

"Whatever. I'll call you later. I got a customer here who's chewing one of my workers' ass off. Gotta go."

"Later."

She placed her phone down, a warm glow spreading through her. *Underneath all Throttle's gruffness, he's a real sweetie. And a damn cute one. Whoa, Kimber, be careful. Remember, he's still a biker.* She opened the screen door. "Blade, I spoke with Throttle. Everything's cool."

Blade looked away, his eyes riveted on the cluster of trees across the street. She knew he'd never engage in conversation with her. He was a prospect, which meant he did the grunt work for all the members all the time. He was basically a nobody until he received his full patch and colors. "You want a cup of coffee?"

"I brought my own." He motioned at his backpack without looking at her.

"Okay." She went back inside to get ready for class.

"DO YOU WANT to come with us to the student center?" Carla, a friend and classmate, asked.

"Not today. I have to talk to Redman about my project, and then I have to go to work. Next time." Kimber watched as Carla and a group of her classmates chatted and laughed as they walked out of the business building. Hanging by the door, Kimber stood up straight when her professor exited the classroom. "Dr. Redman? Can I talk to you about my project?"

Dr. Redman glanced at his watch, then peered over his reading glasses. "I have thirty minutes before my next class. If that's not enough time, you can make an appointment."

"That should be more than enough time," she replied as she followed him to his office around the corner.

Sitting down on a cushy chair near his desk, she glanced at the degrees hanging on the wall. *Damn, I'm thirty years old and just working on an undergraduate degree. Dr. Redman doesn't look more than ten years older than me, and he already has his PhD. I'll never get the fuck out of school.*

"What seems to be the problem you're having with your project? Have you identified the business you want to start?"

They spoke about the specifics she needed to have for an effective business plan, as well as hiring people, healthcare, and all the other issues that went into owning a business with employees. As she closed her notebook, she smiled. "Thank you for sorting all this out for me. I'm really enjoying your class. I signed up for your fall Business Ethics class."

"I'm not sure I'll be able to teach it. It's not common knowledge yet, but I've been appointed dean of the college, and my position starts in the fall school year. I'm not too sure how it will all work out."

Disappointment weaved through her; Dr. Redman was one of the best teachers she'd ever had. "Who'll be teaching the class?"

"I believe it'll be Dr. Donsky. He's very good and students seem to like him."

"I have him for Business Marketing. He's fine." The truth was she thought Dr. Donsky was a bit of a letch, the way he'd stare at the women's legs and chests. He was subtle about it, but she'd caught him checking her out on more than one occasion. He seemed harmless enough, and his kids were pretty cute. One night she actually babysat for them when he and his wife had to attend a school function and their babysitter flaked. She'd needed the money because Hawk had started her out real slow to see how she'd do.

"I'm a teacher at heart, so I'm hoping I can still teach a class a semester. Do you have any other questions or problems you'd like to go over?"

"No. I'm good." She gathered her books and ambled to the door, then stopped and swiveled around. "Congratulations on your promotion. The college is lucky to have you at the helm."

He smiled. "Thank you, Kimber. I look forward to reviewing your project in a few weeks."

She rushed over to her Harley and threw her books in the saddlebags. She was going to be late; it just seemed like she never had enough time.

"Sorry I'm late," she said breathlessly as she dashed to the bathroom to change her clothes.

"No worries. Your security system has been installed," Hawk said.

She stopped and looked at him. "Thank you, but I insist on paying for the installation and the monthly service. You can take my payments out of my check. I want to pay the club back."

He waved his hand. "Forget about it. Throttle told me what happened. You listen to what he tells you, okay? This fucker doesn't sound like an average peeping pervert. Watch yourself, and let Throttle take care of you."

She stiffened. "I don't need a man to take care of me."

"Cara used to tell me that too, and I'm gonna tell you what I told her. It's okay to need a man to help you out, and sometimes it's fucking necessary—like now for you. Just let Throttle lead on this one."

"Okay." She left to change into her uniform. She wasn't stupid, nor was she a martyr; she would let Throttle help her out because she had no intention of being the Lingerie Bandit's next victim. She had a gut feeling that was who'd been watching her, and the thought chilled every nerve in her body. She rushed to the bay, cranked up the radio, and shoved back all thoughts of danger to the recesses of her mind.

By the time the shop closed, Kimber was sweaty, greasy, and totally charged. Three of the customers told Hawk that she'd done the best work they'd ever seen on their bikes. Plus, the one Harley she'd customized for an old, burly dude who didn't trust her near his motorcycle came back to the shop and gave her a case of Coors as a thank you. *That* fucking made her day.

Kimber went to her locker and took out her tote, then slammed it shut. With the overstuffed bag on her shoulder, she passed by the front counter on her way out. Patrick was the only one left, and he was stacking the receipts for Hawk to go over in the morning. "See you," she said, waving at him.

"You going to the clubhouse party tonight? I heard Hawk and a couple of the members talking about it this afternoon. It sounds like it's gonna be a big one. From what I heard, a lot of members from the other Insurgents' chapters are staying at the club for a few days. It sounds like it'd be fun."

"I wasn't invited. Are you going?"

His eyes widened. "No, but I'd love to. If I went, my mom would kill me first and my uncle Banger would do it all over again." He slumped against the back wall. "When I turn eighteen, I wanna prospect for the Insurgents. I know I still got two years to go, but I've wanted it ever since I can remember."

"I'm sure your mom's not too crazy about that plan."

He shook his head. "She's not, but my uncle's thrilled and told me he'd work on her so she'll let *me* make the decision. He said I may even change my mind once I turn eighteen, but I know I won't."

"Prospecting isn't an easy job, and you could end up doing it for two or three years, so I'm with your mom on that one."

He shrugged. "So, are you gonna go tonight?"

"I've been to club parties before back in my hometown, and they can be pretty damn wild, especially for a woman who isn't patched or with one of the members. I don't think it'd be a good idea for me to go."

"You don't have to worry. You're with Throttle."

Pink streaks painted her face as she stared wide-eyed at Patrick. *Damn. I didn't expect* that. "I'm not with *anyone*."

"Really? That's not the word around the shop. All the guys refer to you as Throttle's woman."

"Oh, do they?" *That fucking asshole. He's gone and told every man to keep their distance from me. No wonder all the guys have been acting like I had the damn plague for the last week.* "Well, I'm setting the record straight—I'm no one's woman. I'm my own person."

Patrick lifted one of his shoulders, then went back to stacking the receipts. In that moment, Kimber decided to go to the party. Hawk would be there, and he'd make sure nothing happened to her. She'd show Throttle that she'd go and be anywhere the fuck she wanted. She'd bet he wasn't playing the chaste card at the clubhouse. When she walked in later that night, she'd gamble her Harley that he'd have a few women wrapped around him. He was such a biker stereotype, and she couldn't wait to rub his hypocritical bullshit in his face.

After a long warm shower, she dried her hair and put on her makeup. A while later, she stood before the mirror, assessing her outfit: a short, sleeveless black spandex dress with a low-scoop neck that showed some decent cleavage thanks to a cute push-up bra; three-inch biker boots with gunmetal studs; neon pink polish on the nails and toes that matched the tips in her hair; smoky charcoal eyes; pink lemonade lipstick and gloss; and large silver hoop earrings. *Not bad at all.*

She pulled down on her dress again. She didn't normally dress so provocatively, but she was in the mood for it. Restlessness coursed through her body, and she wanted to have a good time. She could've called her friends and suggested going to a club, but, whether she liked it or not, the biker world was her familiar stomping ground. It'd been a part of her world for a very long time. It would be nice to be back amid all the leather and denim and eavesdrop on some good Harley discussions. She'd missed that ever since she'd left home.

She engaged the security system, hiked up her dress a bit, started her Harley, and headed to the clubhouse, loving the way the wind whipped around her hair. The sun had just set and the street lights had clicked on, dusting the sidewalks and roads in a warm golden glow. The night came to life: the melodious trill of the crickets hidden in the trees, the moths' frenzied flapping against the beam of porch lights, and the fireflies dancing, electrifying the darkness. The heat of the day had been replaced by a cool breeze, and riding at a good clip made goose bumps appear on Kimber's arms.

When she arrived at the clubhouse, several groups of men stood around, thick clouds of smoke encasing them, and the sweet smell of weed hung thickly in the air. A few of the men looked surprised to see a woman on a Harley, and when she walked past them they whistled and called out to her.

"Hey, sweet butt. Come over here and show us what you got," an older man with a long brown beard called out.

"I want you to ride me like you did that Harley," a young biker said. She noticed his cut had "Utah" on the bottom rocker.

Kimber ignored them and walked with her head held high. From nowhere, a man pinched her butt, and she whirled around and clobbered him with her fist. "Don't fuckin' touch me unless I tell you to."

For a couple seconds, there was complete silence, only the hum from inside the clubhouse and the rush of the Colorado River that snaked behind the club penetrating the quietness. Then the bearded older man burst out laughing, the others joining in as the victim of Kimber's ire rubbed his face, glowering at her. Keeping the guys in her peripheral view, she walked through the doors, loud rock music greeting her.

It took her eyes a moment to adjust to the dark; the large room was lit by red bulbs and the bar had a greenish glow from the tube lights around it. The place was packed with people, a sea of black—T-shirts and cuts. Several of the men and scantily clad women grabbed at each other and tottered around in drunken revelry. The club's insignia—a skull wearing a menacing grin with two smoking pistols on either side of its head—covered the length of the back wall, popping out at her as the eyes glowed red. In the far corner, pool tables looked ominous under black lights. She noticed a woman on her knees on one of the pool tables giving a member a blow job while another banged her hard from behind; several hands squeezed and tugged at her swaying tits. Kimber swallowed hard, kept her chin up, and pushed her way to the bar.

She squeezed in and propped her elbow on the wooden surface. Several men stared at a large monitor to the left of the bar, which flashed grainy footage from the security cameras positioned all around the clubhouse. They seemed mesmerized by it, and she was thankful it provided a distraction from her. She recognized the bartender—he was the prospect Throttle had sent to watch over her. She couldn't believe he'd done that. He was an enigma—sweet and thoughtful on one hand, but brutish and too possessive on the other. She knew bikers could be that way, but even her asshole ex waited to show his controlling properties after they dated for a while. And was she even *dating* Throttle?

Blade came over and she smiled broadly at him. "Hi, Blade. Do you have Coors on tap?"

He acted as though he'd never seen her before, turning around without a word. A few seconds later, a frothy mug of beer stood in front of her. Before she could thank him he was gone, serving up more drinks for the members. She scanned the room for Throttle and noticed several pairs of hungry eyes boldly assessing her. Looking around again, she hoped she could see Hawk, but it was too dim and all the guys blended together. She swiveled back around on the barstool and reached for her beer. She took a drink, then jumped when an arm encircled her waist. Kimber turned her head and met the leering eyes of a blond man in his thirties.

"You looking for some fun?" He was so close that his whiskey-scented breath fanned over her face.

"Not really. Just having a drink. From the looks of it, there are plenty of women who are up to having fun with you. I'm just not one of them."

His glassy, unfocused eyes ran over her chest. "You're pretty." He lifted his hand and motioned for Blade to bring him another drink.

She turned away from him, deciding to ignore him, when another man sidled up next to her and pressed real close against her, his excitement obvious against her hip.

Pushing him away as best she could, she shook her head, meeting Blade's gaze. Being a prospect, he'd never tell a patched member to back off, but he did break in by asking her if she wanted anything else. For a moment, it seemed to have given the pushy man some pause, but then he was back to pressing his hardness against her, like that was going to turn her on.

Again, she pushed at him. "Do you mind? I'm trying to drink my beer. Move back a little."

"You a regular?" the man asked thickly.

She shook her head, glancing at his cut. One of his patches said "Itchy" and another spelled out that he was vice president of his chapter. "You?"

He laughed and took out a joint. "Want one?" He handed it to her. The man who had his arm around her waist must have grown bored—or he may have passed out, she wasn't sure—because, much to her relief, he was gone. Itchy lit her joint and his, then inhaled and blew out slowly. "Fuck, that's good stuff." She had to agree with him. "You hitched with someone?"

"Why do you ask that?"

"You're not looking like you wanna fuck." He inhaled again.

She laughed. "I don't. Just having a drink."

He stared at her then shuffled back a step. "Are you fuckin' with me? You came to the party just to drink? Woman, you need a good fuck to set you straight." He came back and rubbed against her. "After your drink, let's go to one of the rooms."

"I don't think so. I'm good right where I am."

"I'm cool with you sucking me off right here." He put his hand on her thigh and squeezed it. "I'll show you a good time." Kimber tried to push his hand away, but it was like a clamp. "You like fun, don't you? I'd like your pink lips around my cock."

"The only cock that's going in her mouth is mine, Itchy. She's with me." Throttle's voice was steely.

All of a sudden he pulled away from her, his hands up in the air. "Fuck, brother, I didn't know she was your woman."

"Now you do." His voice was sharp like broken glass.

She craned her neck and saw him; with his long hair pulled back, his scowling dark brows over his flashing ebony eyes, and his strong jaw tightened, he looked fierce. Her breath caught in her throat, her panties dampened, and the ache between her legs told her she couldn't count on her body to be rational around him.

Lowering his head, he hissed in her ear, "What the fuck are you doing here?"

She smiled sweetly at him. "I heard you were having a party."

"Why didn't you find me? Or did you want another variety of biker cock?"

Without thinking, she slapped him—it was a knee-jerk reaction. "Don't *ever* talk to me that way."

Rubbing the side of his face, he gritted his teeth. "Don't ever let me find you in here again without me by your side." She nodded, then stroked the cheek she'd just smacked.

He grasped her hand and kissed it. "You look pretty," he breathed, his lips grazing her earlobe; she shivered despite the oppressive heat in the great room.

"Thanks. I thought I'd run into you or Hawk. Is Hawk here?"

"He was here just for an hour, then left. He's got an old lady, so he rarely stays that late anymore. Did you come to see me? You should've just called me. I'd have picked you up."

"I was just feeling restless. I needed to get out, and I wanted to be back in the club. I used to hang out at the Demon Riders' parties a lot." She took another sip of beer.

"Were you a hoodrat?" His voice was tight.

"No, not at all. I was with my ex. Being here reminds me of the good times we shared.

You know, it wasn't all bad. I guess I forgot that."

"What he did to you crosses out all the good shit you're remembering."

"I know, but all I'm saying is that things were good for us for a while."

He grunted, then put his arm around her. "You're showing off some fuckin' nice cleavage." He trailed his finger from her throat down to the hollow between her tits, his touch sending sparks of arousal sizzling through her.

She gazed up into his lustful eyes. "Are you happy I came?" She slowly licked her bottom lip.

His gaze lingered on her mouth. "Yeah, but I'm damn surprised you're here. I never would've thought I'd see you tonight." He leaned in and nipped her bottom lip. "But I'm glad you came."

She pulled away. "Do you guys have any food or do you just drink your dinner?"

Still watching her mouth, he smiled. "We got food. Let's go out back and get some." He hooked his arm around her waist and lifted her off the stool. Then, with her securely tucked close to him, they walked to the yard.

A long table housed mounds of ribs, corn on the cob, mashed potatoes, and the biggest bowl of coleslaw she'd ever seen. Her stomach grumbled. "Looks good. Did the old ladies prepare it?"

"I think so. That's usually how it works. I was working all day, so by the time I got back the food was done. Let's grab some food and find a place to sit."

Carrying a plate filled with steaming ribs and the fixings, Kimber followed Throttle through the maze of people, tables and chairs, sitting down next to him on the aluminum picnic bench. Anthrax's "Madhouse" crashed through the outside speakers which surrounded the yard.

A burst of tangy, smoky goodness exploded in her mouth as she sank her teeth into the juicy beef ribs. "Yum." She shook her shoulders and danced in her seat while Throttle watched her through heated eyes. She glanced around and saw a couple of the women sizing her up. "I hope I didn't spoil your plans to have fun with some of these women."

He rubbed his shoulder against hers. "You didn't ruin anything."

She licked her fingers, and he watched her every move. "It must be nice to have women at your disposal twenty-four-seven."

"It can be." He bumped into her. "Don't make a face at me. Everyone here knows the score. The club girls like fuckin' just as much as the brothers. It's the lifestyle everyone craves."

"Is it the one you crave?"

His gaze skimmed over her, landing on her cleavage before moving to her eyes. "I used to, but lately not so much." He slinked his hand around her waist and tugged her close. "I crave you."

She swallowed and curled her fingers around her beer bottle, taking a long pull. His touch was like the spark of a match, igniting all her nerve endings, and she had to cool down. *Isn't this what you wanted? Why else would you have come?* She could kid herself that she wanted a night out, but going to an outlaw biker party was so much more than a night out; it was sheer lunacy if a woman went alone. And she knew she wouldn't be alone. She came for him because she'd missed and wanted him, and she hated her body like hell for its hunger for him.

"Can you get me another beer?" She had every intention of getting sloshed before the night ended. Just looking at his rugged jaw and his black, piercing eyes made her sex throb madly. What was it about this man that had all her best-laid plans all fucked up?

She watched him swagger over to a makeshift bar perpendicular to the buffet table, his firm ass moving oh so right. The minute he stopped at the bar, two women—one of them was the bitchy blonde from the last time she'd been there—wrapped their bony hands around each of his arms, leaning in close and saying something in his ear. Kimber wanted to leap out of her seat and rip the skanks away from him by their hair. He pulled away from them, picked up three bottles of beer, and strode back to the table, setting the beer in front of her.

She looked up at him and that was nearly her undoing; the heated lust in his coal-black eyes nearly melted her panties. She gasped and, in one fluid movement, his fingers were tangled in her hair, pulling her head back. Then he slammed his lips on hers, almost knocking all the breath from her, his tongue pushing into her mouth. She kissed him back, her mouth as hard and demanding as his, and she put her hand on his back, jerking him closer to her. They were a tangle of arms and lips, and each yank of her hair, squeeze on her thigh, and nibble on her lips sent sparks of sensation zinging through her.

"I've missed you, babe," he rasped in her ear as his fingers burned into her tingling skin. "I need to be with you, and you need it too. Are you wet for me?"

"You fucking know I am." She threw her head back, and he showered airy kisses down her throat to the creamy swells that her dress's neckline exposed. Her hardened nipples strained against the thin fabric of her dress and she rubbed them against his muscled chest, burying her moans against his shoulder. Everything about him sent her reeling: his scent, his look, his touch. Her vow not to become involved with him shattered; she wanted him to take her rough and hard and do things to her she'd only dreamed about.

He pulled away slightly and locked his gaze on hers. "You do know what you're doing to me, don't you?" Roughly, he took her hand and placed it on his hard denim-clad dick. It pulsed under her fingertips. "That's right, babe. You did that, and it's all yours."

"What are we waiting for?" She palmed his hard-on and smiled at him, a wicked twinkle in her eyes.

He grabbed her wrist and sprang to his feet, taking her with him. "Let's go," he said huskily, and then he dragged her through the sea of people to the stairway. "My room's on the third floor."

She followed him up the concrete stairs.

CHAPTER EIGHTEEN

B EFORE HE KICKED his door closed, he had her up against the wall, his face buried in her cleavage while his hands slid up her legs. He had a feral, almost dangerous air about him, and she couldn't get enough of him. She bit him on his shoulder and neck, her nails scratching his back. He jerked her head up and covered her mouth with his, his tongue dipping in. She closed her lips over it, sucking it in and out of her mouth, his deep groan setting her on fire. Releasing it, their tongues writhed and twined together as their hands roamed over each other's bodies.

"You like it dark and wild?" he breathed against her lips.

"What do you mean?" she panted as she slipped her hands beneath his T-shirt.

"Some tying up and spanking. You got the perfect ass for it." He peppered kisses along her jawline.

Hell yeah! She'd always wanted to explore the more unconventional side of sex, but she'd never trusted Chewy enough. Plus, for a couple of years before she'd left, he had usually been so drunk or drugged out that their coupling consisted of a few hard squeezes to her breasts and him pounding into her until he came. She didn't know Throttle that well, but she trusted him and knew he wouldn't hurt her.

"Bring it on." She scratched him, hard.

"Fuck, baby." He yanked her away from the wall and walked her over to a closed door, all the while squeezing her ass and kissing the side of her neck. He backed her against it and pulled away. His gaze travelled over her, lingering at her crotch and breasts. "Take off your dress," he ordered.

The tone of his voice made a single shiver zing up her spine. She slowly pulled her dress over her head and tossed it on a chair next to them.

"Turn around and bend over."

She complied, and his shallow breaths behind her tingled her skin as the fire burned in her like a torch.

"Take off your panties and spread your legs wide."

She shimmied out of her lace bikinis and tossed them behind her, hoping they fell on him. "Like this?" she asked innocently, spreading her legs and bending down low so her ass stuck up in the air, giving him a good view of her glistening pussy. She was so damn wet; he was the only man who could make her wet just by a touch or the sound of his voice.

He whistled low. "Damn, woman. You got a beautiful ass." She heard his footsteps as he approached. When he planted his hands on her ass and dug into her soft globes, she thought she was gonna climax.

"You like it? I like the way you touch it."

"Is it a virgin ass?" He kept squeezing her ass cheeks.

"No, but I've only done it a few times and didn't like it."

He bent over her back and his hot breath went over her ear. "When I take your ass, you're gonna love it. We'll have to go slow, but I'll get you ready for me. You want my cock to fuck your ass?"

"I'd like it, but you're so big."

"It'll take time, but I'll stretch you to where you can take all of me. I'm gonna love fucking it, and it belongs to me." He pulled up from her back a bit and unhooked her bra, letting it fall on the floor beneath her. Then he cupped her tits and tugged them, flicking his finger across her nipples until they hardened. "Love the way your nipples get so hard. I'll suck them later."

She moaned and wiggled, her ass swaying and grinding against his dick. "If you keep doing that, I'm gonna come, and I'm not ready to do that yet." He massaged her globes again, then straightened her up and turned her around. He kissed her deep and wet, then went over to a drawer in his nightstand and took out a rope and two padded cuffs.

When she saw them, her nerve endings snapped and sizzled. An ache danced through her breasts and, between her thighs, her mound throbbed wildly. There was something about this man that made a fire rage inside her.

He came back over, the bulge in his pants very large, and opened the door. She saw it was a bathroom, and she wondered if he wanted to take a shower together. "Lift your arms."

When she raised her arms overhead, he grasped her wrists and placed the cuffs on them then placed the rope through the large rings on both of the cuffs, bringing her arms together. Then he looped the rope over an exercise bar, yanking on it hard. The movement lifted her so she was on her tiptoes. He secured the rope and stared at her, his bulge growing bigger. He exhaled. "If it gets to be too much tonight, tell me. Say 'checkers' and I'll stop, okay?"

"Checkers? Okay." Her body tingled with anticipation.

Throttle yanked off his shirt, kicked off his boots, then shrugged out of his jeans and boxers. Her gaze latched on to his rock-hard dick, its tip glistening. She craved to take it all in her mouth and suck on it. He skimmed his hands down the sensitive stretch of her skin along the sides of her body, then kissed her up and down, leaving a trail of goose bumps in his wake. "Keep your legs open," he ordered as he kissed his way down her body. She gasped when he lightly bit and kissed around her belly button, down past her hips, then landed on her inner thighs. She squirmed, the rope holding her in place. With his fingers, he scratched a sweet agony from under her armpits down to where he was kissing so close to her throbbing pussy.

For several minutes he teased her, kissing, licking, and stroking everywhere but where she craved the most. "I need you inside me," she rasped.

He chuckled against her flesh. "Not yet" was all he said, and his wickedly delicious mouth kept torturing her as she twisted above him. When she tried to close her legs to relieve some of the pulsing, he'd order her to keep them open, and she obeyed.

When his tongue finally came very close to her wet, hungry mound, he stood up. "Why'd you stop?" Frustration laced her voice.

"I want to taste your tits."

His hand molded over her breasts and he kneaded them, squeezing them roughly. "I love the way your tits fit in my hand." He pulled a pink nipple into his mouth, swirling his tongue around it before he closed his lips tightly, sucking deeply. She moaned and arched her back, pushing her nipple further into his mouth. He bit on it and, with his other hand, twisted and pinched her other nipple, bringing her a flood of pleasure mixed with pain. She was in sweet agony, and her body was flushed and sensitive to his every touch.

Throttle was breathing heavily as he played with every part of her body except her pussy, which drove her to the edge of lunacy. When she didn't think she could take it any longer, he untied her arms and they fell down, tingling as the feeling came back into them. He led her over to the bed and pushed her on her back as he knelt down, straddling her.

"Suck my cock," he commanded, his dick brushing hot and hard against the smooth skin right under her breasts before coming up to her open mouth. She took him in and sucked him greedily, her eyes fixed on his. "That feels so fuckin' good, baby." He played with her tits while he shoved his cock in and out of her mouth.

Then he pulled out and ordered her to turn around and get on her knees. She did as she was told, and he spread her knees wide and buried his finger into her wet folds.

"Fuck, you really want it, don't you, babe? You're dripping. I love that."

He stroked her over and over, and the pulse in her pussy throbbed with a hungry need to feel him inside her. "Please fuck me," she moaned as the tension built.

"I'm gonna fuck you hard. You're so damn ready, but first I want to bite your soft, round ass." He leaned down and kissed, licked, and bit her ass cheeks while he stroked her sweet spot to marble hardness.

When he smacked her ass hard, the pain from the sting coupled with the delicious flicks of his finger on her clit made her explode, the waves of pleasure spreading through her like a rushing river. She moaned and panted, then turned and looked into Throttle's hunger-filled eyes.

He dug his fingers into her flesh and drove into her hard and fast. She ground her ass hotly against him, taking every inch of his pulsing cock deep inside her. The sound of their bodies slapping into each other fueled her passion, and the flame within her exploded as crashing ecstasy ripped through her. When she came, her grunts and moans filled the room as she lost herself in her orgasm. Soon, Throttle's deep growl pulsed in her ears as thick streams of warmth released inside her clinging walls.

He collapsed on her back, breathing just as hard as she was, then laid down on his side and drew her to him, her back pressed tight against his chest and stomach. He stroked her still trembling body and kissed her head.

"You were fuckin' awesome," he murmured against her hair.

"Wow. I've never experienced anything like that." She placed her hands on top of his. "I'm glad I stopped by. I hope you don't treat all your guests like this." She chuckled.

He hugged her closer to him. "Just you, babe. Only you."

She looked at the way the moonlight filtered in through the slats of the blinds, and she caught a star twinkling in the night sky. As she stared at it, her eyelids drooped and soon she fell fast asleep in his arms.

THE EARLY MORNING rays peeked through the closed blinds, creating thin yellow-white stripes on the floor. Kimber fluttered her eyes open, and for a moment a sense of panic overtook her; she didn't recognize where she was. A warm breath caressed her cheek and she turned over on her side, a big smile spreading over her face when she saw Throttle sleeping soundly. *Of course. I'm in Throttle's room. Damn, I had too much to drink, but I don't regret one damn thing I did.* Her memories of the previous night were clear, and she recalled the ecstasy of being held against his strong arms as they screwed most of the night. Watching him as he slept, she felt a warm glow flow through her. For the first time in the past several years, she was blissfully happy—the giddy and saccharine type.

She looped her arm around his trim waist and snuggled close to him, breathing in his manly scent. Brushing her lips across his side, she remembered how furious he'd made her the first time they'd met. Deep down, she'd known he was danger because he'd evoked such strong feelings in her. At that moment, pressed against his warm body, she couldn't think of wanting to be with anyone else but him. A nagging inner voice kept reminding her that she'd been his new toy, and she couldn't count on him for more than what they'd shared the previous night. Squeezing her eyes shut, she choked down that thought and chose to relive their awesome night together.

"You're up early," he said hoarsely. He nuzzled his face in her hair. "Did you sleep good?"

She tilted her head up and kissed his chin. "Oh yeah. I hope I didn't wake you. You looked so peaceful as you slept."

"You didn't wake me up." He took her hand and put it on his hard shaft. "My dick wants more of your sweet pussy." He rolled her over on her back and loomed over her, lowering his head to capture her lips.

She chuckled. "You're so bad."

"Fuck yeah."

Then his tongue made a searing path down her ribs, to her stomach, and finally to her aching mound. She pushed her head further into the pillow, closed her eyes, and reveled in all the wickedly delicious sensations building in her body, releasing herself completely to his touch.

After a couple hours, Kimber slipped her dress over her head, loving the way Throttle watched her every move. For now, he seemed fascinated with her, and she had to admit she was hooked on him. She wasn't sure if he saw her as something more than a good fuck, but he certainly acted attentive and interested. *Just have a good time and don't put pressure on you or him. You know how his world is.*

"What're you thinking about? Your face is so serious, and you got that cute frown that means something's on your mind."

She smiled. "It's nothing. I was just thinking about school and my project." She turned away so he couldn't see the deception in her eyes. "I need to be going." She zipped up her boots.

"We're gonna go for a ride."

She pointed to her dress. "Like this? I don't think so. Anyway, I have some work to do on my project."

"I'll follow you home to change. I'm not asking you. I'm telling you we're going on a ride. I want you behind me, pressed against me."

"You love giving orders, don't you?" she asked, trying hard to hide the smile whispering on her lips.

Walking past her, he smacked her butt. "Let's go, babe."

SHE SLIPPED HER tool kit into her tote and walked out of her bedroom. "I haven't ridden bitch in years. I love riding on my own."

"I want you against me. I've only let one other woman ride with me, and that was a long time ago."

"So you're telling me I should be honored?"

"Damn straight."

"Were you born with your big-ass ego, or did you develop it as you grew?"

His lips curled in a smirk. "It's in my blood. What about you? Have you always been a smart-ass know-it-all?"

"Yep. My dad raised me the right way. He taught me that I could do anything I ever wanted as long as I believed in myself. For him, it didn't matter if I was a girl or a boy. He was the best."

In a heartbeat, Throttle was at her side, drawing her to him. He kissed her gently on her lips. "You're different from any other woman I've been with."

"How many have you been with?" She pressed closer to him.

"Too many to remember. They all mix together, but none of them held their own like you. The women I've known go out of their way to act stupid and helpless, and you do the opposite. And I like that you let up and realized you *do* need a man in your life."

"And that man is you?" She licked the top of his ear, then drew his earlobe in her mouth and sucked gently.

"Fuck yeah," he gritted. "And don't even think of being with another man." He pushed into her and his hardness poked at her soft flesh. A heated rush of desire flooded her, and she dug her nails in to his back. "Feels good, babe."

Breathless, she pulled away. "If you're trying to have me agree to ride with you, it's working."

"I already decided that. *This* is because I can't get enough of you. I don't know what the fuck you're doing to me, babe, but you're on my mind all the time."

"Even when you didn't call me? Admit you were too proud."

He moved the hair from the side of her neck and lavished the spot with slow, wet kisses. "I don't chase chicks." His lips on her skin vibrated when he spoke, and it sent shivers up her spine.

"Never?" She moved her head further to the side so he had access to all her sensitive spots that drove her wild.

"Nope." He pulled down the strap on her top, exposing her shoulder. Then he kissed it over and over before his mouth trailed up her neck, over her jawline, and landed on her soft lips.

She groaned in pleasure, her fingers tugging on his ponytail, then pushed herself away. "We better get going."

"What the fuck? You gonna leave me like this?" He cupped his hardness in his hand.

"Looks like I am." She laughed, grabbed her sunglasses, and opened the front door. "You coming?"

Shaking his head, he walked over, lowered his head, and kissed her hard, his hand tweaking her nipples. A rush of heat spread over her like a blowtorch and she began to move closer to him, but he opened the screen door and walked out into the brightness of the day. Taking several deep breaths to steady herself, she watched as he strode over to his Harley. Since she first saw his kickass bike, she'd wanted to feel it between her thighs. She'd never let on how stoked she was to ride on it, and she was actually thrilled to ride bitch, which surprised her.

Since she'd bought her own bike, she never wanted to ride behind a man anymore, and that had pissed the hell out of Chewy. She held firm to it, and not until she saw Throttle straddle his Harley had she even considered riding bitch again. The man was just as powerful as his iron machine, and she was falling for him.

"You coming?"

She nodded. "Just need to set the alarm." She didn't move, her body pulsing as she took him in: sunglasses on his tan face, his T-shirt pulled tight across a thickly muscled chest, and inked tattoo lines running out from under the fabric and down his arms. *Damn, he's sexy.* There was something about him that drove her wild, made her do irrational things. He had a dark vibe that gave off raw power, heat, and sinful intent, drawing her to him like a magnet.

"Babe? Did you forget your password? You're just standing in the doorway."

His voice broke through her heated thoughts. "No. I'm good." *Just admiring you, that's all.* She tore herself away from the door and, looking at him, set the alarm and locked the door behind her. "All set." She flashed him a smile while handing him her tote.

"Fuck. What the hell do you have in here?" He placed it in his saddlebag.

"Brought along some tools just in case."

He shook his head, then brushed his lips across hers. "You really are a kook, you know that? Damn, never thought I'd be with a woman who brought her own tools."

"You're getting used to me. That's cool."

"Yeah, pink hair and all."

She laughed and settled on the seat. When he got on, she wrapped her arms around his waist, loving how his hard ripples felt under her fingertips. With a jerk, the Harley roared to life and jumped away from the curb, speeding through the small streets of the town. When he pulled into the parking lot of a strip mall, she wondered what he was doing. After killing the switch, he helped her off the bike.

"What're we doing here?" she asked.

"I wanted to buy some booze for our outing." He grabbed her hand and they walked into the liquor store.

The blast of cold air felt good since the temperature had already crept up to ninety-five degrees. Throttle went straight to the whiskey aisle, Kimber following behind him. While he was looking through the various bottles, she noticed a tall, striking woman staring at them. She had dark brown hair, shapely legs that went on forever, big breasts, and a small waist—a biker's wet dream. She strolled over to Throttle. "Hi again," she said, lightly touching his shoulder and ignoring Kimber.

Throttle spun around, his face turning hard when he saw the woman. "Hey." He turned back to studying the whiskey.

The woman inched closer. "What're you up to?" Her hand moved from his shoulder to his tatted bicep.

His sigh was audible, and Kimber saw him scrub his hand over his face. "We're in a liquor store so it's a no-brainer—getting booze." He gripped a bottle of Jack and grinned at Kimber. "Finally found it. Fuck, they shove the good stuff to the back. Damn weird."

She smiled, encircling her arm around his taut waist. Hating herself for acting like she was back in high school, she wanted this big-busted woman to know that Throttle was hers—at least for today. Kimber wondered if the woman had been one of his bedmates who he hadn't bothered to call back. That I-really-love-you look glimmered in her eyes, and Kimber almost felt sorry for her until the woman finally acknowledged her by sizing her up and turning up her nose in disgust. It was at that moment that Kimber decided the woman was a bitch and deserved whatever it was Throttle had done.

He lowered his head and kissed Kimber on her lips. "You good with whiskey, or do you want something else?"

Right then, Kimber felt a part of her fall in love with this hardened biker who only had eyes for her when a gorgeous, stacked woman stood next to him, fuming. "Whiskey's fine." Her eyes shone and he laughed.

"Excuse me. I'm trying to talk with Throttle." The woman inserted herself in front of them, but Throttle stepped back. "Is that any way to act toward a woman you almost married?" From the glint in her eyes, Kimber knew the bitch enjoyed her look of surprise.

"We don't have anything to talk about. Me and my woman are headed out. Take care of yourself, Mariah." He pushed past her, his arm around Kimber holding her tightly to him.

Even though she knew it was childish, she derived an inordinate amount of satisfaction from Mariah's loud gasp. It was still unclear who she was, and Kimber would ask Throttle about it later, but for that moment, her being attached to his hip pissed the hell out of the snotty bitch and made Kimber's day a bit better.

After paying for the whiskey, Throttle once again helped Kimber on the bike. From her peripheral view, she saw Mariah standing outside the store staring at the way he fussed over her, making sure her feet were on the footrests. If she wasn't enjoying pissing the bitch off so much, she would've been madder than hell at Throttle for acting like she was a newbie rider. *Guiding my feet to the rests? Give me a fuckin' break! He's playing the macho male to a hilt.*

"All good?" His lopsided grin and shining eyes made up for his macho antics; she melted, managing only a nod. "Then let's roll." He revved his powerful engine and, with her arms grasping him tightly, he blasted off.

Half an hour later, Throttle stopped the bike in a beautiful valley lush with pine, aspen, and evergreen trees. Indigo, orange, pink, and red wildflowers lent punches of color to the landscape, carpeting the grass as vibrantly colored butterflies hovered over them. A crystal-clear creek flowed quickly, the bronze rock bed shimmering under the summer sun.

Picking out a nice area near the stream and under a cluster of aspen trees, Throttle spread out a thin blue blanket he retrieved from his saddlebags. Reaching out his hand, he said, "Come on over here, babe." He set down the whiskey and a few bottles of water, then took a seat, his back against the tree trunk and his corded legs stretching in front of him.

Kimber ambled over and kneeled on the blanket, taking his hand. He tugged her to him, settling her between his legs, her back against his chest. He kissed the top of her hair. "You smell real good. I love the perfume you wear. It fuckin' makes my dick twitch every time I get a whiff of it."

She laughed. His blunt, dirty mouth was exactly what she loved. Chewy had been that way in the beginning of their relationship, and that's when she'd realized she loved it. As time went on and Chewy's drinking, drug use, and cruelty escalated, the dirty talking turned into crude, hurtful words. She rested the back of her head on his shoulder. "You want to tell me about Mariah?" she asked softly, her heart thumping in her chest.

He blew out a long, noisy breath and twirled several strands of her hair around his fingers. Then he told her everything about his life with Mariah. When he was finished, he cupped her chin in his hand and craned her neck, gently kissing her.

"Thanks for sharing a glimpse into your past with me." She twisted in his arms so she sat sideways, her back resting against his drawn-up leg. She captured his gaze. "Do you still love her?"

"No. For years I tried to forget her, even punished women for the shit she did to me, but I never could get her out of my system. The bitterness was... fuck, still *is* there. If you're asking if I want to hook up with her again, the answer is no. The funny thing is that, if you weren't around, I'd probably think about using her, but I don't want to hang or be with anyone but you."

Warmth spread through her. Was it possible that she was more than his sex toy? Did he actually care something for her as a person, as a woman? "I don't know why, but what you just said made me real happy.

I know we don't have claims on each other, but I wouldn't want to think of you with her."

"It kicks ass that we're even here holding each other. I love this spot, but I've never shared it with anyone else."

"Not even Mariah?"

"Nope. We were young, and she wasn't interested in anything but partying, shopping, and screwing. I was good with that, so it worked for a while. You're the first woman I've *wanted* to bring here. I don't know… I just wanted to share it with you, and I knew you'd like it. I don't know what the fuck I'm saying."

"I think you're saying that you like me, and I like you too."

"Damn, this is all fuckin' strange. You're a goddamned mechanic, and it bothered the hell outta me, but not so much anymore."

She smiled and ran the back of her hand over his cheek. "That's great. What bothered us before doesn't matter so much now because we're getting to know each other. Like your chauvinistic he-man stomping was beyond annoying when we first met, and now your caveman traits are endearing, in some situations."

He gave her a quizzical look. "Yeah, right. Wait… Did you just fuckin' insult me?"

She kissed his chin. "No. You're too cute." She wanted to ask him if he still had the club girls servicing him, but she didn't want to know the answer, not at that moment. They were having a wonderful day, and knowing he was kissing, touching, and screwing other women the way he did her would break her heart. *Go slowly, Kimber. You guys are having a good time. You're connecting as good friends, but don't let him own your heart. You don't want to go there ever again. At least not with another biker.*

He held her close and she wrapped her arms around him until it was like they were meshed together as one. They stayed like that, enjoying being together, listening to the creek splash over the rocks, and the birds and insects sing and chirp. And, in that solitary moment, they held hope that the pain in their past love affairs had finally healed enough to allow each of them into the other's life.

CHAPTER NINETEEN

SEVERAL STACKS OF paperwork littered Detective McCue's desk. Deputy Manzik sat in a chair, waiting for McCue to finish his phone call. The ceiling lights illuminated the room, but the panel above the detective's desk was dim and flickered intermittently. The deputy looked over her report; the second rape had been very similar to the first, and it definitely had the markings of their Peeping Tom turned burglar turned rapist.

The previous night, she and Bryan had been the first to arrive at the scene, and she made sure she did everything by the book. There was no way she was going to give her sergeant reason to berate her. Deputy Manzik generally liked most people, but she could not stand Sergeant Stichler; he was a bitter, hateful man. Sharon couldn't imagine being the wife or child of such an unpleasant man. She'd met his wife a few times at the department's picnics and Christmas parties, and she looked so downtrodden and miserable that the pretty police officer's heart went out to her.

There was also something very odd about him. His animosity toward her was too much, and she suspected it wasn't entirely because she was a female deputy. She thought it went deeper than that. She'd done some of her hands-on training with him, and she'd seen how he'd shown little sympathy to the victims of domestic abuse, or how he'd condemn the prostitutes who seemed to come out in full force after dark at Elsinor Park on the west side of town. A couple times, the women would protest that he took certain liberties when loading them into the van.

The truth was she didn't feel comfortable at all with her supervisor and wouldn't want to be in a room alone with him. Most of the time, when she'd leave his office, she'd fight the urge to shower off his innuendos, leers, and off-color remarks. When she'd turned in her report that morning, he surprised her by asking if the victim was pretty and stacked while his gaze lingered on her breasts. She couldn't believe he'd asked her that or stared so boldly at her. She'd mumbled something and scooted out of his office as soon as she could. She couldn't wait to put two more years in, then apply for a detective position. If she had to stay under his command for more than that, she'd seriously consider moving over to the next county and applying to its sheriff's department.

"What can I do for you, Sharon?" McCue smiled warmly.

From the minute she became a deputy, the stocky detective had treated her like everyone else. Even though he came off as being gruff and impatient, he didn't fool her; he was nothing but a big old softie with a passion for justice. He'd work tirelessly investigating a case, his prime goal to make sure the bad guy was punished and the victim was vindicated. Sharon admired him for it. Over the five years she'd been on the force, Earl had taken her under his wing and looked out for her, even calling out Sergeant Stichler for the way he spoke to her in his presence. From the glares her supervisor threw at Earl, she suspected he wasn't too fond of the detective.

"I was wondering if CSI found any evidence at the scene of this rape. I'm positive this is the work of our peeping perv. Can you tell me anything?"

He chuckled. "You know I can't, but I will because I know you'll keep it right here at my desk. This time, our sick bastard wasn't so perfect—he left his semen, and a footprint outside the victim's window. We have the rain to thank for that one. If the ground hadn't been so soft that wouldn't have happened. Now we just need a damn suspect to match DNA and the footprint."

"No leads?"

He chomped down on his unlit cigar. "Nope."

"It's amazing how none of the neighbors have seen anything."

"I know. If we could only get *something*. We don't even know if he lives in the area or drives to it. He seems to favor the same area. We'll get something. I feel it. He's getting sloppy. It always happens that way. A perp who doesn't get caught right away becomes a cocky sonofabitch thinking he's invincible, and that's when I get him."

"I hope it's sooner than later."

He sighed and leaned back in his swivel chair. "Me too. He's going to kill someone. Damn." He ran his hand through his graying brown hair. "You look beat. You should go home and rest."

"I'm exhausted. I have to do a briefing with Stichler before my shift ends. But then I have two days off, and I'm totally looking forward to it." She smiled.

"Is he treating you better?"

She shrugged. "What can I say? Stichler is Stichler."

He shook his head. "You let me know if he goes too hard on you."

She pushed up to her feet. "Thanks, but I can handle him. I better go or he'll have my ass, even though he sits for hours in his office not doing much but playing computer games or bullshitting with his cronies. One of the perks of being the boss, I guess."

"He's a goddamned jerk. I'll see you in a couple days. Hopefully I'll have a solid lead to tell you about. Go out and do something fun on your days off."

"Right now, sleeping sounds like a lot of fun."

He laughed, then answered the ringing phone. Sharon walked out of the room, dreading her interaction with Stichler. In a few short hours, she'd be home; she had to focus on that.

Stichler's office was on the second floor, and she entered the area and walked toward it.

"You going in to see the sarge?" one of the deputies asked her.

"Yeah. He asked me to drop by," she said.

"He's gone. He wasn't feeling well so he took off."

Her face beamed. "That's too bad." She turned around and bounced out of the room, heading to the employee cafeteria to find Bryan.

After a few more hours of her and Bryan patrolling the streets of

Pinewood Springs, Sharon clocked out and made her way to her house. She couldn't be happier that she had the next two days off. Her plans were to do absolutely nothing but sleep, catch up on her reading, watch a ton of junk TV, and eat whatever the hell she wanted.

FROM INSIDE THE house, he'd seen the dark-haired woman pull into the driveway—at last. For the past two hours, he'd been learning about her life, looking through her photo albums, smiling at her baby pictures as he imagined her mother and father did, and feeling a sense of admiration when he spotted her in her deputy uniform upon graduation from the sheriff's academy.

He'd also spent time going through her panties and bras, picking out the ones he'd have her model for him before he took her. His pulse quickened and his dick strained against his pants in anticipation of what was to come. He licked his lips and walked to her bedroom, hiding himself between her dresses in her walk-in closet.

She'd taken her time coming into the room, probably sorting through her mail or maybe enjoying a cold drink. It was incredibly hot, so he didn't fault her delay. Then he heard her footsteps on the hardwood floor as she came inside. A few seconds later, he discerned a heavy thud on her nightstand—her gun, he presumed—then the familiar sound of a zipper. He wanted to watch her undress, to see her bra and panties against her skin, but he didn't dare attempt a peek lest he be discovered too soon. So, he imagined her sliding her clothes off, revealing her panties and bra; his pants grew more uncomfortable with each image.

He heard the bathroom door close and he sneaked a peek out of the closet door. Straining to hear over the AC, he relaxed as he realized she was taking a shower. She'd be clean for him; he liked that. The door squeaked open and he stood still, watching her even though he knew he was taking a big chance that she'd see him. He couldn't help it; she was luscious and so pretty, her skin pink from the warm shower and steam.

The close-trimmed strip of hair on her tantalizing mound made him reel.

Then she opened her dresser's top drawer, and he held his breath. She took out the sexiest bubblegum pink hip-hugger panty that he'd ever seen. When she slid it on, the floral lace hugging every curve, he nearly exploded. She stopped for a moment, her body stiff, as if she sensed something. He stepped back, his heart racing so fast he thought he may pass out. He quietly took a few steps to the side and hid himself among her many dresses. The scent of spiced vanilla curled around him, grabbing hold of his hard dick.

Several minutes passed, and then the light from the bedroom window flooded inside; she was so near, and his level of anticipation was off the charts. He swallowed, hoping she hadn't heard him. She grabbed a hanger and her fingers almost touched his chin. She placed some clothes on it, hung it on the closet rod. "Damnit," she said aloud, then turned around and bent down. She wore only a T-shirt, and the cheeks of her butt escaped the skimpy fabric covering it. Not being able to stand it another minute, he pushed out, grabbing her from behind, his large hand clasped over her mouth.

His victim kicked back with her feet, but he'd already anticipated it so he was prepared. Being the hunter always gave him advantage over the hunted, and he liked that *a lot*. She thrashed, pushed against him, and screamed loud when he had to use both hands to subdue her. She twisted around and her eyes bulged, her muscles rigid. "You? What the fuck?"

He smiled and shoved her over to the bed, slamming her down hard. He used those few seconds of shocked recognition to overpower her, sitting on top of her as he tied her hands and feet securely to the bed, duct taping her mouth. He rose up and leaned over to grab her gun on the nightstand, taking out the bullets and slipping them in his pocket. She squirmed, pulling on the rope. She was so pretty; he'd always thought so. Slowly he ran his fingers down her face, marveling at the softness. "They're secure. You're not going anywhere." Her brown eyes pleaded with him not to do what he had to.

He breathed out, knowing they had time—a lot of it. She had two full days off, and that was more than enough to satisfy all his fetishes and cravings. With a detached, cruel smile, he inched up her T-shirt.

DETECTIVE MCCUE CHEWED his gum vigorously as he stared at the lifeless body of Deputy Manzik. A lump formed in his throat and he swallowed it down, a sudden coldness hitting him and spreading through his body. He'd really liked her, and to see the life strangled out of her hit him hard. As many homicides as he'd worked, he still never got used to seeing the dead eyes of the victims.

Murder wasn't the norm in Pinewood Springs; the last homicide had been a year or so before, when the Pinewood Strangler had killed several young women. Since that case, the town had been pretty much homicide-free. He'd been a homicide detective in Denver before relocating to Pinewood Springs, and had seen his share of violent murders. It was at his wife's insistence that he'd traded the smog and noise for fresh air and muted sounds. At first he'd missed the action, the pulse of the city, but in time, he came to appreciate the slower pace of life. A big kudos was that he didn't have to see the opaque eyes of homicide victims very often. After the Pinewood Strangler case was put to rest, he didn't think anything would strike the town again, but he was wrong. What started as a man who peered into women's houses had escalated rapidly in the past couple of months to rape, and now murder.

McCue exhaled. Even though he was a seasoned detective, knowing the victim just punched him in the gut. Sharon was only thirty years old, and she'd had her eyes on being a detective; she would've made a damn good one too. He was proud of how hard she'd worked while always maintaining her compassion. She'd been on the force for five years and had recently completed her degree in criminal justice, a must if she wanted to make detective.

He shook his head. He just couldn't believe she'd become a fucking statistic. Life shouldn't end in violence. Blinking rapidly he turned away, surveying the room. That time, the sonofabitch made a huge mistake—he'd killed someone close to McCue. At that moment, the detective made a silent vow to Sharon as they wheeled her out that he'd find the goddamned killer and make sure he paid for what he'd done.

Seeing the body of a fellow cop, a woman he'd known and guided, was the worst. The previous day, he'd laughed and talked with her, and now she was gone—all the laughter choked out of her. She'd been so excited over having a couple days off, and now she left her home in a body bag. With his jaw working overtime on the gum, he rubbed his eyes, then watched the nondescript burgundy van take away the body of Deputy Sharon Manzik.

CHAPTER TWENTY

KIMBER SAT STARING at her phone, wondering why she gave a shit that Throttle hadn't contacted her in the past several days. She knew the score; she wasn't an ordinary citizen who glamorized bikers, yet she let herself get sucked in *again*. Give her a broad-shouldered, tattooed man with long hair and earrings and she weakened at the knees every damn time. Maybe when she was eighty she'd learn to steer clear of hot bad boys.

She pulled her hair up in a high ponytail to let her neck cool off. It was another scorcher and she knew she should go inside her cool house, but she loved sitting on the front porch, watching how life played out one small step at a time. Her phone alarm rang, tipping her off that it was time to go to work. On lazy summer days, she didn't feel like doing anything but sip on iced tea and sit on her front porch; a good book in her hand was always an extra treat. If only she had enough money to take a trip somewhere—anywhere. She hadn't even been to Denver since she arrived in Colorado. She'd driven through on her way to Silver Ridge, but that didn't really count. What was it about the summer that made her so restless for something new and exciting to happen? She'd thought she'd found her summer fling, but the way Throttle was dissing her now only made her want to kick him in the balls. Hard. Very hard.

She reluctantly stood up and went inside to fix up before going to the shop.

When she arrived at work, Hawk was in a heated discussion with another man who, from the patch on his cut, was from his MC. As she scooted past them, she overheard them say something about the Demon Riders—Chewy's club. *What the hell do the Insurgents have with them?*

She knew the Riders had a chapter in Denver, but as far as she could tell, they didn't have any presence in Insurgents' territory. After changing into her uniform, she walked over to the mini fridge, took out a large can of sweet tea, and made her way to the service garage.

While the music pulsed around her, she buried herself in fixing a rice burner. Normally, they didn't get too many bikes that weren't Harleys, but when they did, she wasn't too crazy about working on them. They didn't have the powerful feel of her beloved Harley-Davidsons, and she always wondered why anyone would buy anything but the American-made bikes. Singing along to "Born in the USA," she worked on replacing the motorcycle's belt. Halfway through the song, she noticed her phone shaking on the work table. She wiped her hands on a towel and picked up her phone, opening the text.

Throttle: *Babe. U good?*

She rolled her eyes even though her stomach fluttered. So he finally contacted her. What she should do was ignore him and go right back to replacing the belt on that bike, but the memory of his lips on hers was too powerful and delicious.

Kimber: *Ya. U been busy?*

Throttle: *Yep. Work & planning road trip to Denver 4 bike expo. Ur coming with me.*

What the hell was he talking about? She didn't remember him telling her about a motorcycle expo. And why in the hell wasn't he asking her if she wanted to go?

Kimber: *U asking or telling?*

Throttle: *If ur answer is yes, then asking—if no, then telling.*

She laughed aloud.

Kimber: *Need to know more about it.*

Throttle: *Let's talk tonite. MC going to Steelers. I'll pick u up @ 8.*

Kimber: *Again ur not asking.*

Throttle: *U don't wanna go?*

Kimber: *I do.*

Throttle: *Then what's the problem?*

She shook her head, a smile whispering on her lips. The whole asking versus telling was inconceivable to him, and she wasn't in the mood to educate him, at least not at that moment. But she was dying to see him—her body ached for him—and she missed talking and hanging out with him.

Kimber: *No problem. See u @ 8. Gotta get back to work.*

For the rest of the afternoon, she hummed and sang along with all the songs on the rock station as she made the rice burner purr like it was brand new. Excited that she wasn't going to spend the night with her computer and leftover Chinese food, she glanced at the clock, wishing it were six o'clock. Closing time couldn't come fast enough.

She was so fucking hooked.

THE JANGLE OF voices greeted them when they arrived at Steelers Bar and Grill. The place was hopping, and the hard rock music jumped and danced in the biker bar. Throttle had his arm around her waist as he wound around warm bodies, making his way to the other side of the bar where all the Insurgents were gathered. She noticed how many of the women checked him out blatantly, like she wasn't there, and winked or giggled at him when they'd catch his eye. He just kept plowing forward until they reached the Insurgents' group.

"Let's get a beer," he said in her ear, his hot breath sending shivers up her spine.

They leaned against the bar, and a burly man with a red, bulbous nose came over and greeted Throttle. His eyes dropped for a brief moment at her low-cut neckline, but then he spun around and poured two beers in large frothy mugs. Kimber touched the hair lying on the shoulder of her black mesh dress, the pink tips a beacon of neon against the dark fabric.

As they approached the gathering, she noticed several women drinking and laughing at two tables that had been put together. Other than Hawk, Cara, and Throttle, she didn't know anyone, and she felt a little bit out of place.

Throttle cupped her chin and kissed her lips softly. "You look beautiful."

She stroked his cheek. "You already told me that when you picked me up."

"I know, and I plan on telling you over and over all night." He squeezed her shoulders and kissed her again. She laughed and laid her head on his shoulder.

"You gonna introduce me to your date?" Rags asked while Rock nodded behind him.

"This is Kimber, and these two losers are Rags and Rock."

"Hi," she said as she tried to avoid their raking eyes.

"Are you the woman mechanic at Hawk's shop?" Rags inquired. Throttle scowled.

"Yes. If you ever need a tune-up or anything, just come on by."

"What does 'anything' include?" Rock asked, a wide smile on his face.

Before she could answer, Throttle's beer mug crashed to the floor and his fist met Rock's jaw, who reacted by throwing a punch in Throttle's face. In a matter of minutes, the two men were cussing, throwing punches, and breathing heavily until Rags, Chas, Jerry, and Jax pulled the two men off one another.

"What the fuck is up with you two?" Jerry asked as he slammed Throttle against the back wall. "We got our old ladies here. Fuck, if you wanna kill yourselves, take it out back."

"I'm fucking standing there, having a goddamned conversation, and this fuckin' asshole takes a punch at me for no reason." Rock wiped the blood from his face with a napkin. "He's a goddamned problem."

"You were fuckin' rude to Kimber, and I won't tolerate that shit."

"Who's Kimber?" Chas asked.

"I am," she replied in a small voice.

They all looked at her, and her neck and face flushed.

"You Throttle's woman?" Jax asked.

"Woman? Uh… no… Not really." *Who the hell am I to Throttle? Fuck buddy, probably.*

"She's the chick who's been messin' with our brother's fucking head for the last month. She's the bitch mechanic at Hawk's shop," Rags said.

The hairs on the back of her neck bristled, and even though she knew the word "bitch" didn't have the same meaning to outlaws as it did to citizens, it still pissed her off. "Yeah, I'm the *woman* who works at the shop. What about it?"

Rags jerked his head back. "Nothing. Just saying."

"Well, quit saying." Kimber crossed her arms over her chest.

"Babe, leave it alone." Throttle put his arm around her, but she twisted out of it.

"I'm not leaving anything alone. If I were a guy, we wouldn't be having this conversation."

"But you ain't a man. You're a bitch, and it's fuckin' weird for a bitch to do a man's job," Wheelie said as Rags opened his mouth.

"Stop calling me a bitch. I'm a woman. How'd you like it if I called you a bastard?"

Several of the brothers had come over when they heard the heated discussion, and many of them grumbled under their breaths that the bitch had a mouth and Throttle better control her before she got her ass thrown out. Kimber met their glowering gazes with a defiant one. Wheelie had taken a few steps toward her, his nostrils flaring. Before he could lay into her, Throttle pulled her to him and whispered in her ear, "Fuckin' leave this alone."

"I can't," she whispered back.

"You gonna let your woman talk to a brother like that, man?" Hoss said as the others voiced their disdain.

"Kimber was just having a good time with me when some of the brothers thought it was okay to disrespect her. That wasn't okay," Throttle explained.

"You're not answering the fuckin' question," Wheelie said, his scowl still fixed on Kimber.

She knew it was huge to lose face in front of the brotherhood, and Throttle's loyalty was to the club first—always first. Citizens just couldn't understand it, and she'd had a hard time with it when she first became acquainted with the outlaw world, but she'd grown to admire the brotherhood and the fierce loyalty they had to each other. Warmth flowed through her as she witnessed Throttle trying to protect her and not lose his brothers' respect. She'd gone too far, had let a couple of assholes turn her evening out into a crusade for feminism. It didn't matter what *they* thought about her, only what *she* thought about herself. She didn't want Throttle to defend her and risk losing his brothers' esteem.

"I was out of line," she said, looking at Wheelie. "I'm sorry."

"You fuckin' better be," he gritted.

"I was disrespectful to the brotherhood. I do apologize." The words sounded hollow to her, but they were what the brothers wanted to hear, so they nodded and shuffled back to the pool tables and bar, a few of them agreeing that "she knew her place." She stiffened but kept her mouth shut. If she were going to continue seeing Throttle—and she *really* wanted to—she'd have to keep her mouth in check. Being a woman involved in the outlaw world meant knowing her place and watching her mouth. From the way Throttle stared at her, she knew he was super pissed, and she hoped she hadn't blown it with him.

"Kimber, do you want to join us for a drink and appetizers?" Cara asked.

She nodded, ready to break away from the tension that filled the air around her and the men. She touched Throttle's arm. "I'm going to join the women for a bit, okay?"

His fierce eyes bored into her. "Come with me." He clutched her hand and dragged her behind him down a hallway, to a back room. Inside, he whirled her around, facing him. "What in the fuck were you thinking by shooting off your mouth like that?"

Her defenses flared up. "I don't like being treated like I'm inferior just because I'm a woman. The way they were calling me 'bitch' and dissing me pissed me off."

"You act like this is the first time you've been around bikers. You know we call women 'bitches.' It doesn't mean shit."

"I know, but it doesn't mean I like it. The fucking respect thing goes two ways. If your brothers want it, they have to give it too. Problem is men are always thinking life is one way with a woman—*their* way. It just got to me, that's all. I probably overreacted, but it's been a shitty week." She flipped her hair over her shoulders.

Throttle's jaw relaxed and he pulled her to him. "I do agree with my brothers about one thing—you've got a mouth on you. And you're right about the respect stuff. The guys were acting like you were a slut, and that's what pissed me off. I wish you would've let me handle it, though."

She shrugged. "I've been handling things ever since I ditched my ex. The day I decided to leave him was the day I swore I wouldn't take any shit from a man ever again."

He pressed her to him. "You're always fighting, sweet one. Relax a bit. Sometimes it's good to have a man take care of you, but you have to let him." He tangled his hand in her hair and jerked her head back. "The way you were sparking out there fuckin' turned me on." He moved his mouth over hers, devouring its softness. His kiss sent new spirals of ecstasy through her. "I need you, babe," he said, his breath hot against her skin.

"Me too," she croaked.

Then his hands were all over her—touching, squeezing, pinching— as he walked her backwards until she was against the wall. With one hand, he pinned her arms above her head as he kissed and nipped the side of her neck, her ears, and her shoulders. He slipped his other hand around her waist, stroking her as his demanding lips seared her skin.

Heat engulfed her, rushing to every corner of her body: her curling toes, her aching nipples, her throbbing mound. Desire saturated every inch of her as she squirmed and rubbed against the wall. In a matter of seconds, her mesh dress was crumpled on the floor next to them, and her hard nipples strained against the thin fabric of her bra, begging to be sucked. He slipped his finger under her bra and brushed the underside of her breasts. "Bite them," she rasped, and he trailed a scorching path from her shoulder to her tits, lightly biting her hardened beads through the fabric.

Twisting her arm behind her, she unhooked her bra, revealing pert breasts with pink, hard nipples. He growled and circled her areolas with his tongue as she yanked his hair, mad with lust as she waited for him to pull her nipple into his mouth. As he bit and sucked her tits, he pulled down her sheer panties and cupped her butt in his hands, squeezing and grunting as he kneaded his hardness against her. Backing up a bit, he unzipped his jeans and tugged them and his boxers down, his erect cock poking at her. She curled her fingers around it; it was hot and pulsing, and her mouth watered.

"I love it when you touch my cock. I'm about ready to explode here, babe. Is you pussy ready for it?"

"It's been ready for you since you picked me up tonight."

"Yeah?" He sucked her breasts hard, leaving red marks as he slid his finger between the folds of her swollen lips. "You're so fuckin' wet. Damn." He brought his finger back up, his smoldering gaze catching hers, and put it in his mouth, slowly licking her juices off. "Fucking delicious."

Surges of electrified passion sparked through her as she watched him lick her off his finger. Right then, she was connected to him through desire and longing, and she had no intention of ever letting him go. "Fuck me," she moaned through parted lips.

He reached under her chin and stroked her jawline. Her lips opened slightly and their breaths mingled. In one movement he lifted her, his hands under her firm ass, and she wrapped her legs around his waist. When he thrust into her heated pussy, she cried out, sliding her hands inside his T-shirt and raking her nails down his back.

Over and over he pumped into her as he bit her breasts, kissed her neck, and sucked her nipples. "You're so beautiful and awesome. What the fuck have you done to me?" he grunted with each thrust.

"What the fuck have you done *to me*?" she panted, the burning desire beginning to uncoil. Sex had never been that intense; Throttle did something to and for her that no man had ever done. He'd gotten into her blood, and even though she knew that was dangerous, as he thumped and shoved into her, she didn't give a damn at all. She just needed and wanted him.

The dam broke, flooding every inch of her with waves of intense rapture she'd never known with a man before she met Throttle. She held on tight for fear of collapsing on the floor. His grunts and groans mixed with the warmth of his come shooting inside her and spilling out. She slid her legs down his corded thighs, and they pressed together as each one of them regained their composure.

He kissed her shoulder. "Fuck."

She kissed the side of his face. "Wow."

As she pulled back, she saw his sparkling eyes and lopsided grin, and she couldn't help but smile back. "I guess we should go back out and join the others. I'll hang at the women's table and let you do the macho thing with the guys."

He laughed and kissed her. "Let's go."

CHAPTER TWENTY-ONE

"I WANT YOU on the back of my bike, babe. I don't want to hear any more argument about it," Throttle said as he sat on Kimber's porch.

"I get that, but I want to ride my own bike to Denver. We're going to a fucking motorcycle expo. Why can't you get that I want my own bike there?" The pink and golden hues from the setting sun illuminated her face.

"I like you pressed against me."

"Not a good enough reason. I can ride with you around the city and some of the trails in the foothills, but I'm going on my own Harley to Denver. If you're going to be pissed off at me and ruin our weekend, that's your choice." She crossed one leg over the other.

Throttle's stare was hard and his twitching jaw told her he was hopping mad, but she wouldn't be bullied. She was tempted to suggest that *he* ride bitch, but she suspected that would be pushing him too far. Why couldn't he understand that she loved riding as much as he did? "Do you want another beer?" The evening breeze was cool, and as it skimmed over her, goose bumps peppered her arms.

He shrugged. *Just great. He's really pissed at me. Men are such babies.* "Have another one. I don't want to drink alone." She stood up and went behind him, wrapped her arms around him, and kissed the top of his head. "Don't be mad at me, okay?"

He stared straight ahead. If anyone should be mad, it was her. He hadn't even asked if she wanted to go to the Denver Motorcycle Expo— he'd just *told* her. The fact that she was over the moon to go wasn't the point; he should have asked her. The expo attracted over two hundred thousand people to its annual event, and since its inception thirty years before, it had grown substantially into a necessary event for bikers. For several years, she'd wanted to go, but she was either too busy or too broke to make the trip. Many members of the Demon Riders went every year and hung out with their Denver chapter. For a brief second, she wondered if Chewy would be at the event; she shuddered at the thought.

"You don't want to talk to me?" she whispered near his ear, licking his earlobe. He shifted a tiny bit in his seat. "I can't wait to spend the whole weekend with you. I can think of a lot of things we can do, you know?" Still no response, but his breathing had deepened. Slipping her hand under his muscle shirt, she scratched her way down over his hard pecs, his abs, his flat stomach, until the waistband of his jeans blocked her. Her kisses on his jawline and throat were hard and then soft, and when a low moan vibrated in his throat, her skin tingled and a jab of desire hit between her legs. Her hand rested on his jeans.

"Don't stop yet," he said huskily.

She chuckled, then undid the button and unzipped his pants, his hard dick throbbing under her touch. "Let's go inside. My mouth needs to take care of that," she breathed in his ear. He jumped up, crushed her against him, and hurried them into the house. Kicking the door closed behind her, she led him to her bedroom.

THE RIDE TO Denver was different, as Kimber had to stay behind all the brothers since she was a female rider. She didn't make a stink about it because she didn't want to start out with any animosity, and she was riding with the Insurgents so their rules applied. Throttle rode at the end, one bike ahead of hers, and each time he'd glance backward at her, her heart turned over. He was turning out to be a real sweetie. Some of the other brothers weren't keen at all on a female riding with them, but they were outvoted so there she was, eating the exhaust of twenty-plus bikes and loving every minute of the ride.

They checked into a two-story motel near the coliseum that held the expo. The yellow neon sign read "Rodeo Motel," and a large cowboy boot with spurs intermittently flashed in blue neon. The motel was a U layout, with all the rooms facing the parking lot, just how the bikers wanted it so they could check on their Harleys to make sure no one messed with them. Of course, the prospects would take turns babysitting the iron and chrome babies, but each biker still wanted to be able to see his machine. Kimber was no exception, and she glanced out the white curtains frequently even though Throttle teased her about it. She caught him checking out his Harley when he thought she wasn't looking. When she called him on it, he began tickling her until tears rolled down her cheeks. Being with him felt so normal and relaxed; it was like they'd known each other for a long time and not for only two short months.

The motel didn't have a restaurant on the premises, but a diner a couple blocks away beckoned the group; they filled the eatery, ordering chicken fried steaks, meatloaf, pork chops, and burgers. Kimber and Throttle sat at a table with Hawk and Cara, Jerry and Kylie, Chas and Addie, Axe and Baylee, and Jax. Kimber had met the old ladies at Steelers Bar and Grill the previous week, and she liked all of them. Since she worked for Hawk, she knew Cara the best, but the others were very friendly and welcomed her into their group right away.

"I have to admit I'm a little nervous about going to the expo tomorrow," Addie said as she cut her chicken fried steak.

"Why, precious?" Chas put his arm around her.

"There're going to be so many different clubs there and all that testosterone going around. I hope nothing happens."

"It's been over fifteen years since shit hit the fan. No reason to be worried about it." Throttle took a gulp of his root beer. The diner didn't have a liquor license so the only beer served was homemade root beer, much to the chagrin of the Insurgents and some of their women.

"I know, but I heard that some rival clubs attend the event. I know you guys are having a booth, and I'm sure others are too." Addie's forehead crinkled.

"It's going to be okay, isn't it, Axe?" Baylee's voice held a note of concern. Of the group, she and Axe were not staying at the motel;

rather, they were staying in her high-rise condo downtown. When she'd fallen in love with Axe, she'd transferred to the architecture firm's Pinewood Springs office, but she'd held on to her condo for weekend trips or if she had to come to the city for business.

"It's gonna be more than fine." Axe kissed her on the cheek. "Addie, eat your damn food and quit worrying about shit that isn't gonna happen."

Addie opened her mouth to reply, but Kimber said, "She has a point. I know the Demon Riders go to the expo. They have a booth every year."

"If they don't start shit, we won't, but if they do, Insurgents won't fuckin' back down." Throttle leaned back in his chair, a scowl on his face.

"I know that. I'm just saying that Addie's right. Whenever you get a bunch of bikers together and a few of the clubs are outlaws, the potential for a problem is real."

"Can we please change the subject?" Baylee said.

Silence fell over the group, and then Cara cleared her throat. "They don't have any leads yet on the deputy who was raped and killed a couple weeks ago."

"Oh, Cara...," Baylee groaned. "I don't want to talk about that either. It's too gruesome and scary. Some fucking pervert is loose in Pinewood Springs, and the cops can't do a damn thing about it. It freaks me out."

"I'm sure they're working hard on it. I knew the victim—Sharon. I saw her a lot in court, and we became work friends. She was very nice. I'm sick about it." Cara's voice hitched and Hawk put his arm around her, tugging her to him and kissing her. He whispered something in her ear, but Kimber couldn't hear it. While Cara spoke about the murdered woman, shivers skated along her nerves as she thought of the man caught watching her on two separate occasions. She was so damn glad Throttle insisted she put in the alarm system.

"Change the subject again." Baylee turned to Jax. "I'm starting to think Cherri had the right idea about staying home."

The group laughed, and Jax said, "Paisley was sick, so she couldn't stay with Chas's mom and dad. She insisted I come, but all this talk about the fuckin' pervert makes me want to haul ass back to Pinewood." He pulled out his phone and began typing.

"That didn't go so well," Addie said softly. "What subject can we talk about that won't bring on any negativity?"

All the guys and Kimber said, "Harleys." And so, for the rest of dinner and during the walk back to the motel, motorcycles were the topic of discussion.

After watching a movie on TV, Throttle turned it off with the remote and pressed Kimber closer to him. She rolled away, smiling when she heard him growl. "I want to check on my bike."

He laughed. "You just checked it an hour ago, babe. Puck's down there making sure your pink baby is doing okay."

"Even so, I want to make sure." She looked through the curtain and saw her Harley, the parking lot light bouncing off the chrome. Puck sat on a chair with his arms crossed, playing sentinel to the powerful machines. She looked up, expecting to see the black sky littered with sparkling stars, but the city's artificial illumination masked the blackness and hid the twinkling lights in the sky. She closed the curtain and crawled into bed.

"All good?"

She nodded and snuggled under the crook of his arm. He reached over and turned off the lamp, then put his thumb under her chin and tilted her head back. Parting her lips, she raised herself to meet his, and she quivered at the sweet tenderness of his kiss. Exhausted from the long ride to the city, they held each other tight as they fell asleep.

KIMBER HAD NEVER seen as many motorcycles in one place as she did at the expo. Her dream had always been to go to Sturgis, and if things continued to go well with Throttle, she'd be joining him that year at one of the largest bike rallies in the country. Of course, if she went, she'd want to ride to South Dakota on her own bike. A knot formed in her stomach just imagining the argument they'd have about that one.

"There's the Insurgents' booth," Throttle said as he guided her through the maze of people and kiosks. Puck and Blade stood guard—one on each side—while Bear, Bruiser, Rock, and Jax spoke with people, handed out literature about the Insurgents MC, and gave away stickers, buttons, and black T-shirts that read "If Riding were a Crime, I'd be on Death Row" and "Respect is Earned, a Beating is Free." A group of women congregated around the booth, flirting and handing out their phone numbers to the members behind and around the kiosk.

"Where's Rags?" Throttle asked as he held up one of the T-shirts.

"He's with Wheelie checking out the wet T-shirt contest," Bear said.

Throttle laughed. "Why aren't you with them?"

Bear lifted his shoulders. "Don't think my ol' lady would like that." He grinned and handed out a few pamphlets to a couple of young guys who wore Harley-Davidson T-shirts.

"Do you want to watch the contest?" Kimber asked Throttle.

He ran his eyes over her body, then tugged her to him. "I wanna see you wiggling your ass in a wet T-shirt," he whispered in her ear, his hot breath singeing her skin.

"You're so damn horny all the time." She smiled as she stroked his cheek.

"You made me that way. I can't get enough of you, babe. The way you smell, the way you sass, and the way you shake your sexy ass is nothing short of a fucking hot wet dream." He kissed the side of her neck, and his fingers skimmed down her arm. Static tingles sizzled under his touch, and a small yelp burst from her throat as she pressed closer to him. Whenever she was near him, it was like she'd stepped on a high tension wire, making their connection magnetized. She looked at him and his gaze shone. "Yeah, baby. I feel it too."

In a place where there were thousands of people and loud noise, no one existed for her but him. It was like a movie where the background receded and the main characters were highlighted. She hooked her arms around his neck, bringing his face to hers, and then she gave him a passionate, loving kiss. At that moment, she cared for him more than she ever had for any other man, and it scared and exhilarated her at the same time.

"Go back to the fuckin' motel," Hoss grumbled as he came up to the booth.

"Don't take it out on me just 'cause no one wants your dried-up dick." Throttle laughed, his arms still around Kimber's waist.

"Fuck you. I could bang more bitches in an hour than you could all night." Hoss cuffed Bruiser on the shoulder; the member nodded, sliding out of the booth and heading toward the wet T-shirt contest.

"Wouldn't want to see you act like a pussy when you lose that bet." Throttle leaned down and kissed Kimber. "You've got me so fuckin' worked up," he said in a low, thick voice.

"Do I?" She squeezed his waist.

"You fuckin' know it. I can't get enough of you."

"You gonna stand there practically fucking your woman or you gonna help? Bear's been manning the booth for the last three hours," Hoss said.

A warm glow spread through her when she heard Hoss refer to her as Throttle's woman. Throttle didn't protest or recoil from her when he heard it, and that made her feel even better. But was she truly *his woman*? They'd never talked about it and he never claimed her while fucking, as was the outlaw's way, but he said stuff to her that made her think she was special and not just some woman he banged for fun. She wasn't sure. She knew he loved the ladies, and she'd gathered from what the other brothers said to him that he loved them back in the way that was only reserved for fucking.

She didn't even know if she was the only one he was screwing. They'd never talked about exclusivity, but she knew if she went out and screwed another man that Throttle would go ballistic, so that was something, wasn't it? Then again, bikers could be very territorial with women, even if the woman wasn't their old lady. The Demon Riders never let their club whores service anyone else but the brothers, and she gathered the Insurgents were the same with their club women.

No, she really didn't know where she stood in Throttle's life.

"Come help me behind the booth. Bear said they've given away a shitload of T-shirts and buttons. The young guys like to put them on their jean vests. I used to do that when I was in high school. I was totally into collecting buttons from my favorite metal bands."

She smiled. "I didn't know that. Do you still have them?"

"Yep. My sister has all my old shit in a big box in her basement. I want you to meet Dawn and Olivia."

"Olivia's your niece, right?"

"Yeah. She's so fucking cute. She cracks me up." A warm smile whispered across his lips.

So the badass biker has a weakness. I love it! "Sure, I'd like to meet them."

"I'm taking them out to dinner next week. I want you to come."

She nodded. *So he wants me to meet his family. That definitely means something. And sharing a glimpse of his past with me—totally huge. Maybe this is more than an affair.* "I'd love to go. Thanks."

"No need to thank me. Fuck, we're beyond that, babe."

"Are we?"

"You know we are." They locked gazes, and the air around them crackled with sexual electricity. A jolt of desire coursed through her like a lightning rod in a savage storm. His dark eyes were molten, making the need between her legs ache more. She bit her inner cheek when she saw the large bulge in his jeans, loving that he wanted her as much as she did him. She licked her lips and began to walk to him when a teenager with long, straggly hair cut in front of her and went up to the booth's table.

"What is the Insurgents MC all about?" he asked Throttle.

With regret etched on his face, he turned to the teen and handed him a leaflet. "The Insurgents MC is a club of brotherhood, the most important aspects being respect and loyalty...."

Kimber turned away, breathing deeply to dispel the desire that was still pulsing through her. Addie and Baylee came up to her. "Hawk told us to come find you. He said there's a killer bike show with over a hundred vintage and high-custom bikes. He said you'd be psyched about it." Addie pointed to the left. "It's over there. Do you see the large neon sign?"

Kimber craned her neck. "Yeah. Hawk's right, I'm totally down for it. You guys going?" They nodded. "Okay, let me tell Throttle where I'll be." She slipped behind the kiosk and told him her plans.

Worry crossed his face. "I don't like you being somewhere I can't see you, especially with so many other bikers around. Why don't you wait and I'll go over with you? I should be able to get a brother to spot me in a couple hours."

"I'll be fine. I know you want to see the bikes too, so I'll go back with you. I'm going over with Addie and Baylee, and Hawk's there. Chill, okay?"

Dipping his head slightly, he said, "All right, but text me when you connect with Hawk, okay?"

"Yes, Dad," she joked, laughing louder when he frowned.

As they walked away, Throttle called out, "Addie, Baylee—you take care of her."

"We will," Baylee replied, the three of them laughing as Throttle frowned.

When Kimber went into the bike show, she couldn't believe how many kickass motorcycles there were. As she was checking out the bikes, someone bumped into her from behind and she felt a pinch on her butt. Enraged, she whirled around, her face blanching as her gaze fell on Chewy. Images of his fist smashing into her face and his boot cracking her ribs flashed through her mind. Without saying a word, she turned away, searching for Hawk.

"Aren't you gonna say hi?" he asked.

She swung her head sideways. "Hi." She walked away, but his hand on her wrist stopped her in her tracks. "Don't touch me."

Chewy let go of her. "You look good, Kimber. It's been a long time. How've you been?"

Every nerve in her body was on edge; she knew his smooth voice and calm demeanor could turn deadly in a heartbeat. "I've been good." *Get away from me, you fucking slime ball. I have nothing to say to you.* She noticed that he'd aged since she last saw him, and his hairline had recessed quite a bit. *That* brought her an enormous amount of satisfaction; Chewy had always been so obsessed with losing his hair. *Karma's a bitch, asshole.*

"You live in Denver now?"

She shook her head. "I have to go."

"Why? You got an old man?"

"Bye." She spotted Hawk and caught his eye, then waved him over. He was there in a few seconds, and she finally relaxed.

"What's up?" he asked.

"I just wanted to show you this 1932 Harley. Bruno, the guy who brought his German vintage in last week, wants me to custom it along these lines." She felt Chewy's glare burning through her.

"Fuck, it looks awesome. Cara and I were admiring this baby earlier. You and I have the same taste when it comes to bikes."

"As the saying goes, 'Great minds think alike.' I so love this motorcycle. If I had the money, I'd collect these vintage babies."

"Is he your old man?" Chewy's voice, laced with irritation, came from behind her.

Why the fuck is he still here?

Before she could answer him, Hawk turned around and, with a hard glint she'd never seen in his eyes before, said, "Who the fuck are you?"

When she saw the vein in Chewy's temple throb, she knew he was on the verge of exploding. Watching Hawk, she saw his gaze harden further when he spotted the Demon Riders patch on Chewy's cut. "You know this fucker?" he asked her.

"A long time ago."

"She was my old lady," Chewy hissed.

From the way Hawk's eyes widened, she knew the comment took him by surprise. He'd definitely have a lot of questions for her later, but for the time being, his stance and taut face indicated he was on the defensive.

"You interested in talking with this asshole?" Hawk said.

"No."

"You heard her. Get the fuck away. Now."

Chewy clenched his fist, and her stomach dropped. *This is bad. Very bad.*

"What if I don't?" Chewy took a step closer to her.

"Then I'll stomp your fuckin' ass."

Their voices had escalated, and several people moved away from the trio as the tension in the air heightened. Kimber was positive a fight was ready to break out, but then Banger, Axe, Chas, Rags, Wheelie, and Rock came over, and relief flooded through her. Chewy was stupid as hell, but he wasn't so stupid to start something with seven Insurgents surrounding him.

"You got trouble with this fucking Demon Rider?" Banger asked.

"Nothing I can't handle," Hawk replied.

"What's the problem, asshole?" Chas said to Chewy.

"He's bothering Kimber, and I told him to get the fuck outta here." Hawk clenched his fists. "Only problem is he's still fucking here."

By the way Chewy's eyes darted around the different members' faces, Kimber knew he was assessing the situation and realizing it was futile to start anything without backup. Stepping back, he disengaged from the group. As he walked away, he said, "This shit isn't over."

"Bring it on, fucker!" Rags's face was red and his nostrils flared.

"Fucking Demon Riders" was muttered by several of the Insurgents.

Kimber turned to Hawk. "Sorry about that. I was hoping not to involve your club."

"No worries. You were a Demon Riders' old lady? You still got shit with the club?"

"Don't worry about it. I haven't had any contact with my ex since I ran away from him a few years ago. I was never that involved with the club. They weren't the nicest to the old ladies. They adhered to the notion that women were beneath second-class citizens."

"You sure you're not with them? Because I don't like the fact you never told Hawk 'bout your connection with them," Banger said, his blue eyes flashing.

"I was never *with* them, as I said. I left, and it never occurred to me to tell Hawk about my broken relationship. I wasn't trying to hide anything."

Banger grunted and Hawk cleared his throat. "Kimber's solid, but we gotta be on alert now. I have a feeling that fucker isn't too happy about what happened. I figure he's gonna want to start some shit."

"Is he with the local chapter?" Axe asked.

"Nah. His patch said 'Iowa.'" Hawk crossed his arms across his chest.

Banger exhaled loudly. "I bet those fuckers Dustin and Shack are here. I want *them* to start something so I can kick their fuckin' asses."

"Yeah. Ever since those bastards joined up with the Demon Riders, I've wanted to kick their asses too. I keep saying we shoulda wasted them when we had them." Chas ran his hand through his hair.

Hawk glared. "We got a citizen here, Chas."

An awkward silence fell over them and Kimber knew it was her time to leave. "I'm going back to the booth to hang with Throttle. He said he wanted to see the bikes, so I'll come back later with him."

Banger nodded, his blue eyes still cold.

"I'll make sure you get back okay," Rags said.

"We better find our women and keep them close. The game has fuckin' changed," Axe said, and all the members nodded in agreement.

As Kimber neared the Insurgents' booth, dread climbed up her spine, and she couldn't shake the feeling that something wasn't right. She chided herself that she was just unnerved because she'd seen Chewy again and he'd stirred up all the old, negative feelings.

When she spotted Throttle talking to a couple guys at the kiosk, an instant wave of relief washed away the dread. She caught his eye and he threw her the sexiest panty-melting smile ever. Her stomach fluttered and she waved at him, returning his smile.

Then a gunshot rang out and all hell broke loose.

CHAPTER TWENTY-TWO

SCREAMS BROKE OUT. The crowd scattered like blowing leaves in a wind storm, rushing the exits, their faces masks of panic and fear. Kimber watched as Throttle and his other brothers whipped around and jumped over the table, running at full speed toward the area behind the booths. She shoved people out of her way as she stood off to the corner and saw more than fifty men fighting, the glint of the overhead lighting bouncing off their chains, industrial flashlights, and knives. Blood was everywhere, and all she could see was a blur of black leather and denim tangled together. The men were shouting and swearing, their jaws clenched, fists flying, stares fevered and intense. From what she could see, it appeared to be a battle between the Insurgents and the Demon Riders, and several men were on the ground, bleeding and writhing in pain.

Then she saw Tiny—a member of the Demon Riders—pull out a gun and aim it at Banger. As his finger moved to pull the trigger, a shot rang out and Tiny fell facedown on the ground. A strained silence hovered over the fighters for a few seconds, but then the fight started up again.

Sirens wailed outside and the men pulled away fleeing, leaving their wounded on the ground in pools of blood. People who had dove under tables slowly crawled out as a swarm of police officers flooded the event center. Kimber ran to the stairwell where palm and footprints painted the floor and bannisters. She rushed down the stairs and when she reached the first landing, someone grabbed her from behind. She screamed and kicked, but he held her firmly. Twisting around, she stared into Chewy's menacing face.

"Leave me the fuck alone!" She tried to pull away from his grip.

"You owe me, bitch! Nobody takes off on me the way you did. You were my fuckin' ol' lady. Disrespect gets fuckin' punished." He punched the side of her face. "And being an Insurgents whore makes you a dead bitch after I have some fun with you."

"Please, Chewy. Let me go. You don't want to do this. We used to love each other, remember?"

"You took care of that, didn't you? Fuckin' slut." He delivered a blow to her stomach, knocking the wind out of her.

The metal door banged open a flight above them, and Chewy yanked her behind him and took her out of the building. Stumbling as she tried to keep up with him, her eye already swelling, she tried to figure out how to get away from him. Chaos was everywhere around them, and she and Chewy were lost within it.

She saw his Harley and her stomach dropped. *If he takes me away, I'll never be found. I'd rather die here than later after he hurts me real bad.* Figuring she had nothing to lose, a loud and piercing scream broke from deep inside her. And she kept screaming until he punched her in the mouth, the taste of copper trickling down her throat.

When Throttle slammed a large padlock tied to a bandana against the side of Chewy's head, knocking the hell out of him, she knew her screams had been heard. He crushed Kimber to him and tilted her head back, his eyes darkening when they landed on her beaten face. With eyebrows squeezed together in a crease and jaw thrust forward, he moved Kimber aside and picked up Chewy by the back of his neck.

"You fuckin' piece of shit. You like beating up women, you god-damned pussy? Let's see how you do with a man."

Chewy held up his head to look at Throttle, the blood running down the side of his face from where the padlock had hit him. For several seconds, a strange stillness settled over them, even though mayhem was still going on around them. They stared at each other, and if hatred were visible the air would have been crimson. Then Throttle slammed the other side of Chewy's head with the padlock, and the man yelled out as he crumpled to his knees on the ground. With a quick succession of punches, Chewy lay flat on the asphalt as blood from his open wounds stained the tarmac.

Throttle slammed his steel-toed boot repeatedly against Chewy's broken body, the spittle flying from his mouth as he continued his deadly assault. Kimber watched in horror knowing he didn't just want to teach Chewy a lesson; he wanted to smash and obliterate him. "Throttle, enough. Stop. Let's go. The cops are everywhere. It's just a matter of minutes before they come out here. Leave him alone. He's not worth a fucking murder rap." She pulled at him, trying to halt his frenzy, but he was unstoppable. Scanning the area, she spotted Jax and yelled for him to come over.

Jax, his face bruised and swelling, rushed to her side. "What's going on?" he yelled.

"Stop him. He's going to fucking kill him."

Jax looped his arms around Throttle's waist and jerked him away. "Fuck, man, what the hell are you doing? The fuckin' badges are everywhere. We gotta get outta here."

"Leave me the fuck alone. I'm gonna kill this sonofabitch!" Spittle flew while Throttle yelled.

"We gotta go now. The badges already nabbed Wheelie and Rock. Let's go." He dragged Throttle away. "Come on, Kimber. Fucking move it!"

She stared at Chewy, wondering if he were alive, then breathed out when she saw his chest rise and fall. The cops would find him and send him to the hospital. She hated him for what he did to her, but she didn't want him dead. How had a day that held so much promise turned into such a violent melee? She followed Jax and Throttle to their bikes. So many people were outside that the cops were having a hard time controlling who came and went from the complex. Taking off their cuts, Jax and Throttle placed them neatly in her saddlebags. Then the three of them mixed in with the non-outlaw bikers and rode away from the coliseum, leaving the fracas behind them.

They arrived at the motel and went immediately to their room so Throttle could wash off the blood from the fight. Placing ice cubes wrapped in a washcloth over her swollen eyes, she leaned against the headboard.

"What the fuck happened back there?" she asked when he came out of the shower.

The mattress sagged when he crawled over to her, cradling her in his arms. "The fuckin' Demon Riders started that shit. They were pissed about something Hawk and some brothers said to one of their members, so they started in on us. And there's no fuckin' way Insurgents let anyone disrespect them. We never back down from a fight." He kissed the top of her head. "Who the fuck was the sonofabitch who hit you?"

She traced the tattoos on his chest with her finger. "Chewy—my ex. I hadn't seen him since I ran out on him a few years ago. I wondered if he'd be at the expo because I know his club went in the past. It was my bad luck that they were there this year. He was pissed I ran out on him, and he wanted to teach me a lesson. I'm glad you came when you did. I couldn't fight him off... I never could." She hugged him.

"I hope I killed his pussy ass. You should've told me your concerns. You need to open up to me more, baby."

"It's hard for me to trust any man because of the bad experience I had with Chewy, but I'm getting there." Silence spread between them, and then she said in a small voice, "One of your members killed Tiny."

He stiffened under her touch. "Who the fuck's Tiny?"

"A Demon Rider. He was one of the older dudes. He could be a mean SOB."

"Not anymore." He laughed. "I don't know who did it. I didn't see it."

She knew he was lying, and that was okay; after all, it was club business, and she really didn't want to know. "What a mess, huh?"

"Yep, but the fuckers started it. You gonna be okay for an hour or so? Banger's called an emergency church in his room. You want me to ask a couple of the old ladies to keep you company?"

"I'll be okay. I'd rather be alone until you come back. I'm so tired."

He kissed the side of her face that Chewy hadn't battered and stood up. "Be back soon, and then we can order a pizza or something. I think it's best if we head back tomorrow morning."

"Okay." She watched him close the door behind her, then turned on the TV searching for the local news. On four channels, the mayhem at the Denver Motorcycle Expo was the breaking story. She watched the videotape of the fight as if seeing it for the first time; the whole incident seemed surreal. In the end, Tiny was dead, and three Demon Riders and two Insurgents were in serious condition at a local hospital. Many of the others who were injured fled the scene. *Throttle and I are among them.* She turned the TV to mute, watching the images of the fight over and over as they flickered on the screen until her eyes grew heavy and sleep blocked out everything.

SOMETHING WARM AND soft made her skin tingle. She fluttered her eyes open and Throttle's lustful eyes met hers. "Did I wake you?" he whispered against her soft cheek as his nose nuzzled against it.

"Yeah, but I think it's going to be worth it." She circled her arms around his waist, bringing his body closer to her. When his dick poked her, she laughed.

"You think it's funny that you make me harder than a goddamned rock whenever I'm around you?" He pretended to be annoyed, but the smile tugging at the corners of his mouth gave him away. He yanked at her pajama top, hoisting it above her head, as she unzipped his jeans, shoving them down over his hips. "You make me crazy, baby. I can't get enough of you. Every time I see you I want to touch you, taste you, and be inside you. You fuckin' rule my head and cock." He gently covered his mouth over hers.

Sparks of white heat popped from her nipples to her wet, throbbing sex as he held her close, his hands skimming over her flesh. His tongue trailed down to her sex, and he spread her wide and buried his face into her wetness, breathing in deeply. "I love the way you smell when you're turned on. Fuckin' sweet." He dipped his head and licked her clit while he dragged his finger up and down the length of her seam.

Hot heat coiled tighter inside her as the tension built. She laced her fingers through his hair, pulling it hard as she groaned and writhed beneath him. He leaned over and kissed her hard, tasting herself on his tongue.

"Do you like the way you taste? Sweet and addictive. Damn."

The pressure continued to build, and she could only groan her answer as he resumed his wicked lapping on her clit. "I want you inside me," she panted.

He pulled back then shoved into her, her scream filling the room. As he pistoned in and out, he claimed her. "Your sweet pussy belongs only to me." He dipped his head and sucked in one of her tight nipples. "Your tits are mine." He slid his hands under her ass and squeezed her cheeks hard. "And your luscious ass is all mine. The only cock you'll come all over is mine and it's the only one that'll fill your pussy. You understand?" His finger swirled around her hardened nub as he grunted and slammed into her over and over.

Fisting the sheets, she nodded as her head thrashed against the pillow. Then the scorching heat uncoiled, coursing through her veins like liquid fire as she shattered into a million pieces. Through the euphoria, she heard him yell, "Kimber. Fuck!" His fingers dug into her hips before he collapsed on top of her, his face buried in the crook of her neck.

After a while, he rolled over and pulled her to him, wrapping her in his arms. The drone of big-rig trucks on the interstate hung over them as they lay sated, their legs tangled together.

"You make me happy," Kimber said as she kissed his chest.

He didn't answer. His steady breathing told her he'd already fallen asleep. Smiling, she burrowed herself closer to his warm body; she felt safe and protected. She hadn't felt that way in a very long time, and she liked it.

He'd claimed her, and the memory of his passion-filled words made her stomach flutter. He'd slipped into her heart and life when she least expected him to. And she liked that.

A lot.

CHAPTER TWENTY-THREE

"CARA'S TRYING TO help out some of the brothers the fuckin' badges nabbed on Saturday. She doesn't think anyone's gonna be charged, including the filthy Demon Riders." Hawk stood rigid, his face flushed.

"What about your female mechanic?" Rags called out. "She saw the whole mess go down. She even saw me shoot the fuckin' Demon Rider."

"She didn't see shit. Leave her out of it." Throttle jumped to his feet, the vein in his neck pulsing like hell.

"The fuck she didn't. Anyway, she got herself in this by not telling us she was a Demon Riders' whore!" Rags slammed his fist on the table while his brothers yelled out their agreement.

Throttle was on the table in no time, lunging at Rags. Before the brothers could stop him, he and Rags were punching each other like they were in a boxing match. "You fuckin' asshole," Throttle panted as he threw his fist against Rags's left jaw. Rags returned the punches as good as he got.

"Will someone pull these two apart? We got shit to discuss!" Banger's voice boomed inside the crowded room.

Several brothers rushed over and separated the two. Hawk came over and roughly jerked Throttle to the other side of the room. "Stop fighting with the brothers whenever they say shit about Kimber. You're acting like a pussy-whipped asshole."

"You know damn well you wouldn't sit still if the brothers said shit about Cara."

"That's different. She's my old lady. We're getting married."

"What about before? You were plenty pissed when someone even looked at her. Don't fuckin' lecture me now about this."

Hawk scowled. "You making her your old lady?"

Throttle stared, his chin held high in defiance. "That's no one's fuckin' business."

"That's what I thought. We got some serious shit going on with the club, and you're acting like a fuckin' teenager with outta-control hormones. Get your shit together. Now."

Throttle kicked the chair with his boot and sat down, the fire still raging inside him. He couldn't even look at Rags because he'd be over the table and in his face again in a second. He didn't want anyone disrespecting his woman. And Kimber was his—he'd claimed her. Was he ready to make her his old lady? He wasn't sure how she felt about him. He wanted her to tell him she loved him. *Fuck, listen to me. I'm acting just like a girl. I'm so fucking obsessed with her.* Not only obsessed but addicted to her scent, her taste, her soft skin, and her laugh. She consumed his heart and his every thought; she was the spark to his flame. How could he not beat the shit out of anyone who dared to diss her?

"You know damn good and well that if she weren't fuckin' Throttle and working for Hawk, we'd make sure she disappeared," Hoss said. Jax and Axe held Throttle down.

"Calm the fuck down, will you?" Banger stared fiercely at him. "How involved is your woman with the Demon Riders?"

"She's not," he gritted. "She's from Iowa, and she hooked up with one of the fuckers and became his old lady. She ran away after he beat the shit outta her, and she hasn't been back since. That was a few years ago. She cut all contact with him. She didn't even want to get involved with bikers again."

"Did your cock change her mind?" Bones made sucking sounds and the brothers broke out in raucous laughter.

"Easy, man," Jax said as Throttle started to rise.

Banger slammed the gavel down. "Enough of this shit. You trust her, Hawk?"

Hawk nodded.

"That's good enough for me. Jax, you're gonna be back in your Sergeant-At-Arms position 'til Rock gets his ass outta jail. Cara and one of her lawyer friends in Denver are sorting all this shit out. Once he's back, he gets his position back. Got it?"

Jax nodded. "I didn't think Banger would ever let me near an officer's patch again," he said in a low voice to Jerry and Throttle.

"He's mellowed since Harley was born," Jerry said. "Instead of yelling at me and giving me dirty looks each time I come over when Kylie's home from college, he does it every other time. I'm making some damn progress." Jax and Throttle chuckled.

"There's gonna be retaliation for killing one of the fuckers. The Demon Riders won't forget it, even though they were aiming to kill me," Banger said.

"It was self-defense all the way," Axe replied.

"The bastard deserved to die. He was playing dirty, so he got snuffed out. We have our brother Rags to thank for saving our president's life." Hawk jerked his chin at Rags and all the members jumped to their feet, chanting, "Insurgents Forever, Forever Insurgents." A swell of pride filled Throttle as he chanted along with his brothers, his fist held high.

After they settled down, they looked to Banger. "Dustin and Shack were there, and I wouldn't put it past them to have been the instigators behind the fight. They've been aiming to kick our asses and kill me since we beat and ousted them from the Insurgents MC. We gotta watch them and keep our ears finely tuned to the grapevine. They will retaliate."

The brothers nodded in agreement. "You think the Deadly Demons knew about this?" Jerry asked.

Hawk and Banger shook their heads. "Nah, I don't think Reaper wants to break the truce we have. He's a sharp president, and a fight at an expo wouldn't be worth starting a war," Hawk said. "Besides, they know we got a shitload more money than them, so we can buy the big-ass weapons." He laughed.

"I saw Reaper earlier in the morning, and we acknowledged each other. I don't think he knew the Demon Riders were gonna start shit, even if they are affiliated with the Deadly Demons." Banger took out his bandana and wiped his forehead. "We're on high alert. Hawk will be fielding the communications to see what pops up, but we all gotta make sure we keep our women and kids safe. If something comes up or escalates, we'll have to do a lockdown."

Lockdowns were common when the Insurgents were embroiled in a conflict or war with a rival club. It was a necessary evil in the outlaw world, and hated by the women who loved the outlaw bikers. Until a volatile situation was deactivated, the old ladies, children, and girlfriends were moved into the clubhouse for protection. They couldn't venture one step outside the walls unless accompanied by one or two of the brothers. In times of war, they weren't allowed out at all. The Insurgents hoped it wouldn't come to that, but they had to be prepared for it; retaliation for killing a member of a rival club was inevitable. The only thing to figure out was when it would occur.

"Seems like that's all we got to discuss for now. If something comes up, we'll call an emergency church. Go on, grab a drink, and get some pussy. Church is adjourned." Banger tapped the gavel on the table. The brothers shuffled out of the room and headed to the great room, where the prospects had their drinks waiting and the club girls had their legs spread.

Hunched over on a barstool, staring at the mirrors behind the bar, Throttle threw back his shot, the rich amber liquid sliding down his throat like a fiery caress. Sturgis was in one month, and he knew it would be a powder keg when the Insurgents and Demon Riders crossed paths again. He was up for the fight, but he didn't want Kimber getting caught in the cross-fire. He knew he should tell her to stay home because it was too risky. *Yeah, like she's really gonna listen to me.* Sometimes her stubbornness was too much. They could always go next year. *So I'm planning for us to still be together next year? Of course I am. She's in my fuckin' blood.*

"You wanna come by tonight to play some poker?" Jax asked as he popped a green olive in his mouth.

"Can't. I'm taking Dawn, Olivia, and Kimber out to dinner."

"I fuckin' can't believe that the brother who was the most cynical 'bout our old ladies is lovesick over a mechanic." Jax chuckled and popped in another olive. "These are damn good. Usually the olives we get taste like ass. You should try them."

Throttle chomped on a couple. "They are good. One of the old ladies is responsible for this. Whoever it was probably tasted the shit we had and thought we deserved something better. I bet it was Belle." The prospect ran over and filled the nearly empty bowl with more olives.

"What of it, man? Jax is right. You gave me so much shit about Addie, and here you are fighting any brother who even jokes about Kimber. Never thought I'd see the day you had an old lady." Chas laughed.

"She's not my old lady." He narrowed his eyes.

"Yet," Jax said, and Chas, Jerry, and Axe broke out laughing.

"Don't sweat it, bro. Once you take the step, you'll wonder how you ever thought easy pussy was enough." Axe took a handful of peanuts from the bowl next to Throttle.

"I'd like to stay here and chat with you about the pros and cons of easy pussy, but I gotta change and head out to Kimber's."

As he walked away, he heard the guys say, "Definitely gonna make her his old lady. He's so pussy-whipped." He gritted his teeth and climbed the stairs to his room.

WHEN SHE OPENED the door, Throttle's gaze traveled up her body, caressing every inch of her. Her halter top, tropical print sundress hugged her in just the right places, and he felt his jeans tighten when he saw her pink-painted toenails in the strappy high heels. The image of her legs wrapped around his waist with her heels digging into his ass made his pants snugger.

"You're early," she said as she stepped aside. "I have to put on my lipstick and change out my purse."

He drew her to him and dug his fingers in her inner thighs. Burying his face in the space between her ear and neck, he nibbled her soft skin, whispering against it, "Seeing you in your short dress and fuck-me heels drives me crazy. Your scent, your body, your look make me hard as hell. What're you doing to me, babe?" He covered her mouth and plunged his tongue deep inside, pressing her even closer to him.

She pulled away slightly. "Oh, Throttle," she murmured on his lips before he pushed in deeper, swallowing her moans.

In and out he thrust his tongue inside her warm mouth, and she fisted his muscle shirt and rubbed her knee against his throbbing dick. She arched her back and pushed against him, her hard and erect nipples burning his skin. "You're so fuckin' irresistible," he breathed. His hand glided underneath her dress and he slipped his finger inside her panties, tucking it between her wet folds.

"I love it when you touch me there," she panted, then groaned when he inserted his finger in her heat.

"And I love it when you're wet. It tells me how badly you want me." He shoved his finger deeper.

Each groan, whimper, and yelp of pleasure hit him like a Taser straight to his dick. He couldn't remember ever wanting a woman as badly as he wanted her. His fingers stretched and twisted inside her heated wetness while his thumb stroked her hardened nub, and he felt her skin tremble beneath his touch.

"You're driving me crazy," she said, then zipped down his jeans, freeing his throbbing dick. While she squeezed and moved her hand up and down, they kissed hotly, the fire in him raging.

"How do you make me so wild? All I ever want to do is touch you, fuck you, and just be with you."

A whimper of enjoyment escaped from her throat, and he felt her walls clamp around his fingers. With her head thrown back, she screamed out, her body trembling in his arms. He held her close as he stiffened, a surge of tension ripping through him before he released his warm streams. He grunted, and they held each other as their climaxes peaked and then descended, pressed together as one. They panted softly into each other's ears.

After several minutes, Kimber kissed him tenderly and broke away, pulling down her dress. "That was some greeting." Her eyes sparkled.

"Yeah." He looked down at the wet spot on his jeans and grimaced. "Fuck."

Kimber laughed and held out her hand. "Give them to me. I'll throw them in the dryer for a few minutes." She took his jeans. "I have to freshen up. Grab a beer and I'll be back soon."

While he sat on the couch in his boxers, drinking a beer, his phone pinged. He looked down and smiled.

Dawn: *U coming?*

Throttle: *Soon.*

Dawn: *When?*

Throttle: *20 to 30 minutes.*

Dawn: *K. Livi's been asking.*

Throttle smiled.

Throttle: *Tell her to hold on. I'm coming. I'm bringing someone.*

Dawn: *Who?*

Throttle: *Her name's Kimber.*

He braced himself for the onslaught of questions his sister would ask. He should have mentioned it when they'd spoken a few days before, but he wasn't up to explaining what he had with Kimber. And all the shit that happened at the expo clouded everything else. He also suspected his sister was in cahoots with Mariah to get him back together with her. Another ping.

Dawn: *She must be someone special for you to bring her. Never met* *any woman u know since Mariah.*

Throttle: *She is special. B nice.*

Dawn: *What about Mariah?*

Throttle: *What about her?*

Dawn: *Thought u 2 would hook up again.*

Throttle: *Fuck no!*

"Your jeans are all dry—not a trace of evidence of any fucking." Kimber handed him his warm pants and kissed him on the cheek. "Who're you texting?"

He pulled her down next to him and kissed her shoulder. "My sister. Olivia's freaking 'cause I'm late."

"Then we better go. I hope your sister likes me."

"She will, and if she doesn't, I don't give a fuck." He glanced down at his phone.

Dawn: *U loved her a lot. She's a changed woman. Don't throw something good away because u can't let go of ur anger.*

Throttle: *Not talkin' about this. Done with Mariah. We're leaving now. See you in 5.*

He stood up and slipped his pants on, then put his vibrating phone in his pocket. "You ready?" he asked Kimber.

She nodded and, after setting the alarm and locking up, they walked to his pickup truck. "Where're we going for dinner? I'm really hungry. I've been so busy with my small-business project that I haven't eaten since last night." She kneaded the back of his neck as he drove. "I'm taking tonight off. I'm free to do whatever."

Throttle glanced at her from under hooded lids, a devilish smile dancing on his lips. "That's good to know. I can fill up your free time real good." He turned the corner and in less than ten minutes, he pulled up in front of Dawn's house.

Before he could come around to the passenger's side to help Kimber out, Olivia came barreling down the sidewalk, yelling, "Uncle Throttle!" He caught her in his arms, scooped her up, and hugged her close, planting a big kiss on her soft cheek. "You're late," she said, then giggled when he kissed her again.

"I know, sorry. I had shit to do, but I'm here now." He put her down and grasped her small hand in his. Kimber closed the truck's door and he turned to her, reaching out for her hand. "Kimber, this is Olivia, the cutest, smartest, and sometimes most ornery girl in Pinewood Springs." He smiled as his niece giggled. "And Olivia, this is Kimber, the sweetest, prettiest, and most of the time most stubborn woman in Pinewood Springs." Kimber swatted him on the arm as she smiled at him and Olivia.

"Where's your mom?" Throttle asked as the three of them walked up to the house.

"She's coming. She's just finishing a phone call. Where are we going for dinner?" Olivia twirled around on the porch.

"I've been trying to find that out myself," Kimber said softly.

"We're going to Burgers & Beer Joint."

"I love that place," Olivia squealed, her dark eyes bright.

"You're such a goofball," Throttle said as he pulled her on his lap. "But that's why I love you so much."

"I love you too, Uncle Throttle. Mommy said you're going to take us to the carnival next week."

"Yep. It'll kick ass. You can ask a friend to come along."

"I already asked Ella and she said yes. I lost another tooth. See?" She pulled back her bottom lip, revealing a space.

"Pretty soon you're gonna be toothless," he said. She laughed loud like it was the funniest thing she'd ever heard.

Olivia wiggled off his lap. "I'm going to see what's taking Mommy so long."

When the screen door slammed behind the girl, Kimber brought Throttle's hand to her lips and kissed it. "Thanks."

"For what?"

"For sharing a part of you I didn't think existed. Even though you don't want anyone to know, you're a real sweetheart." She leaned over and kissed him gently on the lips.

Something deep inside him stirred and it twisted around his groin, moved up his stomach, and filled his heart. It scared the shit out of him; the biker who had blood on his hands from years with the brotherhood was afraid of love. He'd given his heart completely to Mariah, and she'd trampled on it. How could he be certain Kimber wouldn't do the same? Even though she wasn't anything at all like Mariah, she was still a woman, and women, in his experience, were fickle. Kimber hadn't voiced her feelings for him other than having a good time when they hung out and loving the mind-blowing orgasms he gave her.

Looking at her right then, he saw something different in her eyes. Love? He wasn't sure, but he didn't want to go there until he sorted out whatever the fuck was coursing through him. He smiled weakly. "You know your ass is going to the carnival too."

She burst out laughing. "Damn. I used to love going when I was a kid. I wouldn't miss it."

They locked gazes and a comfortable silence fell around them, only lifting when the screen door banged open and Olivia and Dawn came out. Throttle noticed the way Dawn checked out Kimber before he introduced them, and the way she kept staring at her began to irk him. He figured Dawn would have to get to know Kimber, and when she did, she'd see that his woman complemented him in a way Mariah never did. They settled in the truck, laughing and chatting all the way to the restaurant.

After dinner, he took them to Red Spot Creamery for ice cream. Kimber smiled and squeezed his hand, and he knew she was happy that he remembered it was her favorite ice cream place in town. He and Dawn waited to place their orders while Olivia and Kimber held their table.

"She's real nice and pretty," Dawn said as they waited in line. He nodded. "She seems so confident and driven. Damn, I don't think I ever met a woman who was a mechanic. I've read about them, but I'm sure she's the only one in town. I'm surprised you were attracted to her for that reason alone."

"I gave her a hard time about it in the beginning. Fuck, I'm surprised too, but I like her confidence and independence. I was getting sick of all the chicks who acted like they couldn't change a fuckin' lightbulb."

Dawn smiled, her gaze fixed on his. "You're in love with her, aren't you?"

Throttle darted his eyes from hers. "No... Fuck, I don't know. I like being with her. That's all."

"You're not fooling me. I know you better than anyone, and I can see by the way you act and look at her that you're in all the way. I think it's wonderful. You deserve to be happy and to have someone really love you. And she does love you. You know that, right?"

He shrugged. "Enough of this. What kind of ice cream do you want?"

"You're not getting off that easily. You two need to stop hiding and tell each other how you feel. I want the mocha almond fudge, and Olivia wants the birthday cake. And you were right, Mariah is definitely not the right one for you. She couldn't hold a candle to Kimber. Don't fucking blow this."

"You done now?"

"Yes." She chuckled.

Dawn's right. Kimber is the best thing that's come into my life. And she's the fuckin' real deal. He placed their orders and helped carry the cones over to Kimber and Olivia. Sitting there eating ice cream with his three favorite women made him feel like he had all the pieces in his life. Since the day Mariah had shattered his heart, he finally felt like it had been put back together again, stronger and better.

After he dropped Olivia and Dawn off, he and Kimber went to her place. He didn't want to watch TV, or listen to music on the computer, or even talk. All he wanted was to make love to the woman who'd slipped into his life and heart. He'd claimed her; she was his woman in every sense of the word.

She came out of the bathroom, and her eyes widened. "Don't you want to watch TV?"

He patted the spot beside him on the bed. "Come here," he said thickly.

A wide smile broke out over her face. "You're so bad." She padded over and slipped in next to him, his stiff dick poking against her thighs. She chuckled. "Seems like you're ready."

"I've been ready for you for a long time, baby." He wrapped his arms around her, kissing her deeply.

The moonlight spilled into the room, its soft, shimmering glow encasing the couple as they kissed, touched, and drove each other to ecstasy.

CHAPTER TWENTY-FOUR

KIMBER SCRUBBED THE grease off her hands; she normally wore tight-fitting gloves, but sometimes she had to use her bare hands to get the job done. She had to hustle otherwise she'd be late for her classes. As she brushed under her fingernails, she thought of Throttle—as she often did—and a surge of heat shot through her. Each time she thought she had him figured out, he'd go and do something that threw her for a loop.

Over the weekend, at the expo, he was the quintessential badass biker—hard, loyal, and tough. Then a few days later, he picked her up, introduced her to his sister and niece, and played the doting uncle to a tee. Later that night, he hadn't fucked her; he'd *made love* to her, and that blew her away. Since then, he'd been so loving toward her, treating her like an actual girlfriend and not a fuck buddy. He'd claimed her the night of the horrible fight in Denver, but she'd figured it was the rhetoric all bikers used. Hell, she'd heard it often enough since she started screwing around with them over the years and it didn't mean crap. The thought of him actually being in love with her made her skin pebble and her insides twist.

It also made her nerves scream warnings. He wasn't a one-woman man; he'd been used to such freedom and variety when it came to women, so how could he ever be content with just one? Although, he'd given his heart to one woman before, but that was a long time ago.

"You working tomorrow?" Darren, one of the mechanics, asked.

"Huh…? Oh yeah, I come in at ten."

"How do you keep your hands so clean? My girlfriend's always bitching at me about how stained my hands are."

"I use gloves most of the time, but the best thing you can use is a stiff brush, raw sugar, water, and a bit of liquid detergent. Then a ton of cream to keep your hands soft. Works like a charm."

"Yeah? I'll have to try that. Dirty hands don't get you too much action." He laughed.

Kimber smiled weakly. One of the pros of being the only female in a traditionally male job was that, after time, she was treated as one of the guys. But it became a con when she was included in all the raunchy jokes, innuendos, and details of her fellow employee's sex lives— something she could definitely live without.

"I have to go to class. See you tomorrow." She dashed out of the shop and left the parking lot with a trail of noise behind her.

After her two classes, she went to the student center to have an iced tea with her friends. They talked for a couple hours about classes, the worst professors, and guys. She didn't reveal that her guy was an outlaw biker, since they'd probably conjure up images of movies and television programs about the outlaw world.

Kimber glanced at the wall clock and stood. "I better get going. I have a bunch of stuff to finish for Donsky's class. I can't wait for the summer session to end."

"Me too. It seems like it's really dragging. Then when we get out, we only have a two-week break before the fall semester starts." Carla stood from the table and slung her backpack over her shoulder. "I'm heading out too. I'll walk with you."

Kimber gathered her books, then noticed her laptop wasn't there. She looked under the table, on the floor, and searched her tote again. Her stomach sank when she couldn't find it. "Does anyone remember if I had my laptop with me when we sat down?"

"I didn't see it," Carla replied.

"Sorry, I wasn't paying attention," Mitzi said.

"Same here," Terri and Nikki voiced.

"Did you leave it in class?" Carla asked.

"I must have. I thought I had it in Donsky's class, but I don't remember. I have to go back and check." Kimber stuffed all her things in her tote and threw it on her shoulder.

"I'd go with you, but I have somewhere I have to be," Carla said.

"That's okay. I'll see you tomorrow. I have to fly." Kimber rushed out of the student center and zipped across the campus to the business building. Grateful that a class wasn't in session, she went into the two rooms she'd sat in a few hours before and searched for her laptop. It was nowhere. Tears stung at her eyes; she had just bought the laptop after saving up for it for a year, and she didn't have the budget to buy a new one. Her class project was safe since she'd backed up her work, but she had all her music, photos, and other personal stuff on it.

She went to the faculty offices and was happy to see Dr. Redman and Dr. Donsky still in their offices. Another student was there, but she poked her head in anyway. "I'm sorry to bother you, but did you find a laptop after our class? I can't find mine and was thinking I may have left it in the classroom." She crossed her fingers.

Dr. Redman slowly shook his head. "No. I didn't find anything after class, and no one turned it in at my office." A knot formed in the pit of her stomach, and hot tears burned behind her eyes.

"Did you lose something?" Dr. Donsky came out of his office and stood by her. "I overheard you."

"A laptop." Her face held hope.

"No. I didn't see it. I can't believe someone would take it."

Her hope shattered, and she tried not to lose it in front of her professors. "I don't think someone would do that either, but it's gone and I can't find it." Her voice hitched.

"Check lost and found. If it's not there, go over to security to file a report. I'm sure it'll turn up. Did you back up all your work?" Dr. Redman asked.

She nodded, eager to get away before she broke down and cried like a baby. "Thanks for the advice." She stumbled away, but Dr. Donsky grabbed her elbow.

When she flashed him a confused, pissed look, he quickly said, "I thought you were going to fall. I'm sorry."

"That's okay," she mumbled. "I have to go." She hurried out of the building and made her way to lost and found.

Twenty minutes later, she stormed to her bike, tears threatening to spill down her face. No one had turned in her laptop; she knew they wouldn't. Someone probably found it and kept it. *Fuck! This sucks!* She tried so hard to do everything right, but life just kept kicking her in the gut. Throwing her tote in the saddlebags, she jumped on her bike and sped away to the nearest grocery store for a junk food run. She needed macaroni and cheese, chocolate cupcakes with thick dark chocolate frosting, a bag of spicy nacho cheese chips, and a two-liter bottle of regular—not diet—Coke. That should make her feel a little bit better. She swung her bike into the store's parking lot and went in to execute her plan.

As she sat on her couch, crunching on chips and slugging Coke down her throat, her phone vibrated. She picked it up.

Throttle: Hey, babe. U wanna hang out? Ribs?

Kimber: Sorry. Not 2nite. Had a shitty day.

Throttle: I'll come over. I can pick up something.

Blowing out a long breath, she bit down on another chip, wiping the fake cheese powder on her napkin. She didn't want to hurt his feelings, but she wanted to be alone. She wasn't in the mood to play girlfriend or lover. She was fucking pissed and upset about her computer, and the only thing she wanted to spend time with was her stash of junk food.

Kimber: Don't B mad. Not in the mood. Want 2 B alone.

Throttle: I'm coming over.

She threw the remote across the table. *He's so fucking exasperating!*

Kimber: Do u ever take no for an answer?

Throttle: No. What happened today?

Kimber: *Lost my laptop. Saved up to buy it. Very upset.*

Throttle: *Fuck. I'll see u in 30 minutes.*

Kimber: *It's ok. I won't be good company.*

He didn't reply, and she knew he was going to come by. Why couldn't he understand that she wanted to wallow in self-pity, watch a brainless show, and eat her stash? *If he thinks I'm going to be fucked out of my mood, he's damn wrong. He wants to come, fine, but he better not expect me to play the goddamned hostess.* She reached over, grabbed the remote, and stared at the TV screen.

As she watched a hokey love story, a noise outside caught her attention. She lowered the volume on the TV and turned her head toward the window on the side of her house. There it was again, like something scratching on the wood. And again. That time, it was like something dragging across her screen. *Fuck! It sounds like someone is trying to open my window.* Her adrenaline spiked and her knees went weak as she slowly inched her way to the front door. When she spotted Riley's cherry-red truck, her hand flew to her mouth, suppressing a scream. She hadn't heard from him for a couple weeks, so she'd figured he'd finally given up.

Slowly pulling the drapes closed on her living room window, she tiptoed over to the window where she'd heard the noise and stood to the side, looking through the small sliver in the blinds. She discerned a black hat, and knew for sure it was Riley who was trying to break into her house. Cursing herself for forgetting to set the alarm, she rushed over to the alarm box and, with shaking fingers, plugged in the code. Nothing. She had the code wrong. She racked her brain to remember what it was, but she couldn't. *I better call the police.* As she picked up the phone, she heard the low rumble of Throttle's Harley. Relief flooded over her, and she breathed again.

From the corner of the curtain, she watched his bike glide to the curb before he leapt off his bike and ran to the side of her house. She flung open the front door and stepped out on her porch. Loud yelling and cussing accompanied loud thuds against her siding. She jumped off the porch and came around the corner; a red-faced Riley sputtered and gasped for air while pinned against the wall by Throttle, who had his hands around his neck.

"Throttle, stop!" She rushed over to him and grabbed his arm, trying in vain to pull him off Riley. "You're going to kill him."

"That's my fuckin' intention." He squeezed harder as Riley unsuccessfully attempted to push him away.

"Please, Throttle. Stop." Her voice hitched, and he looked at her before finally pulling his hands away. Riley rubbed his neck as he inhaled large gulps of air, his face beginning to return to its normal color.

Inches from the cowboy's face, Throttle said, "I fuckin' caught you peeking in my woman's windows, asshole."

"I was just trying—"

"Shut the fuck up!" Throttle punched Riley in the face.

Kimber crossed her arms. "I'll call the police."

"I don't need any fuckin' badges around. I'll take care of this in my own way." He slammed the cowboy against the house again.

"I didn't mean any harm. I was only seeing if you were home. I was in the neighborhood—my good friend lives a few blocks from here—and I wanted to say hi. I didn't mean to scare you, Kimber. Honest. I swear on the Bible and my grandmother's grave that I didn't mean any harm. I just wanted to see if there was any hope we could have another try at dating."

When he said "dating," Throttle banged him against the house again. Then in a low, cruel voice, he said, "Kimber's my woman. You stay the fuck away from her. I don't want anyone messing with her. I don't want you to look at her, talk to her, or even fucking dream about her." He slammed him again. "'Cause if you do, you're dead. You won't know where I'll be or when I'll come, but I will come for you. Do you get my drift?" Another slam against the wall.

Riley bobbed his head up and down.

Throttle pushed him to the ground and kicked him in the stomach.

"Get the fuck outta here before I change my mind and get rid of you right now."

Riley stumbled to his feet and, with his hand over his stomach, staggered to his truck. Climbing in quickly, he drove away. Throttle watched him leave, then turned to Kimber. "You okay, babe?"

Clutching at her arm, she said in a voice choked with tears, "No." Then the tears she had fought for so long broke through and flowed down her face. Since her dad had died, she'd tried to be brave, tough, and let life slide off her back, but in that one moment everything caught up to her. Even though she hated crying in front of people—especially men—she sobbed unabashedly. Throttle pulled her to him and looped his arms around her, and she clung to him, never wanting to let go.

He scooped her up and carried her into the house, placing her down on the couch with him. He held her close while she let out all the anger about her father dying too young, her ex beating her, her loneliness, her constant struggle to pay the bills, her fear that the Lingerie Bandit has focused on her, and the loss of her laptop—the catalyst. Throttle didn't placate her with meaningless words; rather, he held her and let her cry.

When she was spent, he pushed back a little and tilted her chin up, showering kisses on her damp cheeks. "Feel better?" he whispered as he brushed his lips across hers.

She nodded and he reached for the box of tissues on the coffee table. He pulled out some and handed them to her. "Blow," he said as he swept away the black tendrils clinging to her cheeks. A few minutes later, she looked at him, her eyelids swollen, her nose red, and she kissed him gently on his lips. "Thanks for that."

He smiled. "Hey, you up for shopping?"

"Shopping? For what?" Her voice sounded nasally.

"A laptop."

She groaned. "I told you I can't afford one."

"I can. Come on." He put a finger against her lips when she started to protest. "I'm not gonna take no for an answer. I want to do this, so let's get going, woman."

She smiled, her heart bursting. Standing up, she went to the mirror in her hallway, trying to fix her hair and look somewhat decent as she reapplied her lipstick. "You believed Riley's story, didn't you?"

"Why do you say that?"

"Because if you didn't, he'd be six feet under somewhere."

He chuckled. "You know me well, babe. Yeah, I believed him. He wasn't the fucker I chased from your house that night. The asshole was not as tall or broad. Cowboy's just a lovesick shit who needed some straightening out."

"I think you accomplished that. Thanks."

He came over to her and held her close. "You never have to thank me, babe. I'd do anything for you. Remember that I always have your back. And put your goddamned alarm on. I installed it for a reason."

"Yes sir." She saluted him, then hugged him close to her. "I forgot the code," she whispered. He burst out laughing, then went over to her kitchen counter, scribbled down something on a Post-It, and handed it to her. She glanced at it and saw four numbers. "My code, right?"

"Yeah. Memorize it. You gotta use the alarm. Let's go." He tucked her under his arm and they walked over to his Harley.

"How are we going to bring the laptop home on your bike? Won't the box be too big to fit in your saddlebags?"

"That's what prospects are for, babe."

She hooked her arms around his waist and kissed his shoulder. He turned sideways and they kissed briefly before his iron machine jumped to life and took off.

WHEN THEY GOT back from their shopping trip, Kimber set her new laptop with the shiny pink cover on her table, eager to try it out. Throttle grabbed a beer and flopped on the couch, turning on the TV.

"Pizza and salad?" he asked as he flipped through the channels.

"If you want. I'm not that hungry." She didn't share the fact that she'd stuffed her face with chips and cupcakes before the Riley incident happened. "Just order a medium. I only want one slice."

He ordered the pizza and while they waited, she played around on her new computer and he cussed at the boxing match on the television. When the pizza came, she sat near him on the couch and they watched an action movie. After it was over, she cleaned up and they went to her bedroom, where they kissed and touched. But before he could roll her over, her eyelids had grown heavy and she fell asleep with his arms cradling her close to him.

A SCOWL CROSSED the man's face as he watched the dark house. He knew the biker was spending the night with her. He ground his teeth, his heart pounding. The man breathed noisily as the anticipation of what he could have had consumed him. Molten rage burned within him.

He wanted her. He'd targeted her a while back, and that night was the time to be with her, but the motorcycle man thwarted his plans. He wasn't happy about that at all; he couldn't chance entering with the outlaw in there. Everything was ruined.

His nostrils flared. He couldn't just go home; his wife would ask too many questions, and besides, the desire was too strong. The man stood for a long time hidden behind the cluster of trees staring at the house. He glanced at the biker's Harley on the street and considered cutting the tires as punishment for screwing up his plans. But the more he thought about it, the more he realized what a bad idea it would be. The biker probably had a sixth sense about his motorcycle and would be on top of him in no time. As tempting as it was to slash the bike's tires, he couldn't risk being caught.

He sucked in a deep breath and let it out slowly before he strode away from his hiding place, walking the two blocks to an unlit street where he'd parked his SUV. The man took off without turning his headlights on until he was on the main street. He roamed up and down the neighborhoods until he spied a woman in her mid-twenties exercising on her treadmill. Her blinds and windows were open; he surmised that she probably didn't have AC, so she was letting the light nighttime breeze in.

He watched her for a long while, excited by the way her toned body moved. No one else appeared to be in her small carriage house that backed up to a dark alley. It was a perfect location for him to slip in and out without detection.

After an hour, the woman went to a back room, closed her blinds, and soon the lights switched off. He became a part of the shadows in the inky blackness. Only a sliver of moon hung in the dark sky; it was a perfect night for hunting.

As an owl hooted, its cry—forlorn and dismal—piercing the stillness of the night, he walked around back and cut her window screen. Like a lion on the prowl, he silently slipped into the small home. Waiting for his eyes to adjust to the darkness, he illuminated his way with his cell phone, his ears pricked for any sound. The soft, even breathing from a room to the right told him she was in there. His brown eyes blinked rapidly, and he wet his lips as a tightness formed in his pants.

He padded over to the room and stood in the doorway, his lust-filled gaze raking over her figure. From the sound of her breathing, he knew she was sleeping. A large smile broke out over his face as he stalked to her. In one movement, he had her on her back, duct tape over her mouth before he quickly secured her hands, her bulging eyes and trembling chin giving him a rush. He tied her legs to the bed, then relaxed. He now had a few hours before sunrise, and he could do a lot. Taking out his pocket knife, he slowly cut away her nightgown.

Small whimpers emitted from Amber Hewett's throat. She'd woken up to a nightmare where the bogeyman was real, and happy endings didn't happen.

CHAPTER TWENTY-FIVE

KIMBER SHUDDERED WHEN she read about the previous night's rape and murder of another woman not too far away from her neighborhood. *Why can't the cops find this psycho?* A weighted feeling came over her as she thought of the woman who'd lost her life to a madman. The poor woman never would have imagined when she'd gone to bed that she wouldn't see the sunrise; her life was at the mercy of the killer.

Sighing, she closed the paper and poured herself another cup of coffee. The previous night, a woman had lost her life and Kimber had gained one. She'd been floundering ever since her dad had been killed on his motorcycle, and Chewy had not even come close to filling her life. And then she'd met Throttle, a man she'd thought would be the least likely to occupy her heart and soul. Little did she know when she'd first met him—pissed as hell at her for working on Banger's bike—that he'd invade her dreams and her life.

Since she'd left Chewy, she'd tried to forget about bikers and their world, but the truth was she loved them and their way of life. She loved living against the grain, not conforming to what society dictated. Since she'd ridden her first Harley, she'd been hooked on the machine, the men who rode them, and the men who gave the finger to socially accepted standards.

She'd fought her attraction and feelings for a long time and it didn't work; she was in love with Throttle. Just thinking those words made her giddy and jittery. She was pretty sure he cared about her, but she wasn't sure if he was in love with her. But she didn't care. For the first time in her life, she'd found a good-hearted, tough, kickass guy who treated her like a lady—no man had ever treated her like that.

She stared out her window and watched the sprinkler water her neighbor's grass, the drops dancing in the air before they came down and were absorbed by the thirsty lawn. Throttle had been an angel the night before—*never thought "Throttle" and "angel" would be in the same sentence*—and she wanted to have him over for a nice dinner. She'd tell him she loved him even if he balked and ran from her. She picked up her phone and sent him a text.

Kimber: *Hi. Thinking about u.*

Throttle: *I like that. Thinking bout u too.*

Kimber: *Come over for dinner 2nite. Making something good.*

Throttle: *Yeah? I'm in. Would love to taste your cooking and other things.*

Kimber smiled and reread the text. That simple message went straight to the throb between her legs. *Damn. There's something about him that gets me all hot and bothered.*

Kimber: *Bad boy. I hope u stay that way.*

Throttle: *No plans on changing.*

Kimber: *See you at 7ish?*

Throttle: *Can't wait, babe.*

Butterflies swarmed her stomach, and she placed her hand on it and pressed hard to quell the fluttering. What if Throttle didn't want anything more than casual sex and some laughs? She was taking a big chance revealing her love to him, but she couldn't contain it any longer. If he bolted, then at least she'd had the best time in her life for a couple months.

She ambled over to the cupboard and pulled out her mother's recipe box—the one thing she cherished the most from her—and flipped through the cards until she found the one for crispy oven fried chicken. In her opinion, her mom's fried chicken recipe was the best she'd ever tasted. Mashed potatoes with sour cream and chives, a crisp cucumber and tomato salad, and her father's bacon baked beans should take care of Throttle's stomach. Later, she'd take care of the rest of him. With a devilish grin curling her lips, she sat down and made out her grocery list.

"STEEL'S ASKED FOR our help down south. Seems that punk club, the Skull Crushers, is infringing on their turf. Since the Night Rebels are our affiliates, we gotta help 'em. Anyway, I don't like the punk shits for nothing." Banger jutted out his chin.

"They don't think we're in with the Night Rebels, otherwise they'd leave it alone. I heard their fuckin' prez 'bout died when he got the care package we sent them." Throttle laughed.

"Heard one of the fuckers we eliminated was the prez's brother. Guess he wants to join him." Chas narrowed his eyes. "I can't stand these wannabe outlaws who don't know shit about what the brotherhood means."

"Me neither," echoed Jax. "What are we gonna do?"

Banger narrowed his eyes. "Also, the word's out that the sonsofbitches are wearing a 'Colorado' bottom rocker."

The membership exploded. The bottom rocker always stated the location of the territory belonging to an outlaw club, and Colorado was Insurgents territory; it had been since 1976 when the MC staked its claim. The importance of it was that no other club could use the state on its bottom rocker—no exceptions. The Skull Crushers, either through ignorance, sheer stupidity, or arrogance, had violated that rule. When an offending club wore the bottom rocker, they were asking for a violent confrontation. The Insurgents were more than ready and willing to defend their territory.

"Fuck *that*!" many members yelled, their fists pounding walls, tables, and chairs. Several members threw their chairs against the concrete walls, splintering the wood frames. For an MC to even consider wearing a bottom rocker claiming the Insurgents territory was an offense that called for immediate, violent punishment.

Hawk held up his hands. "A few days ago, several of these fuckers forced an Insurgent in northern Colorado off the road and beat him with chains, hammers, and pipes, and then they stole his bike. We can't let that shit go unpunished."

"When the fuck we gonna straighten these fuckers out?" Jax asked, the vein in his neck throbbing. "We should leave after church."

"I say we annihilate 'em. There's no mercy for fuckers who pull that shit." Rags stood tall, his shoulders straight. "No way is that gonna be tolerated."

"Steel thinks they got the support of the Demon Riders, which means indirect support from the Deadly Demons." Hawk crossed his arms.

"I know I keep saying it every time the bastards' club comes up, but we shoulda fuckin' killed Dustin and Shack when we were in Nebraska," Chas said.

"You're right, and we've had nothin' but fuckin' problems with them and the renegade Insurgents who followed those two to the Demon Riders. Fuck, we never had troubles with the club before. They stayed in Iowa and we stayed in Colorado. Now there's all kinds of shit going down. I wouldn't be surprised if these Skull Crusher assholes were put together by the Demon Riders. They just popped up after Dustin and Shack patched in with 'em. We gotta show them we don't take shit from nobody." Banger pounded his fist on the table.

"Banger and I talked some, and the best way to handle this is for a group of us to go down to Alina and pay them a surprise visit. We'll beat their asses good, rip off their patches, and burn them. Then—"

"We need to blow their clubhouse to hell and back, and not give a fuck if one or all of them dies. They can't mess with the Insurgents." Throttle's nostrils flared as his face heated.

"As much as I agree with Throttle, we can't kill any of the fuckers. Maiming is okay, but killing will bring the fuckin' badges breathing down our backs. With the shit we got going in Denver, we can't risk any more attention. We gotta make sure we beat them good, but keep them breathing."

"When do we leave?" Throttle asked as he cracked his knuckles.

"I want to send about ten of our brothers: Hawk, Throttle, Jax, Axe, Jerry, Bear, Bones, Ace, Tigger, and Hoss. Steel and his brothers will also be helping out on this mission. You'll be leaving in about an hour or two. I'll leave the particulars of the attack to Hawk and Jax, who'll be coordinating with Steel. Any questions?"

With his boot, Throttle pushed away from the wall. "Can the club spare one of the prospects to watch out for my woman?" The members sniggered. "I don't feel comfortable leaving her unprotected since it seems like someone's targeted her."

Banger scrubbed his face and tugged his beard. "I didn't know you had a woman."

Some of the guys yelled, "A woman who can fix his Harley." Then a group of them made sucking noises. Throttle clenched his jaw and stared at his president.

Banger narrowed his eyes. "Is this the woman you made all the fuss about at Hawk's shop?" Throttle grumbled his assent. "I can have one of the prospects watch her until you get back, but tell her you're doing that. I don't want her calling the badges on him. Anymore questions?" The membership stayed silent. "Church adjourned." The gavel echoed in the quiet room. The brothers slowly stood from their chairs and filed out of the room.

Throttle took the stairs two at a time and rushed into his room. He threw a few necessities in a small bag and dashed down the stairs, bumping in to Hawk. "Sorry, man. When do we leave?"

Hawk glanced at his watch. "It's twelve thirty now. Say two o'clock. Everyone's to meet in the club parking lot."

"Sounds good. I'll be there." He hustled out of the club, placed his bag in his saddlebags, and took off, leaving a trail of dust behind him.

When he pulled into Kimber's driveway, he texted Dawn to let her know he'd be gone for a few days. She didn't ask any questions—after seventeen years of dealing with his outlaw biker ways, she knew he wouldn't answer them. It'd taken him a while to have her understand his world, but she'd finally caught on and it made things a lot easier and smoother.

He rang the doorbell and in a few seconds, the door flew open and Kimber burst through the screen door, falling into his arms and peppering his face with kisses. "You're here. I didn't expect you in the middle of the day. What a great surprise. I was just getting ready to go to the grocery store."

"Babe,"—he turned her face to his and placed his nose on hers—"I gotta take a raincheck on that dinner. I'm gonna be gone for a few days on club business." His heart lurched when he saw her face morph from extreme bliss to sadness. Her small pout was damn cute, and he caught it with his mouth and kissed her deeply.

"Is the club business dangerous?"

The hitch in her voice surprised him. He pressed her closer to him. "No, babe. You smell amazing, and the way you feel in my arms is making me fucking horny." Her small laugh landed right on his dick. "I got a little bit of time. I want to taste you so I have you on my lips when I leave."

She squeezed him and traced circles on his back with her fingertips. Burying her face in his chest, she murmured, "I don't want you to go."

He kissed her head. "I know, babe, but I'll be back before you know it. And one of the prospects is gonna keep an eye on you while I'm gone. I don't want anything to happen to you. I don't know who it'll be, but you'll know him by his cut." She nodded, her head still snug against him. The way she clung to him made him feel warm inside. She was acting different, but he couldn't quite pinpoint why. "Babe? You gonna give me something sweet before I leave?" He tilted her chin up, then kissed her softly on her lips.

She nodded. "Just promise me you'll come home safe, okay?"

"Okay." He kissed her again, that time more urgently and much wetter. Taking her hand, he entered the house, kicking the door closed behind him. He slowly stripped off her clothes and laid her naked body on the bed, his gaze raking over her ripeness. Her nipples were hard, her desire for him making them that way; it grabbed his dick hard. Very hard.

He quickly shrugged off his boots and clothes and slid next to her. With his finger, he traced a trail from her forehead down to her feet, blowing lightly. Tiny bumps appeared on her skin as he felt her shiver under his touch. "You are so beautiful," he said softly.

He bent his head down and kissed her, his tongue entering her mouth, twisting and plunging deep. She hooked her arms around his neck and returned the kiss as he swallowed her small moans. Then he nipped, licked, and kissed his way to her tits, where he massaged and played with them as he sucked deeply on her hard nipples. She writhed underneath him, moaning, "Oh, Throttle." Hearing her say his name fueled his desire.

He pushed up and pulled her toward him. "I want you to sit on my face. I want to eat your sweet pussy."

He lay back and she crawled up to him. Then he positioned her over his face and, with his fingers digging into her soft flesh, he guided her hips down until she was a couple inches away, her sweet sex right over his mouth. "That's it." He massaged her wet mound. "This is all for me."

"Always and forever," she breathed as she threw her head back.

He swept his tongue over her wet folds and she gasped, igniting his fire even more. As he licked her, he squeezed her ass with one hand and tweaked and pinched her nipple with another. He couldn't get enough of her taste, her touch—just *her*. Never had he experienced such a longing for a woman. She reached back and clasped her hand around his hard-as-fuck dick. Bolts of pleasure zinged through him. "I love the way you touch my cock, babe."

"I want to take it in my mouth. All of it," she panted as she continued to move her hand up and down.

"I can fix that." He gently pushed her away. "Bend over me so your mouth has my cock, and I can finish licking your tasty pussy." And it *was* tasty, like almonds and honey, and it was fast becoming his favorite flavor. He craved her—she lived in his dreams and thoughts. He went to bed thinking of her and woke up wanting her. Even when they were together, eating, watching TV, or talking, he craved her. All of her, all the time. She was the only woman who ever commanded such attention. And he was fucking hooked. All the way.

As she sucked his cock and played with his balls, he lapped her juicy sweetness in long strokes while two fingers sank into her, moving in and out. Her moans vibrated against his dick and he wanted to stay like that forever, licking her pussy while finger-fucking her as she sucked his cock. Her nub was swollen and peeking from its hood, and he flicked the tip of his tongue over it, loving the way it hardened under his touch. Savoring her scent and taste, he slid his tongue over her again and again as he tugged and played with her tits. She moaned loudly, her breathing growing shallow.

Then she took his hardness all the way back in her mouth as far as it would go and began swallowing, taking his head even further into her throat. A feral grunt broke through his lips, and every nerve in his body was fired up. Each swallow took his dick further, and the muscles of her throat felt like she was milking his cock.

"Fuck, Kimber. You're killing me. Fuckin' love it." His voice was so hoarse, he didn't even recognize it.

Her juicy walls clamped around his fingers, and her low guttural groan pulsed in his ears. She went over the edge just as the tension surged through his dick, releasing ribbons of hotness into her tight mouth. Her thighs seemed to have given out and she collapsed on him, his softened dick still inside her mouth. "Babe," he croaked. "Get the fuck up here." She turned around and scooted up to him and he held her close, kissing her forehead as she held his spent dick in her warm hand. A cozy feeling surrounded him, and he knew what he had with her was special and something he wanted for a very long time. "You're incredible." He raked his fingers through her hair.

"No one has ever made me come like you have." She snuggled closer to him.

Was that all he was to her, someone to make her come good and hard? He wanted her to feel more for him than that. When he came back, they'd have to talk. He didn't want her to walk away from him after the desire waned. For him, he knew he'd always desire her—she was the perfect complement to him.

His phone vibrated and he glanced at the clock on the nightstand. It was almost two o'clock. He picked up his phone.

"On my way," he said.

"We're leaving in twenty minutes. Make sure your ass is here." Hawk's gruff voice told Throttle he was irritated, but he didn't care; he'd had a burn only Kimber could've put out. She fucking rocked his world.

He grunted and then hung up the phone, sitting up. "Gotta go, babe." He put on his clothes and watched as she went over to the dresser, loving the way she jiggled in all the right places. She slipped a long T-shirt over her head before they padded out of the bedroom and went to the front door. He drew her to him and kissed her deeply, the taste of both of them in their mouths. "You take care of yourself. Tell the prospect if something spooks you. Got it?"

She nodded, her blue orbs shining. *Fuck. I can't see her cry. If I do, it'll kill me.* He turned around quickly. "Be back in a few days. I'll text or call if I can."

Panic shone in her gaze. "You have to at least text me once so I know you're safe. I don't want to sit here and worry."

He jutted out his jaw. "I'll try, babe. I can't promise it. I'll be fine. Be back soon." He hurried over to his Harley and jumped on. He looked at her, his heart cracking. "Put the goddamned alarm on. The prospect's coming now."

He jerked his head to the street where a black and chrome motorcycle pulled into the driveway beside him. "You watch my woman," he said to Puck. The big man nodded.

Then he sped away.

CHAPTER TWENTY-SIX

AFTER FIVE AND a half hours, the bikers finally pulled into Alina, a small southwestern town near the Four Corners area at the foot of the San Juan Mountains. A dry desert wind blew over them as they steered their Harleys into the secluded Night Rebels clubhouse. Steel rushed out to meet them. Several other members walked out and held up their fists in the air, then pounded them against their chests in greeting.

"How was the ride?" Steel asked the men as they walked into the clubhouse.

"Good," Hawk replied.

Throttle stayed back and walked around the corner of the building, taking out his phone. He plugged in Kimber's number.

"Hey, babe. I'm here."

"Hi." Her voice pulled his heart. "Where are you?"

"I can't say. Club business, remember? Whatcha doin'?"

"Just finished some Chinese food and watching a show. What about you?"

"Just talking to you."

"I know you can't tell me anything, but if you're at a club I'm sure there'll be a lot of women. Bikers and women seem to go hand in hand."

He chuckled. "You telling me not to fuck around?"

"Yes. Am I stepping over a line with us?"

Was she? He would kill any guy who even tried to touch her, let alone fuck her, but he'd realized he was crazy about her. Maybe she was about him too. Why would she care if he fucked someone else unless she had feelings for him? "No."

"No, I'm not overstepping? I mean, I don't want you to think I'm a possessive witch, you know?" She laughed. "But it'd kill me if you fucked another woman." Her voice was low.

"I don't wanna fuck anyone but you."

"Really?" Joy replaced the insecurity he'd heard in her voice.

"Yeah. Puck been doing his job?"

"Keeping watch since you left this afternoon."

"Good."

"I miss you already," she whispered.

"Me too. Gotta go. We got shit to discuss."

"Okay. Take care of yourself."

He slid his phone into his pocket and walked into the clubhouse. Was it possible that Kimber felt the same way about him as he did about her? When he returned, they were going to talk no matter what the hell was going on around them.

He spotted some of his brothers by the bar, a few of them cozying up to the club girls. Throttle slipped onto a barstool and ordered a beer, gulping it in one long drink. "Damn, that was good," he said aloud. The ride had been hot and dusty, and a frothy beer made all the difference.

"How've you been, Steel?" Throttle asked.

"Okay. Yourself?"

"Busy as hell." Throttle liked Steel a lot. Part Navajo, part Irish, he was a fierce leader who also ruled by reason. He'd been to Pinewood Springs many times, and they'd come to Alina to hang out on various occasions. The president was a typical biker in that he fucked hard and left the satisfied women easily. The Night Rebels kept the southern part of the state in order, and they were an asset to the Insurgents.

"Let's all go make plans to teach these assholes a lesson. Grab a few beers." Steel motioned to one of the prospects to get the bottles.

Inside the meeting room, Steel laid out the problems they'd been having with the Skull Crushers ever since the day they'd just sprung up in the Night Rebels' backyard. "The fuckers think they can just set up shop, elect officers, and ride around wearing a 'Colorado' bottom rocker.

They also think they can deal meth and weed in your territory." He picked up his beer and took a drink.

"They should be stomped to death for having rice burners alone," Bones said, and all the Insurgents' and Night Rebels' members laughed.

"We have to teach them that they're not wanted in Insurgents' or Night Rebels' territory. These fuckin' punks don't know shit. They have to ask permission to have a club in our territory. Then, if we approve, they have to pay us for doing business in Colorado. They started their shit in Pinewood Springs and we took care of them." Hawk leaned back in his chair.

"They don't give a shit about the time-honored rules of MC clubs. All they give a fuck about is making money, getting high, and acting like they're badass." Steel spread his hands out on the table. "I say we strike tomorrow night. If we wait too long, they'll get wind you're all here."

"I agree," said Hawk. He glanced at his brothers. "You?" They all voiced their agreements by nods, grunts, and "yeahs."

"Then we hit them tomorrow night at Teasers—their favorite strip bar. It's a weeknight, so it should be quiet in there. Chaco, Pino, and Stretch have been watching them for a couple weeks. They're pretty predictable. We should have no problem surprising them."

Hawk leaned forward. "What about citizens? Is this strip bar just for bikers? I don't want any citizens getting hurt over this shit we got going with these assholes."

"It's a seedy strip bar on the outskirts of town. The fuckers drove out the citizens and made it their own, so it's basically them."

"Bartenders and barmaids aligned with them?" Throttle asked.

Steel turned to Chaco, gesturing him to answer. He nodded. "Yep. They aren't members of the group, but they are definitely sympathizers."

"We gotta isolate them as soon as we get there. If there are any citizens, we do the same with them. A couple of your brothers can watch them in a back room. We don't want anyone hurt who isn't part of the disrespect. Understood?" Hawk said.

"We're with you on that brother," Steel replied.

"We don't want anyone calling the fuckin' badges either," said Throttle. "We got enough shit going on in Denver."

"Heard about that. Fuck. We were gonna go, but we had some club business that came up. Your guys going down on a murder rap?"

Hawk shrugged. "We got some lawyers trying to make sure that shit doesn't happen. Anyway, Rock and Wheelie didn't shoot the bastard. But we don't want any interference with the badges tomorrow night. We don't have to worry about the Skull Crushers, but the citizens are another story. We gotta watch them."

Steel nodded in agreement. "We shouldn't have a problem with that. There's a back room we can keep them in. Anyway, the badges hate the Skull Crushers as much as we do. Since they came into the county, they've thrown off the balance. There's been a long-time understanding between the badges and our club. They'll overlook some things if we make sure certain shit doesn't go down in their backyard. Keeping crystal and crank outta the county is one, and not beating the shit outta citizens is another. The Skull Crushers have disrupted the flow, and they're looking to us to make it right."

"Hell, if they could, the badges would join us in kicking the fuckers' asses." Chaco chuckled along with the other members.

"Sounds like we pretty much have free reign. Okay, let's decide how this is gonna go down," Hawk said.

The two clubs talked well into the night, strategizing. When they'd finally cemented everything, the members from both clubs walked into a large room. One of the back tables had steaming burritos, enchiladas, tamales, rice, guacamole, and chips. "Eat up and have some fun. Our club whores and hang-arounds love tasting new biker cock," Steel said. "Enjoy."

As Throttle sat at one of the tables, shoveling a forkful of rice in his mouth, a busty, dark-haired beauty cozied up to him. "Aren't you a good-looking man. You wanna have some fun?" She was exactly the type of woman Throttle went for, and pre-Kimber, he'd be sucking and fucking her big tits while he finger-fucked one of the other dark-haired club girls. He wasn't interested anymore. The petite, sassy mechanic had taken down the ripped, arrogant biker. He couldn't imagine it any other way.

"You want me to ask some of my friends to join us?" the woman asked.

He shook his head. "I got a woman."

A tall blonde with legs that went on for miles sat on the chair next to him. "That doesn't seem to bother a lot of the brothers."

Throttle knew some of the brothers like Ruben and Tigger were married, but they both had two hot chicks straddling their laps, their hands roaming over their bodies. Ruben's old lady, Doris, let her man have his fun once in a while, claiming it kept their fourteen-year marriage better than ever. But Tigger's old lady, Sofia, was not into sharing her husband; the only problem was Tigger was always panting over the club whores and hoodrats every chance he got. Sofia was only twenty-four years old, and she was so pretty and fragile that most of the members felt sorry for the way Tigger treated her.

"I'm one of the brothers it does bother." He turned away, dismissing them. All he could think about was Kimber, not easy pussy from a couple of chicks who'd been around the block more times than they could count. They knew the score just like the brothers did. It didn't matter if they were partying in Pinewood Springs or Alina, it was all the same: booze and easy sex.

"You have it bad for Kimber, don't you?" Hawk said as he sat down. Throttle shrugged. "I know you do because you're not even looking at the women in the room." Hawk threw a shot back.

"Fuck. She's all I think about, dude. I never thought I'd feel like this about a woman, but your smart-assed employee grabbed my dick bad."

Nodding, Hawk curled up the corners of his mouth in a wide grin. "You know, I thought I'd be single my whole life. I didn't want to settle down—easy pussy was the way I lived. You were the same. I thought we'd be like Rob and Packer—old but still banging away. Then I met Cara and she fuckin' blew me away. I couldn't even remember why I thought easy pussy was so great." He threw back another shot. "Now you got bit, and after all the shit you gave me about Cara, I gotta say I'm enjoying this."

Throttle chuckled. "I can't believe I'm even having this pansy-assed conversation with you."

"That's the point, man. It feels real good when a woman enters your life. A woman who grabs hold of all of you and takes you on the wildest ride ever. Nothing fuckin' compares to that."

"You're damn right about that."

Hawk stood from the table and clasped Throttle's shoulder. "I'm gonna call Cara and then get some sleep. We got a long twenty-four hours ahead of us." He walked out of the room.

Shortly after Hawk left, Throttle drained his beer and made his way to one of the guest rooms in the club's basement. He stripped off his clothes and lay on the bed, wishing like hell Kimber were there to hold. He closed his eyes and, in a matter of seconds, fell fast asleep.

TEASERS WAS A small, squat club that sat on a stretch of road five miles away from town. The windows were painted black, and a couple of low-watt lightbulbs hung over the entrance, attracting a swarm of moths that flapped their wings incessantly against them. The loud clash of black metal seeped out from the door cracks. Several Insurgents and Night Rebels positioned themselves at the back exit while the rest of the brothers entered the seedy joint.

Inside, the light was dim, but they could see a bar to one side and a stage at the other. A few tables scattered near a pool table in the back. A large sign on the bar read "Special—Tacos $1.00" in blue magic marker. "War" by Burzum played on the overhead speakers as two women moved around on the stage: one so skinny it looked like her G-string would fall off, the other with a tiny waist and huge fake tits. Under the pulsing black light, she looked grim and worn out as she danced around a pole—badly—and the skinny one looked bored as she swayed, staring at one of the ceiling panels.

The sour smell of the joint mingled with a faint scent of a Febreze-style spray that curled around Throttle's nostrils. He noted the place had all the markings of a dive: worn carpet, cigarette burns, and patched upholstery. His assessment revealed two strippers, one bartender, and one barmaid; the rest of the patrons were Skull Crushers.

A tall man with short, spiked blond hair and two shorter men sporting the same hair color and style walked up to the newly arrived men. Sneers and numerous piercings marked their faces. The name on the tall man's cut read "Hitler," and he also sported a swastika patch and one that said "President." Darting his eyes between Throttle and Hawk, his brows rose when his gaze landed on their "Insurgents" patch. His pale blue eyes darted to Steel, and Throttle swore he noticed a sliver of fear creep into the dirtbag's eyes.

"Can we help you?" he yelled over the music.

Throttle went over to the bartender. "Turn the fuckin' music down."

"Who the fuck do you think you are? I'm not turning shit down."

"I'm the guy who's gonna kick your ass good if you don't do as I ask. We got business here."

The bartender stared at Throttle and then threw his rag down, bent over, and fiddled with something in a cupboard. The noise level decreased, and Throttle walked back over to where Hawk stood. Two Night Rebels went behind the bar on either side of the bartender.

"That's better," Hawk said.

"What the fuck do you want?" Hitler asked.

"Your bottom rocker, and then my fist in your fuckin' face."

"You're on our turf. You should think—"

"Fuckin' correction, asshole. You're on *our* turf, and that's the problem," Throttle hissed.

Hawk took a step toward the president. "Why the fuck you wearing the bottom rocker? You didn't get permission from the Insurgents. You're doing business in our state and our territory. Night Rebels are with us. You've been doing all kinds of shit on their turf."

Hitler sneered at Steel. "We don't recognize Injuns as anything but trash."

The tension in the air hissed.

Hawk gestured to Ace and Hoss to help the two Night Rebels members, Doc and Pokey, take the citizens to the back room. They complied, pushing the four angry people out of the main area.

Hawk pushed Hitler.

The two men with him stepped forward, their shoulders thrown back, their faces distorted and blotchy, as they clenched their fists.

Throttle shoved them, and one of them fell to the right.

The rest of the Skull Crushers came over, some carrying pool cues, all of them taking out their chains and knives. Throttle and the others kept their eyes peeled for any handguns, knowing that if anyone drew, the scene would turn from a violent fight to a bloodbath.

Most of the Insurgents and Night Rebels had thick rings with their insignia on them on all of their fingers. They provided the same effect as brass knuckles. In Throttle's estimation there were about fifteen Skull Crushers and, with the two clubs combined, there were about twenty on his side. His blood was pumping as adrenaline shot through him in anticipation of the fight. Each and every time a rumble was about to begin, he'd get a real big charge which fueled him throughout the fight.

"We're gonna let you off with a warning. Don't ever wear a 'Colorado' bottom rocker. Just remember, next time you're all fuckin' dead."

Like lightning, Hawk punched Hitler's face.

One of the Skull Crushers slammed his fist into Throttle's back. Rage surged through him.

He whirled around, grabbed the fucker by his T-shirt, and forced him down. He could hear the rasp of ripping material. Once on the ground, the Skull Crusher slammed his brass knuckles into Throttle's shin.

He lifted his steel-toed boot and pummeled the guy with it.

Black metal music thumped as the men shoved, kicked, stomped, and punched each other. Rough hands pulled at cuts and T-shirts. From the other side of the room, Throttle saw three guys attacking Tigger as he lay on the ground.

Rushing over and leaping like a panther, Throttle landed on one of the Skull Crushers' back. He smashed his industrial flashlight over the man's head, his blood sticky and warm on Throttle's fingers.

In that moment, from the right, a fist of metal crashed against him. "Fuck!" His voice was tight with rage, his tongue soaked in the taste of blood.

He swung around and sank his balled fist into his attacker's gut.

The Skull Crusher grunted, then fell to his knees.

Throttle lifted his leg and shoved his foot into the man's face. He heard the crunch of bone. "You fuckin' asshole!"

He swung around and met the crazed gaze of a burly, tall man.

"We're going to teach you a lesson, you fuckin' pieces of trash. When we're done, we'll be wearing whatever the hell we want on our patch!" The Skull Crusher's balled fist collided with Throttle's cheek-bone.

His head flailed like a branch caught in the wind. As he staggered backward, he nearly fell over the table. Red spilled out from his open wound.

The Skull Crusher came in for round two.

Regaining his balance, Throttle bent low and then came up high, clipping the burly man in his Adam's apple. The man howled, then dropped to the floor, where Throttle whacked the back of his back with the flashlight. Hard. Then he turned the Skull Crusher over and punched him in the face, snapping his nose into a mangled mess.

The fight lasted only six minutes, but the stench of sweat, urine, and rusting iron permeated the joint. Pools of red were scattered around the room, flies already buzzing above them. Throttle, bruised and cut, stumbled over to the bar where the others wiped off the remnants of the brawl.

All the Skull Crushers had been subdued and their cuts ripped from them. Jerry took them and sliced off the bottom rockers with his hunting knife. "Let's burn these."

Hawk nodded, and several members of the two clubs hollered as Jerry doused them in lighter fluid from behind the bar and lit them up. Many of the members looked like they'd been thrown through a windshield at a high speed. The swelling of cheeks, broken noses, busted lips, and black eyes began to appear.

After the bottom rockers were burned, Hawk went over to Hitler who lay on the ground, holding his battered head and face in his hands. "You ever wear a 'Colorado' rocker again, you're fuckin' dead. You get the fuck out of this county. If you don't, we'll blow up your goddamned clubhouse."

Throttle kicked him in the ribs. "Now you've been fuckin' told."

The two clubs shuffled out of the bar. Hawk gave some money to the bartender to cover the cost of damages and cleanup; then they revved their Harleys and headed back to the Night Rebels' clubhouse. They'd need plenty of whiskey, the club girls to clean and patch them up, and the doctor on call to stitch up the wounds.

The distaste in their mouths and cores had been washed away by the Skull Crushers' blood.

They would be no more.

Mission accomplished.

CHAPTER TWENTY-SEVEN

ON DAY THREE of not hearing from Throttle, Kimber decided that instead of overanalyzing, she'd simply ask one of the prospects who were stationed outside her house. She hadn't been able to focus, which wasn't good for the customers or her studies, and as much as she attempted to stay positive, worst-case scenarios kept flitting through her mind.

She stepped out on her porch and recognized Puck as the one on duty. "Hi," she said casually.

He stretched his neck toward her and grunted. She wondered if grunting was one of the requirements of becoming a full-patched member. She made a mental note to ask Throttle about it after she wrung his neck for worrying her; that was if he were okay. *He has to be okay.*

She held out a can of Coors to Puck. "Do you want one? It's so damn hot out here."

He shook his head, his eyes darting back to the cluster of trees across the street from her. "Why don't you come inside? I know Throttle would be cool with that. I mean, you're here to make sure no one breaks in, so being in or out really makes no difference. Right?"

He didn't answer, just kept staring. *Guess the answer's no.* "Do you know when Throttle is supposed to get back?"

He shook his head, and she resisted the temptation to clobber him with her potted plants. "He's okay, isn't he? I mean, I haven't heard from him in three days. I'm worried. Can't you give me *something* to ease my mind?"

"Don't know anything."

So he can *talk. Good to know.* "Is there any way you can find out?"

He shook his head, jaw jutted out, then turned his chair so his back faced her. Taking that as her cue that the "conversation" was over, she walked back inside the house and put the beer in the refrigerator. Then she sat down on the couch, wishing Throttle would call or text her. An empty feeling in the pit of her stomach frayed all her nerves. She couldn't just sit around, glancing at her phone, wondering if he was going to contact her.

She leapt up, grabbed her keys, and jumped on her Harley. Swinging a right at the stop sign, she headed to the Insurgents' clubhouse to find someone who could answer her questions.

When she pulled up to the electrified gate, Blade was the member on duty. She threw him a smile. "Can you open the gate, please?"

He stared stone-faced and picked up a receiver. Her eyes widened. "Are you serious? You have to call to see if *I* can come in?"

"You have ties with the Demon Riders. Gotta check."

She couldn't believe her connection to Chewy a few years back put her on the "Do Not Enter" list with the club. Why she didn't just live a normal life in the citizen's world escaped her; it'd be a lot simpler. But she knew the danger and edge the outlaw world had were what attracted her. Besides, she was hopelessly in love with Throttle.

"Okay. Got it." Blade set the receiver back in its cradle and opened the gate, stepping aside to make room for her bike.

"Thanks." She drove through, not expecting him to answer. She pulled into a spot near the front entrance. Brushing back her hair, she walked inside. Each time she had come to the club, the great room was dimly lit, so she was surprised when she entered a brightly lit room. The usual black curtains were open, letting the natural light through all the windows.

Johnnie was at the bar, and it seemed like he was taking inventory of the bottles; he had a notebook and pen and was jotting something in it when she approached. He didn't look up. Exasperation at all outlaw bikers fell over her. She was not in the mood for this crap.

"Where's Banger's office?"

"He expecting you?"

"You didn't answer my question. Where is it?"

"He expecting you?" The repeated question grated on her nerves.

"Look, you can tell me, or I can walk down the hallway and open every door until I find it."

"I'm thinking he's not expecting you. Wait." He slipped away from the hall and swaggered down the hall.

Kimber counted the liquor bottles while she waited for him to come back. When she left her house, she'd made the decision that she wasn't going to leave the clubhouse until she found out if Throttle was all right. She may end up bruised and bloody, but she was going to find out the answers to her questions one way or the other.

"Down the hall, last door on the left," he said as Johnnie went behind the bar once more, picked up his notebook, and turned his back to her.

She walked away, her stomach clenching. When she was at Banger's door, she knocked and entered when he yelled out. She saw an attractive older man with a beard and piercing blue eyes. Her insides quivered, but she willed her frazzled nerves to calm down as she stood in front of his desk.

"Sit down." He held her gaze as she settled into the chair. "What can I do for you?"

He acted like he'd never seen her before, and she wondered if he'd forgotten her even though they spent time together as a group at the expo a couple weeks before. She swallowed, then caught his gaze. "I don't know if you remember me but—"

"I know who you are. What do you want?" His voice was gruff and mixed with impatience.

"I haven't heard from Throttle in three days, and I'm worried sick. I can't concentrate, and I'm doing a shitty job at work. I don't need to know where he is, but I need to know if he's safe. That's all." She broke eye contact and wrung her hands in her lap.

Banger's eyes narrowed. "He's on club business."

"I know that," she snapped. "I just want to know how he is."

"Fine." He bent his head down and reviewed a document in front of him.

That's it? Fine? She sat there, the silence squeezing against her.

With his head still bent, he said, "You still here?"

"I was hoping you could add something more to 'fine'." Her heartbeat thumped against her rib cage.

He looked up, his gaze penetrating. "I gotta admit you got guts coming in here. But you better never fuckin' come in here again when Throttle's out on club business. We're done here." He lowered his head again in a dismissive way.

She stood from the chair and padded to the door. Kimber looked over her shoulder at the president. "Thank you for seeing me and easing my mind. I'm sorry I disturbed you."

He grunted and she left the office, heading straight for her motorcycle. When she put the key in the ignition, her phone pinged. Her stomach leapt as she opened the text.

Throttle: *Headed back. Should be there around 9.*

Kimber: *Is everything okay?*

She waited for a while, but there was no response. She knew he'd have to come back to the clubhouse to brief Banger on what went on during their "club business." Smiling, she rushed home and packed an overnight bag. She'd surprise him when he came back.

"Throttle's on his way home, so I'm going to meet him at the clubhouse in a couple hours. You don't need to stay," she told Puck.

"I stay until one of the brothers tells me not to."

She shrugged and went inside to take a long bath; after worrying for three days, it'd feel good to relax. She slathered on her rose-patchouli cream to make her skin extra soft for her man. Humming, she lit a couple of sandalwood incense sticks before she slipped into the tub, the warm water and bubbles splashing around her.

After one of the best baths she'd had in a long time, she gathered all her belongings and checked herself out in the mirror one last time. Her yellow crochet crop top complemented the tattoos on her arms and shoulder. Straightening her short jean skirt, she fluffed her damp hair with her fingers and then set the alarm.

"I'm off, Puck. Call Banger or someone so you can leave." She waved and placed her bag in the saddlebags. She knew he wouldn't call anyone. Prospects weren't allowed to do any of that; he'd stay on the porch until he was told to leave. She made a mental note to tell one of the brothers that Puck didn't have to finish out the night at her house.

When she walked into the clubhouse, the sun was just setting, and more brothers and women were around than when she'd been there earlier. The men glanced in her direction, but the minute they recognized her, they turned around. Relief spread over her—being Throttle's woman had its advantages. She ordered a whiskey sour and sipped it as she waited for Throttle to walk through the door.

An hour later, a low rumble—anyone not familiar with Harleys would have mistaken it for thunder—thrummed in her ears. A jolt of adrenaline surged through her as she stared at the door, a wide grin on her face. When the roar became deafening, she knew Throttle was minutes from coming in. She rose from the barstool and planted herself near the front door.

It swung open and Jerry, Hawk, Axe, and Jax came in first, their faces and arms banged up in varying degrees of hideousness. Then Bear, Bones, Tigger, and Throttle came in and she flew to him, wrapping her arms around him, kissing his battered face. From the way he stepped back, she figured he hadn't expected her to be there. Recovering, he picked her up and swung her around. She looped her legs around his trim waist and buried her head in his neck, inhaling the scent of him mixed with the wind and the night.

He carried her up to his room and placed her on the bed, kissing her deeply like he was a starved man and she was his only sustenance. "I missed you so fuckin' much," he whispered against her lips.

"Me too. I thought I'd die when I didn't hear from you."

"I couldn't call. It wasn't because I didn't want to."

"It doesn't matter now. You're home. I'm so happy." She ran her fingers through his windblown hair, tugging them through the tangles.

"I'll be back, babe. We got church, but it shouldn't be too long."

"You better go. I'm already on Banger's shit list."

"How come?" He kissed her shoulders.

"I came here to ask if you were okay. He didn't take too kindly to that."

He burst out laughing. "You fuckin' did that? That's gutsy and downright insane. I know Banger's gonna give me shit for *that* one."

"Sorry. I was just so worried, I didn't think."

"No worries, babe. It's too fuckin' funny." He hovered over her, and that's when she saw how badly bruised and swollen his face was.

"Damn! What the hell happened to you?" She reached out and gently caressed him. "Are you all right?"

"It looks worse than it is. I'm good. Nothing broken or requiring stitches." He kissed her hard on the lips. "I gotta go. When I get back, we'll have some fun." He hoisted himself off the bed and walked out of the room.

Kimber was shocked when she saw the condition of his face. She wondered what the other guy looked like. Knowing Throttle, he gave better than he got. She decided to bring in her overnight bag and change into something sexy before he came back to the room. For the past few days, she'd ached something terrible for Throttle; her body was already tingling in anticipation of what was to come. She hoped church would be short, because she had a hunger that nothing but Throttle could satisfy.

When the doorknob turned a half hour later, Kimber was ready to tackle him and take him on the floor. Her whole body hummed with desire, and the throbbing between her legs had started when she pictured him touching her in her mind. She saw the haze of lust in his dark eyes the minute they roamed over her body, encased in a black stretch fishnet and lace-trim halter teddy with bows. The teddy had front and side ribbon ties, and the back exposed her ass with a ribbon acting as a thong.

"Fuck," he whispered under his breath. He rushed to her, crushing her to him, grabbing her ass cheeks. "Damn. You're so soft and you smell amazing."

They kissed deeply, their hands touching, scratching, and groping each other as though they hadn't been together in years. She unzipped his jeans and shoved them past his narrow hips, and he kicked off his boots and stepped out of his pants and boxers. He yanked his shirt over his head and stood before her naked, his pulsing cock begging for attention.

She dropped to her knees and, catching his eyes, she ran the tip of her tongue over his smooth, warm head, loving the brine of his pre-come. He groaned and dug his fingers into her hair as she licked him up and down, wanting all of him in her mouth. She never broke her sultry eye contact with him.

When he was close to coming, he pulled out and looped his hands under her arms, lifting her up. "I want to taste your sweet pussy," he rasped against her ear, his lips tickling her. "And I wanna fuckin' untie all those bows." He nudged her down on the bed and devoured her lips.

She arched her back, her pert tits straining against the fishnet material, a pink, hardened nipple peeking out from one of the eyelets. He ran his thumb over it and electrified pleasure zapped her like thousands of live wires. She dug her nails in his taut skin, wanting to melt into him, to become as one.

"I want to unwrap you," he said huskily as his mouth trailed down past her collarbone. When he arrived at the tie that kept her breasts covered, he tugged on it with his teeth and it came undone, revealing her small, high tits. He lowered his head and captured her aching nipples in his mouth, sucking deeply, biting them just enough to cause a bit of pain to mix with the pleasure surging through her.

"That feels so good, Throttle. You can bite them harder."

"You like the pain, babe?"

"Uh-huh. So good."

He leaned over, took out a plastic bag, then came back to her, feathering kisses all over her neck and shoulders. "You ever tried nipple clamps?"

She paused. She'd heard about them and had always been intrigued since her nipples were one of her most erogenous zones on her body, but she'd never used them. "No," she breathed, her stomach doing small flips.

"You wanna do it? I won't put them on too tight. You can tell me how much pressure you want. They'll make you feel fuckin' awesome." He kissed her, slipping his tongue through her parted lips, his hands playing with her tits.

"Put them on," she whispered against his mouth, her body at an insane level of passion mixed with apprehension.

He tore open the package with his teeth and a long chain with two clamps on either side fell out. When she saw the clamps, they reminded her of something medieval, and her mouth went dry.

"You okay?" he asked softly, kissing her jawline.

"It looks like it could hurt."

"These have rubber tips so they'll be fine. There will be some pain, but that's the point. If you don't like it, I'll take them off. You tell me the pressure you want. You wanna try?"

She swallowed and nodded. He moved down and flicked his tongue over one of her nipples, his fingers playing with the other one until they were hard points. Then he opened the clamps and put them over her nipples. The tantalizing pinch made her gasp. "Too tight?" he asked.

"No. I want it tighter."

He smiled. "You're perfect for me, babe." He tightened the tension screws until she told him it was enough. When he leaned back, his hungry eyes devoured her. Her nipples tingled with extreme pleasure and a nip of pain, but when he pulled on the chain, her ass jumped up from the mattress; the gratification was so intense. Each time she moved, the weighted chain would pull on her sensitive nipples, causing waves of rapture flooding through her. Never had she felt something so mind-blowing. The more she moaned, the faster he undid her ribbons until she was finally naked beneath him, thrashing under his expert touch.

As he licked her closer to climax, he tugged on her chain, driving her wild with pleasure. Just when she was ready to lose it, he pulled back. "I want you on your knees. I have another surprise for you that'll give you a lot of pleasure." He pulled her up by her chain, and the act of him leading her to her knees by using it turned her on to no end. She felt submissive to him, and she let him take control. Sometimes she liked it after having to defend herself for her choice of profession. And she worked in a male-dominated arena, so letting go was a real treat.

She knelt on the bed, her ass facing him as the dangling chain swung, pulling at her nipples. When he buried his fingers between her slick folds, she cried out and he gently yanked her chain and kissed her lower back.

"You must love the clamps because you're sopping. Fuck, I love the way your juices feel against my fingers. I fuckin' love your pussy." His tongue dove into her heated slit while his fingers worked her clit, and she didn't think she could hold on anymore. "Don't come yet," he ordered, then dipped his tongue inside her.

"I don't think I can hold it any longer," she panted.

"Don't come." He pulled away.

Her throbbing mound felt empty. She was mad with desire, and he kept teasing her. Did he want to drive her crazy? He sure was doing a good job of it. "I need to come and feel you inside me," she whined.

He smacked her ass and she jumped, the sting making her hornier. Then his warm tongue licking her ass cheek soothed the sting, and her sex throbbed like mad. She heard rustling and turned to look over her shoulder. He had another plastic bag in his hands. "What's that?" she asked.

He smiled devilishly and took out a bright pink object that she recognized immediately as a butt plug. Chewy had put one in her a few times, but he'd been so rough that she didn't find the experience pleasant. "You ever try a butt plug?" He pulled out a tube of lube.

"Yeah. I hated it. Do you always keep sex toys in your drawers?"

He laughed. "I got this one for you. Notice the color? I bet the asshole who tried one on you didn't know what the hell he was doing."

"You're right on that."

"I know what to do. If it gets too painful, let me know. Remember, our word is 'checkers.' You say that and I stop, okay?"

He seemed fascinated with her ass, so she'd allow him this one time to prove it was worth her giving it to him. If she didn't like it, she'd definitely let him know. "Okay, but be gentle."

She watched him slather lube on the pink plug before he leaned over and kissed, bit, and licked her firm globes, kneading them with his hands.

"I love your ass, babe. I'm not gonna fuck it tonight, but I'm getting you ready for when I do. Your ass turns me way the hell on." He slapped her cheeks a few more times, then pulled on her chain. She ground her butt against his rock-hard dick as she moaned and threw her head back. Tangling her hair around his hand, he jerked her head back and kissed her neck. "I love watching you squirm and wiggle from pleasure. You like the pain, don't you?"

"Yeah." He yanked hard on her chain and she cried out, the sweet agony hitting her drenched mound.

"Here we go, babe. Just relax and breathe. It'll be good, I promise." She felt him part her cheeks. When the slippery tip of the plug entered her puckered opening, it felt so good. "Your hole is so damn tight. Love that." He pushed further until it was inside her ass. "How's it feel?" he asked as he rubbed his hands over her rounded globes.

"It feels good but weird. Like I'm all full up."

"Wait 'til you come. You're gonna love it." He wiggled the base and her insides lit up like a blowtorch. Then he slipped his finger between her swollen lips and stroked her sweet spot as he pushed his cock through her slit.

"Oh fuck, that feels good," she rasped, pushing her ass higher.

In and out he thrust while his finger stroked the side of her hardened nub. She slipped her hand under her and tugged the chain, her nipples bursting with sweet pain.

"You want it harder?" he growled.

"Yeah. Harder."

He rode her rough and hard, and each time his balls slapped against her ass it felt amazing with the plug inside. The scent of their arousal surrounded them, and her moans and cries filled the room as they both neared their climax. Then her pussy and ass pulsed and her wet walls clung to his stiff dick as she burst in thousands of pieces, her muscles contracting, her nerves zapping crazily. As she rode her orgasmic rapture, she felt Throttle stiffen, then grunt deep and loud as his hot streams filled her up and her muscles tightened around him, milking every last drop. Not able to stop the quivering in her legs, she collapsed on the bed with Throttle covering her back as he came down from his own euphoria.

They panted in rhythm and soon their breathing returned to normal. She couldn't believe how intense her orgasm was; she'd never experienced one of such magnitude before. He rolled to his side and moved her to her back. Smiling, he kissed her deeply. "How was it?" he asked as he nuzzled her neck.

"Fucking awesome. The butt plug rules."

He laughed and mussed her hair. She reached to take off the clamps but he grabbed her hand. "You can't just take them off because you'll be in a lot of pain as the blood rushes back in. Let me do it. It'll hurt for a second, but then it'll be okay." He gently took off the first clamp and a searing pain stabbed her nipple and she yelled out, but it went away as he sucked it in his mouth, licking it. He did the same with the second clamp. "Do you wanna take out the butt plug?"

"No. I'll leave it in until tomorrow. I like the way it feels."

He kissed her. "Good girl."

She turned toward him, kissed his chin, and hooked her arm around his waist. That night was perfect; they'd been connected through passion, understanding, respect, and love... at least for her. Kimber still wasn't sure if Throttle was in love with her, but the way they connected that night made her suspect he was. If only he'd tell her.

She leaned over and turned off the lamp, then snuggled back against him. The moonlight lit up his face. Even with the swelling, bruising, and cuts, he was still the most handsome man she'd ever met. She couldn't lose him—she'd waited thirty years to have him in her life. He'd fallen asleep right away, and she'd presumed it was from the long trip and their intense lovemaking.

She closed her eyes, happy he was back and she was in his arms—exactly where she belonged.

CHAPTER TWENTY-EIGHT

Detective McCue chewed his gum as he looked at his board listing the similarities of the women who'd been killed. He was stumped; they all appeared to be random. The glaring inconsistency was that two of the women who'd been murdered had been out of the killer's usual area. There had to be a clue in that. *It's probably staring at me, ready to bite me in the ass. Damnit! I know there's something here that links some of the victims.* He sat on his desk staring at the board, willing the murdered victims to tell him something.

The women who had been raped or sexually molested had not proved to be much help in aiding the artist in drawing a composite of the perpetrator. The attacks had been at night, usually moonless ones, and the women had been so terrified that all they could remember was that he was about five eleven and had a soothing voice. Not a whole lot to go on. He poured another cup of coffee and went over the facts of each case again.

The evidence they'd collected—a couple footprints and some semen—didn't pan out either. The DNA results were plugged into CODIS—the National DNA Index System—but there wasn't a hit, indicating the murderer wasn't in the criminal justice system, which stumped him more. How could someone burst onto the crime scene with that level of depravity and never have come in contact with law enforcement?

McCue's gaze stopped on Deputy Manzik. Every time he looked at her picture, his chest would grow tight. She didn't deserve to die the way she did; none of the victims did.

"Find out anything?" a voice asked from behind him.

He craned his neck and his gaze fell on Sergeant Stichler—Sharon's nemesis. A knot of muscles on the side of his jaw pulsed. "Nope."

"The case stumping the big-city detective?" Stichler laughed, and McCue gripped the side of his desk to keep from punching him.

"You want something?"

"I had to talk to the chief about something. I knew being a police woman was going to get her in trouble." He pointed to Deputy Manzik's photo. "Men don't like it when women take on their roles. It's not natural, you know? Like that woman who works at Thunderbird Motorcycle Repair shop. She's a mechanic. Now that's just crazy."

He wanted the ignorant sergeant to get the hell away from him. "What's your point?"

"Men don't like that shit. It makes them feel like less than a man. You know. I can't think of the word I want to say."

"Emasculated?"

The sergeant's face lit up. "Yep, that's the word. I think women should stick to what they know and let the men do the hard, tough jobs. Like how can this woman mechanic be better at fixing Harleys than a man? It's all messed up. The place is owned by an Insurgent, so I'm surprised he's allowing that. Probably doing a favor for a buddy's daughter."

"I don't ride so I don't know the shop, but are you saying Deputy Manzik didn't do her job as well as the other deputies in the department?"

"I cut her a lot of slack because she was a woman. She was always leaning on the guys to do the tougher stuff. She didn't belong here." His eyes narrowed.

"That isn't what I heard from her colleagues."

"People feel funny talking shit about the dead."

"And you obviously don't." They locked gazes, both of the hard and steely variety. "I'm busy." McCue pushed away from the desk and went over to his filing cabinet to pull the robbery case he'd worked on the previous day.

"Okay. Just wondering what was new with the investigation." The sergeant picked up a muffin from the tray the clerical staff had brought to the investigators, unwrapped it and took a large bite, then ambled out of the office.

Sparks burned through McCue as he watched the sexist man leave. It was people like Stichler who gave the department a bad name. He shook his head and opened the robbery file. After many phone calls, computer searches, and reviews of the file, the detective believed he had a couple suspects in the rash of robberies at several gas stations in and on the outskirts of town.

"How're things going?" Carlos asked. Detective Ibuado and McCue worked well together, both of them bringing different perspectives to the cases that fell into their laps.

"Good on the gas stations robberies. I'm about to leave to interview one of the witnesses we spoke to the other day. Randy Hillman, remember him?"

"Oh, yeah. He was the one who was bending over backwards to be helpful. I never buy that shit."

"Me neither."

"Did you talk to Josh down in the evidence room?"

"Josh? No. Should I?"

"He's got a theory about the murders. Something he spotted when he was cataloguing all the evidence."

"Really? I could use all the help I can get. I know not all of these murders are random, especially the one outside his usual area. I've been obsessing so much about this case that I can't figure anything out."

"You need to take a break from it for one day. I can field anything that may come in. You'll have a fresher look in a day."

"Good advice. I'm going to visit Josh and then see what Randy has to say about the robberies. I think a day away from the Lingerie Bandit should give me a fresher perspective." He picked up his notepad and grabbed a poppy seed muffin. "By the way, how well do you know Sergeant Stichler?"

Carlos shook his head. "Not very well. Why?"

"The guy's a real asshole. How long has he worked for the department?

"Long time. Before I came, and I've been here for almost seventeen years. I think he came in when he was like eighteen or nineteen years old. What's going on with him?"

"I'm not sure. The gals brought muffins. Help yourself. Later."

McCue walked the four flights to the basement and flashed his identification to the clerk. "Josh Sender," he said to the woman. She buzzed him in, and he made his way down the narrow hallway until he stopped in front of the evidence room. He turned the doorknob and went in.

The room smelled dank and musty, and the overhead fluorescent lights flicked and hummed. A man in his late twenties with a mop of dark hair came out. "May I help you?"

"I'm looking for Josh Sender." McCue shoved a stick of gum in his mouth.

"I'm Josh."

"I'm Detective McCue. My colleague, Detective Ibuado, said you got some theory or something about these murders?"

Josh's eyes lit up with excitement. "Yes, the Lingerie Bandit murders. Don't you just hate that, when the press comes up with these names? It trivializes the victims."

"Agreed. So, what've you got?"

Josh motioned for McCue to sit down, and then he shared his ideas and findings.

An hour later, McCue rushed back up to his office, adrenaline coursing through him. He headed over to the board with all the victims on it. "I think I just got my first major lead in the case. If this pans out, we may catch this sonofabitch before he kills again."

"I thought you were taking a break?" Carlos said as he came near McCue.

"No time. You busy?"

"Not for this."

"Good. We got our work cut out for us." He rolled up his sleeves and settled in his chair in anticipation of a long day.

CHAPTER TWENTY-NINE

"I'M BANKING ON you understanding that, until finals week is over, I can only see you for a few hours. Absolutely no sleepovers. I have to ace these tests to keep my scholarship in place."

"Okay," Throttle said.

"Yeah, you say that so easily, but last night, the night before, and the night before that, you stayed all night."

"I don't remember any complaints from you." He chuckled, the deep tone making her skin pebble.

"I know," she groaned. "That's the problem."

"I don't see any problem in it."

"Of course you wouldn't." She smiled; she was just as guilty as he was because whenever he was near, she couldn't stay away from him. She craved him and wanted her skin pressed to his as they slept. He was her elixir, and she needed it like an alcoholic needed a drink.

"You gotta eat, right? I'll come in a few hours and bring your favorite Chinese food. You can take a break, and then I'll leave so you can study."

The only reason he was acting so nonchalant about not spending the night, was because he knew she'd cave in like she had for the past three nights. But she had to study; she'd blown off too much time. "Okay, but come a little later. I'm going to start studying now."

"No problem. I have church, and then I'm gonna play a game or two of pool. Do you want egg rolls and Kung Pao chicken?"

"Yes, but make sure the egg rolls are veggie this time. Tell them extra spicy on the Kung Pao."

"You're extra spicy, babe. Can't wait for dessert."

"You see? That kind of talk is deadly to a student during finals week. Dessert tonight will have to be a fortune cookie."

He chuckled. "Be there in a few hours. If you need anything, call me."

She placed her phone on the coffee table and slumped on the couch. She was hopeless; she knew damn well he'd crumble the fortune cookie over her naked body and nibble it up. Sighing, she decided to get a hard few hours of studying in before her good-intentioned plans went to hell.

The sun shining through her large window blinded her and she went over to close the curtains. As she pulled them, she noticed a police car driving slowly by her house. It was the second time she'd spotted the car in the last hour. A shiver ran up her spine. She closed the drapes and set the alarm. Taking out a bottle of sweet tea, she plopped down on the kitchen chair, opened her new laptop, and began to study.

Two hours later, she rose from the table and stretched, lolling her head from side to side to work out the kinks in her neck. She walked around for a few minutes before heading back to her studies when the doorbell rang. For a split second, her nerves snapped and her pulse quickened. *I'm not expecting anyone.* She padded to the door and looked out the peephole, relief washing over her. A big smile replaced her tight look, and she disengaged the alarm and swung the door open.

"Dr. Redman, how are you?"

He smiled. "I was hoping you'd be home. I knew I wasn't going to see you until your final exam on Friday. I have good news. I found your laptop." He produced her computer, his beaming face infectious.

"Great! Where did you find it? Did someone turn it in?"

"No. I found it in one of the supply cabinets in the classroom. Isn't that strange? I have no idea how it got there."

"That is strange. Maybe someone was taking it and stashed it when they were interrupted." She shrugged. "I don't know. I watch too much TV." She opened the screen door and took her computer. "Thank you so much for bringing it to me. I had a bunch of notes on it that I didn't backup. This is great timing."

"Glad I could help." He turned and began to walk down the stairs.

"Would you like an iced tea? I was just taking my study break."

He glanced at his watch. "I guess I can spare twenty minutes. I told my wife I'd help her with one of the committees she's on." He came back up the stairs. "Should we have it out here?" He pointed to the wicker chairs.

"It's too hot out, and the mosquitoes are awful in August. We can go inside. It's nice and cool." He followed her inside. "When you're dean of the college, your wife will have to be on a lot of committees, won't she? That's what I've heard."

He sat on the couch. "Yes. It'll be demanding, but she loves all the social stuff. Much more than I do."

From the kitchen, she called out, "I also have lemonade. Would you rather have that?"

"Lemonade is great. You have a nice place here."

"It's comfortable."

"Are you doing okay with your studying? Do you have any questions?"

"As a matter of fact, I do." She handed him his drink, grabbed her notebook, then flopped on the couch at the other end. "Let's see. Oh yeah, how do you get the formula for productivity to balance out? I'm still confused about that."

Dr. Redman explained how to arrive at the answer, and Kimber wondered if she'd ever be as smart and knowledgeable as her professor.

"YOU MIGHT AS well give me the thousand bucks 'cause I'm gonna win the game," Throttle said as he sank two more balls in the far-left pocket.

"Fuck," Bones said under his breath. "Just a damn lucky shot."

"Like the last five have been? Own up to it—I kicked your ass in this game."

The other brothers laughed, and Rosie and Wendy yelled out accolades to Throttle as he sank another ball. Hawk came up beside him after his shot. "I need to talk with you."

"Fuck, dude. I'm in the middle of kicking Bones's ass. Hang tight."

"It's urgent. Now."

From the tight look on his brother's face, Throttle knew something was up. He handed his cue stick to Rags. "Make me proud, brother. We'll split the dough." He followed Hawk to his office.

"What the fuck's up?" he asked as he leaned against the wall.

"A real good friend of Cara's works for the sheriff's department, and he and Cara were talking shop about the murders happening in town."

"So?"

"Cara mentioned how Kimber thought she'd been targeted and how the Insurgents beefed up the security, and he told her something that had her spooked like hell."

Icy fingers grabbed his spine. "Go on." His face was tight, and a dull throb banged against his temples.

"Josh thinks he found a common denominator with some of the murdered women. Three out of the six murdered so far have gone to Pinewood Springs Community College. He also went back through the cases of the women who were assaulted only and found four of them were also students."

Throttle felt the color drain from his face. "Fuck," he muttered. "Kimber goes there. Fuck!"

"Yeah." Hawk spread out his hands on his desk.

Throttle pulled out his phone and dialed Kimber.

"Hiya," she said.

"You okay?"

"Yeah. Oh, my laptop was found. Isn't that cool?"

"You didn't mention that to me a couple hours ago."

"That's because I didn't know. Dr. Redman brought it over. Wasn't that nice? He thought I might need it for finals."

His heart raced, nearly exploding as his adrenaline spiked. "Is he still with you?"

"Uh-huh."

Fuck! "Babe, listen to me. Act totally normal and don't freak out. Don't interrupt me either. You're in extreme danger, and you gotta keep the prof talking until I get there. You got it?" He looked at Hawk and mouthed, "I'm outta here. Call the fuckin' badges." He knew the cops were ten minutes away to his twenty-five. Even if he hauled ass—which he planned on doing—he was still fifteen minutes further. A lot of harm could happen in a few minutes.

"Not really."

"Just act normal. Keep talking to me about whatever the hell you want but don't ask me any questions about what I'm telling you." He ran out to the parking lot; he had to get to her.

"That's just great."

"Good, babe. You got it. Don't tell the prof I'm coming, okay?"

"Yes, I'd like that a lot."

"Try to go over and punch the panic button on the alarm system. Just keep calm. If you punch it, you'll get some rough guys over in a flash to help you out." He jumped on his bike.

"You want me to look up the number?"

"Yeah. Get over there and push it."

"I'll see if I can find the number."

In the background, he heard a male voice. "What are you doing, Kimber?"

"My boyfriend wants me to give him a number. It's on the table by the door."

"The biker?"

"How did you know he's a biker?"

Throttle yelled, "Push the fuckin' button!" He hauled ass down the highway.

"He's giving you instructions, isn't he?"

"What? No. Stop it. What are you doing?"

"Babe, push the button. Run if you have to."

A sinister laugh echoed through the phone.

Then it went dead.

CHAPTER THIRTY

"**W**HAT THE FUCK are you doing? Let go of me!" Kimber pushed at her professor, but his grip was too tight. "Why'd you hang up my phone?"

"You think I'm stupid? He told you, didn't he?"

"Told me what?"

He chuckled, easing up a bit on her arm. She pulled away and made a mad dash for the alarm system to hit the panic button, but he lunged for her, knocking her against the wall. He was strong, and as she tried to kick and scratch him, she realized she was no match for him.

After she hit him in the chest with her elbow, he took out a hunting knife and brought it close to her throat. "I normally don't bring such a big knife to my targets' homes, but I brought extra security because of the biker."

Dizziness overtook her and her limbs grew shaky and weak. *Dr. Redman is the monster who's been killing and raping all the women. And the underwear thing? He's a fucking psycho. Don't panic—that's for later. You have to keep your head straight or you'll never survive.*

"How'd you know I was dating a biker?" she asked casually as though they were chatting after dinner.

He licked his lips, his gaze lingering on her chest. "I've watched you all semester." With a strong pull, he dragged her to the bedroom and tied her hands behind her back, his knife aimed at her body the whole time. Then he pushed her on her back.

"Throttle's going to be here any minute, and he's got a lot of his friends coming with him. Please don't do this. It's over. You don't have to do this."

With an incredulous look, he shook his head. "I can't stop. I *have* to have you. See you in your panties and bra. You don't understand. No one does."

Cold clamminess chilled her to her core, and the sound of her heartbeat thrashed in her ears as she struggled to loosen the ties. No luck. He opened her top drawer, picked up a handful of her undies, and brought them to his nose, breathing in deeply. Softly, he said, "I've been to your house before, when you were at work. I love the lime-green panties I took."

She watched in horror as he took her cherry-red bikini bottoms and sniffed the crotch while he grabbed his erection and moved his hand up and down.

"The biker tried to spoil everything for me, but I didn't give up—I never do. My wife tells me that's one of my strengths. When he had you put the alarm in, it ended my visits when you weren't home. Then he had a series of goons watching you when he wasn't around. It took me a while to figure out how I was going to please you. Then I thought about taking your computer. It was ingenious. And here we are, together... at last." He came over and ran his finger down her the face. "My only regret is that I can't savor you. I know he's coming. It's a shame, but life can't always be perfect, can it, Kimber?"

"You're a fucking sicko. Why do you do this shit? You're not going to walk out of here alive." A primal scream ripped from her throat, and the way his eyes widened, she knew she'd startled him.

He pulled a roll of duct tape from his pocket, cut a piece, held her flailing head still, and slapped the tape across her mouth. "I can't have you making a scene. You understand." He walked back to the dresser and picked up the knife, then came over to the bed. He cut off her T-shirt and bra, then gazed at her breasts as he licked his lips. He put the knife on the mattress and grasped the waist of her shorts. When he started pulling them down, she bent her knees and shoved her legs against him with all her might. Taken by surprise, he lost his balance and fell off the bed. In that second of opportunity, she pushed herself up and ran out of the room.

Her blood pumped as she tried to get to the panic button, her hands tingling from the lack of circulation caused by the tightly bound rope. All she could think of was survival. Just as she reached the alarm panel, she was jerked backward by her arms. The pain ripping through them made her think he'd pulled them from their sockets, but compared to the terror weaving around her nerves, the pain was minimal.

"That wasn't too smart. I pegged you as one of my brighter students." He began pulling her backward to the bedroom.

Frantically, she tried to free her hands, but she couldn't.

She heard loud footsteps on her porch. Her heart leapt as hope replaced terror.

The duct tape across her mouth prevented her from screaming out. With renewed vigor, she kicked behind her, hitting his shin. He released her and she dashed to the front door, throwing her body against it.

"Police. Open up!" The loud voice cut through the wooden door. Once again, she threw herself against the door.

Then the madman yanked her by the hair and dragged her to him. It felt like her scalp was ripping away from her skull.

When they entered her bedroom again, she heard the front door splinter. Then the rush of footsteps. He released his grip and she dashed out, tears streaming down her face as she gazed into the faces of several deputies.

He was behind her, the knife blade cool on the back of her neck.

"Sir, put the knife down," one of the deputies said.

"Stay away or I'll kill her." His voice hitched. He whispered against her hair, "I *needed* you." He pushed her forward a bit and let out a despairing scream as he plunged the knife in the base of her neck.

Searing pain tore through her and she screamed against the tape, her eyes tearing. As blood seeped out from her wound, dizziness overcame her, and she began to go down. It was in that moment that she saw Throttle pushing his way in, his face tight and blanched.

She slammed face down on the hardwood floor.

And then everything went black.

CHAPTER THIRTY-ONE

THROUGH THE HAZE of the night, Throttle followed the flashing lights until they turned into the ER driveway at Pinewood Springs Hospital. He secured his bike and ran inside only to be stopped by security.

"Sir, you can't go back there. You have to wait in the lobby."

"Fuck that. My woman was stabbed. I need to be with her." He rushed through the metal detectors, the alarms beeping at a high pitch. When he came up to the massive metal doors that led to the emergency area, he reached a roadblock—the doors were locked.

The security officer ran over to him. "Sir, I'm going to have to ask you to step back out. I need to check you for weapons."

"Fuck off!" Throttle pounded on the metal doors. "Open the god-damned doors!" From the corner of his eye, he saw the technician pick up the phone. Figuring she was calling the badges, he decided to calm the hell down; if he got a courtesy ride to the town jail, he wouldn't be there for Kimber. He whirled around. "Where do you want me to go?"

The security guard's face relaxed a bit. "You have to go back out and come through the detectors again."

Throttle followed him and placed his chains, rings, money clip, belt, and pocket knife in the yellow basket. He took off his biker boots, then walked through without setting off the detector. He'd left his gun and two knives back in the saddlebags in his Harley; he didn't have time to fuck around with the badges over a few simple weapons.

As he slid his belt in the belt hoops, a round-faced woman with short hair smiled at him. "Who are you here to see?"

"Kimber Descourts. She was just brought in."

"Let's have a look." She stared at the computer screen. "Yes, she's being put into a room right now. I'll let you know when you can go back. Please have a seat."

Not able to stay still, Throttle paced the length of the room, his eyes darting to the large wall clock every few seconds.

On his tenth lap around the waiting room, Hawk and Cara came through security with Banger and Rags behind them. A warm feeling spread through him when he saw his brothers. He tilted his chin to them.

"Do you know anything?" Cara asked.

He shook his head, and Hawk, Banger, and Rags came over and clasped his shoulder, striking their chests with their fists in a show of solidarity. Throttle returned the gesture. Cara brought him a cup of coffee and he gulped it, the bitterness making his lips pucker. They sat in silence, the three men staring at the television on a shelf in the corner of the room while Cara leafed through a magazine.

Images of Kimber's face, bloated from fear, and the blood streaming down her shoulders assaulted him. If he'd only been there with her, none of it would've happened. She was his woman and he was supposed to protect her, but he'd failed her. Over and over his mind played out the events—he couldn't stop the images. He sat with his elbows propped on his thighs, his head in his hands. After a few minutes, he felt a hand on his arm, and he looked up into Hawk's face.

"I'm here for you, brother. We all are. Lean on us." Hawk squeezed Throttle's arm once, then let go.

"Fuck. I don't know what I'm gonna do if something happens to Kimber. I should've been there." His voice broke and he turned away.

"I understand what you're going through. I went through the same thing with Cara. It fuckin' sucks, but don't be blaming this shit on yourself. We can all say we should've done something, but we never know what would've happened or not. It seems like this motherfucker was aiming for her and would've struck another time. Sometimes shit just happens. The strength comes in how we deal with the shit when it's thrown at us."

"Yeah, you're right. It's just that I wanted to protect her. I didn't want this to have happened."

"None of us wants our women hurt, but you did your best. You're here for her now. She'll do okay. She's tough. She's got a helluva lot of fight in her. You know that."

Throttle smiled weakly. "Yeah, she's quite a woman."

"Sir, you can go back now," the round-faced woman said. Throttle rushed up to the counter. "It's room fifteen. Go through the door, turn left and it'll be at the end of the hall, to your left." She pushed a button and a loud buzzer sounded.

Throttle walked through and searched for Kimber's room. When he arrived, he saw the curtain drawn around her bed. He waited outside her room until two people exited. A blonde woman stopped and asked, "Are you here for Ms. Descourts?" He nodded. She smiled and extended her hand. "I'm Dr. Haines."

Throttle shook her hand. "Is she gonna be okay?"

"She's going to be fine. There will be a bit of recovery time, but she should be back on her feet in two to three weeks. You can see her." The doctor opened the curtain.

Kimber lay under a white blanket, her black hair a stark contrast against the pillowcase. "Babe?" Throttle approached the bed, then took her cold hand in his warm one. Her eyes fluttered open, a glassy look covering them. "You gonna get outta here fast for me?"

A smile tugged at her mouth.

"She's very groggy due to the sedatives we gave her. She is one lucky lady. The knife didn't cut any arteries, and the wound wasn't so deep. I stitched it up. I'll keep her in the hospital for a week to make sure she's free from infection. When she does go home, she'll need help cleaning and changing the bandages. Will she have help with that?" Throttle nodded. "Excellent. I'll leave you alone with her. Since she's being admitted to the hospital, we're waiting for a room so she can be transported there from the ER. It shouldn't take more than an hour. Do you have any questions?"

"No." He watched as the doctor left; then he walked over to the bed and kissed Kimber on her forehead. "You scared the fuck outta me, babe," he said in a low voice as he held her hand tight.

She looked at him, her eyes not entirely focused. "Sorry," she rasped.

"I know you got some strong drugs in you, so go ahead and sleep. I'll be here when you wake up and after that."

"Come closer," she whispered. He leaned down, his ear next to her mouth. "I love you."

Her declaration made his heart soar, and for the first time since he'd learned she was in serious danger, lightness descended on him, pushing away all the heaviness from the past twelve hours. "That's good to know because I've been in love with you for a long while." She closed her eyes, and he brushed his lips over hers as she drifted to sleep.

THE ROOM'S WALLS were concrete and painted a steel-blue. A cheap light fixture hung down from the paneled ceiling, casting dark shadows in the corner of the windowless room. Detective McCue sat on one of the plastic chairs opposite to Dr. Redman. The Lingerie Bandit sat with his hands folded on the metal table, a cocky smile played on his lips.

McCue blew out a long breath and locked eyes with him. Instead of apprehension, the detective saw confidence in the man's brown orbs. *He thinks he's going to beat this.* Shaking his head, he leaned back in his chair. "You're in quite a jam, aren't you?"

Redman chuckled then leaned back, crossing his leg over his thigh. "Why do you say that?"

"You stabbed one of your students in front of me and several deputies." He took a sip of his coffee.

"I was driven to the brink of insanity by Ms. Descourts. She'd invited me to come over to help her with some problems she was having in my business class. She threw herself at me then threatened to expose me to the school's Board of Directors and to my wife. I don't know why she wanted to destroy everything I worked so hard for, but she did. I think she was in love with me and became vindictive when I spurned her." He shook his head. "I feel sorry for her."

"So you stabbed her?"

"I felt cornered. It was like she was toying with me. You know, like a cat does with a mouse. I lost it. Women can be that way. Twisting and turning men inside out. They know they have that power and they enjoy it." He placed his hands behind his head and smiled.

White rage shot through McCue but he knew he had to keep his anger at bay if he ever hoped to garner a confession on the other murders. "You sure you don't want a lawyer?"

"No reason for one. I went insane for several moments. I'm a family man with children."

"Is that right? Does your wife know about your late night strolls?"

Redman scrunched his face. "Night strolls? I don't know what you're talking about."

"The walks you take when you want to watch women undress. I'm sure it's pretty exciting."

The man's face turned bright red as his nostrils flared "I know what you're doing. You're trying to pin the break-ins and murders of that pervert the papers have named the Lingerie Bandit. I won't stand for this." He began to stand up.

"Sit down. You're not going anywhere." It was McCue's turn to smile. "You sure you don't want that lawyer?"

"No."

"Your shoe prints match the ones found at several of the crime scenes, many of the victims were either former students of yours or attended the college during the time you were employed there, and I'm more than sure your DNA is going to match the one we collected at the crime scenes." The detective's gaze never wandered from the killer's.

Redman's cocky demeanor crumbled. Looking stunned, he stared at McCue. "I don't know what to say."

"Just tell me what happened. We're going to find out. We have search warrants in our hands and are ready to execute them at your residence and place of work."

Panic spread over his face. "My wife likes an orderly house. You can't have your men tearing it apart. It'll just crush her if the house is out of order."

"You're the one controlling this. You can tell me about Deputy Manzik, and it'll make things a lot better for your family. You don't want them plastered across the breaking news, do you?"

"No," he said in a low voice.

The detective sat sipping his coffee waiting for Redman to take the lead.

"It's hard to believe this is happening. I didn't mean for any of it to go this way. I only wanted to watch the women, but it got to be that it wasn't enough." He raised his eyes searching McCue's for understanding.

Nodding his head, the detective said, "So you wanted to kick it up a bit to get the thrill back."

"Yes. I wanted so much more." He bowed his head, his shoulders slumping. "I always felt shame and disgust when I'd be home sleeping next to my wife. I'd promise myself that it would be the last time, but it never was. The urge was too strong...."

"So if you hadn't been caught you would've continued raping and murdering women?"

"I was hoping not but I can't really answer the question... I only know that I struggled with it daily."

"And Deputy Manzik?"

"She was beautiful. I desired her when she was at the college. I'd seen her photo recently in the paper, and it reminded me how pretty she was and how much I wanted her. I took it as a sign, and I sought her out." He rested his head between his hands. "I had a lot of time with her. I filmed our time together. I'm sure your deputies will find it. It's about three hours, I think." A long pause ensued before he cleared his throat. "I'm so horribly ashamed of the despicable crimes I've committed." His voice broke and deep sobs shook his body and filled the small room.

Several hours later, Detective McCue exited the room, tape recorder in hand and nodded to the waiting deputy. "Take him to holding and start the process. I'll send the charges over." He walked out into the cool night air and breathed in deeply. Looking at the winking stars he whispered under his breath, "He'll never hurt anyone ever again, Sharon. I'm just sorry I couldn't have caught the sick sonofabitch before he killed you. Rest in peace."

He turned around and went back into the building.

Chapter Thirty-Two

A COUPLE OF days later, Kimber sat in a chair by the window when Detective McCue entered her room. She loved looking out at the Rocky Mountains, the leaves on the aspen trees swayed in the breeze.

"What can I do for you?" she asked, gesturing for him to sit down.

McCue took a chair across from her. "How are you getting along?"

"Good. I should be able to go home in a few more days. I can't wait. I'm going crazy in here."

The detective looked around the room. "I bet you are. You're looking good. Better than you did several days ago."

"Has it only been a few days? It seems like a lifetime ago. I still can't wrap my head around it, that Dr. Redman was the one who killed and raped all those women. And he was the one breaking into women's houses—my house—to steal underwear? It doesn't seem real. It's like I dreamed it all. He was such a beloved professor and academic. He was going to be dean for the upcoming school year. It's unfathomable. I can't even imagine how his wife and kids feel. I'm just so grateful to be alive."

She shivered knowing that if Throttle hadn't called her when he did, she most probably wouldn't be talking to McCue. The series of circumstances from Josh to Cara to Hawk made her sure her father had a hand in protecting her. Even from beyond the grave, he was still looking out for her. Her eyes shimmered as she focused on what the detective was saying.

"He never even had a parking ticket. No one can believe it. The Board of Directors is in shock, as well as his colleagues, friends, and, of course, his wife and kids."

"I heard he pled guilty to all charges."

McCue nodded in agreement. "He wanted to save his family from a trial. His wife is moving back to Connecticut to be with her parents."

"So several of the other women went to the same college as me?"

"Yep. That's how we got the lead—a guy who works for us went to school with a few of the women. He also knew Deputy Manzik had gone there. Funny thing is no one recognized him. I can't understand that."

"Why did he do all those horrible, depraved things?" she asked softly.

"I don't know. I just solve cases and make sure the bad guy is punished. The head stuff is left for the mental health people."

A silence fell between them, and the clatter of trays and metal utensils signaled that lunch was ready to be served. The detective stood from the chair. "I just wanted to stop by to update you. I thought you'd like to know you don't have to rehash that night on a witness stand. Take care of yourself."

"I will. Thanks for stopping by."

Kimber watched Detective McCue walk out of the room, a feeling of intense relief washing over her. Later that afternoon, she'd meet with her counselor to work on the anger she'd felt since she began feeling better. It'd take time for her to come to terms with that night, but she'd have to be patient if she ever wanted to feel safe and whole again.

"Lunch, miss." The service woman placed the tray in front of Kimber, then left the room.

Kimber removed the metal domes and grimaced: soggy green beans, a piece of chicken, mashed potatoes with congealed yellow gravy, and red Jell-O. She replaced the domes over the food.

I can't wait to go home. I can't wait to be with Throttle.

THE DAY AFTER she came home from the hospital, Throttle moved his things into her house. He immediately insisted that she didn't need a visiting nurse to clean and change her bandages. Two times every day, he'd take off her bandage, wash her wound, apply the medicated salve, and redress it. His gentle hands soothed her and made her fall in love with him all over again. When he was tied up with church or work, one of the old ladies would come over.

Cherri and Addie were the ones who usually came over because they didn't work outside the home. Whenever Cherri came by to help, she'd bring her darling daughter, Paisley, who was such a good assistant to her mother. On the days Addie came by, she brought her daughter Hope, who was still shaky on her chubby little legs. She was so precious, and the love Kimber saw in both Cherri's and Addie's eyes when they looked at their children made her consider—for the first time ever—about starting a family. She wondered if Throttle wanted marriage and kids. She wasn't sure how he'd feel about it.

She was over-the-moon in love with him, and the fact that he loved her too—and *told* her—made her life complete. She never thought she'd hear those words from him, being that he was a hardcore biker and soft, romantic words weren't in his vocabulary very often.

Kimber was blown away at how the club pulled together to help her during her recovery. The old ladies were a godsend. Each night, one of them would bring over a dish for dinner. Cara always brought over wonderful Italian dishes, while Cherri's specialties were delicious chili and enchiladas. Addie was the casserole queen; Kylie made simple, healthy dinners; Baylee delivered takeout from Big Rocky's and Imperial Garden; and Belle made the best fried chicken Kimber had ever eaten.

Some of the other old ladies, like Doris, Bernie, Marlene, and Sofia, came by to help with the house cleaning and the laundry. For the first time since her father died, she didn't feel alone; she had Throttle and the Insurgent family behind her.

After dinner that night, Throttle pulled her close to him and kissed the top of her head. "What did the doctor tell you today?"

"That I'm doing great and can go back to work next week. She wants me to limit my heavy lifting for another month, but I can start working full time. I can't wait. I've been so damn antsy this past week."

"You sure you should go back to full time so soon? Why don't you start back at part time and see how you do?"

"You worry too much. I'll be fine. If it seems like too much, I'll lessen my hours."

"I worry about you because you're important to me. You're part of me."

She turned her head up, looped her arm around his neck, and drew him to her. "I love you so much. I'm so grateful you came into my life."

"I'm the lucky one. I was alone and didn't even realize it until you entered my life. When I saw you with the knife in you... Fuck, babe, I was seized with fear for the first time in my life. I realized I want you in my life. Not just for the summer or a year, but forever. You're the only one for me. I want you to wear my patch."

Tears sprang into her eyes as she looked into his love-filled ones. "I'd be honored to be your old lady and ride beside you."

"And sometimes behind me. I gotta have you pressed against me."

She shook her head. "Okay. Sometimes I'll ride behind you and press my boobs to your back. Does that work?"

"Fuck yeah. And give me some hand action in the front too," he teased. He ruffled her hair. "You make me proud. You're a kickass mechanic. Hell, you fix a bike better than I do. Even better than a lot of the brothers can, and if you ever tell anyone I said that, I'll deny it. And you totally know how to handle a Harley. I haven't seen a woman handle a Harley the way you do. You're independent and strong, but you're a soft, sexy lioness in the bedroom. I love you, babe—every fuckin' part of you."

Her insides exploded from his words and for a minute she couldn't talk, she was that overcome. "Throttle, I love your rough side, and your soft side that most people don't see. I love that you care about your sister and play silly games and have tea parties with Olivia. You are the best thing that has happened to me and I'm never letting you go."

"No worries there 'cause I'm not leaving."

She drew him close to her and kissed him, parting her lips to allow his tongue in.

And he kissed back. Wet. Deep. Hard.

"It's been so long, babe. Did the doc say we could fuck? I miss being inside you."

Since the stabbing, she hadn't been able to do much because she was groggy most of the time with pain meds and the stitches were healing. As she became stronger, they fooled around, but he hadn't been inside her since before the incident. Her body craved him and the connection they had every time they fused together. They shared something fierce and hot, and she wanted him all the time, which worked out perfectly because he wanted her just as much.

"She gave me the okay." She smiled seductively at him.

His eyes brightened, and she burst out laughing. He acted like he won the lottery or something. Shivers spread through her; it was always a turn-on to know how much he desired her. And only her. The club women, the hoodrats, the one-night stands—all the trappings of easy sex were gone. He was hers, and only hers, forever.

He stood up and pulled her with him. "Let's go to the bedroom. We gotta make up for some lost time here." He nuzzled her neck, licking her favorite spot right under her ear.

"What're we waiting for?" she breathed.

He lifted her and carried her into the bedroom while she peppered his face and neck with kisses. He laid her on the bed and slowly unbuttoned her shirt while she quivered under his touch.

She adored him, and their love amazed them both.

It came when they'd given up on asking for it to come.

The End

Make sure you sign up for my newsletter so you can keep up with my new releases, special sales, free short stories, and other treats only available to newsletter readers. When you sign up, you will receive a FREE hot and steamy novella. Sign up at:

http://eepurl.com/bACCL1

Visit me on Facebook
facebook.com/Chiah-Wilder-1625397261063989

Check out my other books at my Author Page
amazon.com/author/chiahwilder

Acknowledgments

I have so many people to thank who have made my writing endeavors a reality. It is the support, hard work, laughs, and love of reading that have made my dreams come true.

Thank you to my amazing Personal Assistant Amanda Faulkner who keeps me sane with all the social media, ideas, and know how in running the non-writing part smoothly. So happy YOU are on my team!

Thank you to my editor, Kristin, for all your insightful edits, excitement with the Insurgents MC series, and encouragement during the writing and editing process. I truly value your editorial eyes and suggestions as well as the time you've spent with the series. You're the best!

Thank you to my wonderful beta readers, Kolleen, Paula, Jessica, and Barb—my final-eyes reader. Your enthusiasm for the Insurgents Motorcycle Club series has pushed me to strive and set the bar higher with each book. Your dedication is amazing!

Thank you to my proofreader, Amber, whose last set of eyes before the last once over I do, is invaluable. I appreciate the time and attention to detail you always give to each book.

Thank you to the bloggers for your support in reading my book, sharing it, reviewing it, and getting my name out there. I so appreciate all your efforts.

Thank you to Carrie from Cheeky Covers. You put up with numerous revisions, especially the color of Kylie's fingernails and the tattoos until I said, "Yes, that's the cover!" Your patience is amazing. You totally rock. I love your artistic vision.

Thank you to the readers who support the Insurgents MC series. You have made the hours of typing on the computer and the frustrations that come with the territory of writing books so worth it. You make it possible for writers to write because without you reading the books, we wouldn't exist. Thank you, thank you!

Throttle's Seduction: Insurgents Motorcycle Club (Book 7)

Dear Readers,

Thank you for reading my book. I hope you enjoyed the seventh book in the Insurgents MC series as much as I enjoyed writing Kimber and Throttle's story. This rough motorcycle club has a lot more to say, so I hope you will look for the upcoming books in the series. Romance makes life so much more colorful, and a rough, sexy bad boy makes life a whole lot more interesting.

If you enjoyed the book, please consider leaving a review on Amazon. I read all of them and appreciate the time taken out of busy schedules to do that.

I love hearing from my fans, so if you have any comments or questions, please email me at chiahwilder@gmail.com or visit my facebook page.

To hear of **new releases**, **special sales**, **free short stories**, and **ARC opportunities**, please sign up for my **Newsletter** at http://eepurl.com/bACCL1.

A big thank you to my readers whose love of stories and words enables authors to continue weaving stories. Without the love of words, books wouldn't exist.

Happy Reading,

Chiah

ROCK'S REDEMPTION

Book 8 in the Insurgents MC Series

Coming in October 23, 2016

Rock is the ripped, handsome Sergeant-At-Arms for the Insurgents MC. Being one of the club's officers, women clamor to share his bed. The biker's more than willing to oblige as long it's a short-time hookup; *long-term relationship* is not part of his vocabulary.

He's only been in love once—a long time ago—and the end result was shattering. He learned his lesson: keep his heart encased in steel.

The tragic night that sent him to prison is over even though it still simmers inside him. But once he joined the Insurgents MC, he vowed to leave the past darkness and disappointments back in Louisiana. He's embraced his new life of brotherhood, booze, easy women, and Harleys. It suits him just fine. Some things are best left alone, especially a pretty brunette who destroyed his heart.

Easy sex has become his mantra.

Until his past crashes into his life....

Clotille Boucher is the wealthy, spoiled girl who'd stolen Rock's heart many years ago. From a young age, family loyalty was drilled into her, so when darkness engulfed her and Rock, fleeing seemed to be the only way out for her. Deciding to make a new life for herself, she didn't count on having to pay for the sins of her brother.

Just when her life doesn't seem like it could get worse, a face from her past gives her a glimmer of hope. Shamed that Rock has to see how far she's fallen, she pretends her life is exactly what she wants, but his penetrating stare tells her he's not buying her act.

Fearful that the secrets of the past will catch up with her and Rock, her inclination is to do what she does best—run away. Only problem is,

Rock's not letting her slip away so easily this time.

Can two damaged people learn to trust one another again? Will Rock be able to reconcile the demons that have plagued him since that tragic night? Does Clotille offer him redemption or destruction?

As Rock and Clotille maneuver the treacherous waters of their past and present, someone is lurking behind the shadows to make sure the truth never comes out.

The Insurgents MC series are standalone romance novels. This is Rock and Clotille's love story. This book contains violence, sexual assault (not graphic), strong language, and steamy/graphic sexual scenes. It describes the life and actions of an outlaw motorcycle club. If any of these issues offend you, please do not read the book. HEA. No cliffhangers! The book is intended for readers over the age of 18.

Chiah Wilder's Other Books

Hawk's Property: Insurgents Motorcycle Club Book 1
Jax's Dilemma: Insurgents Motorcycle Club Book 2
Chas's Fervor: Insurgents Motorcycle Club Book 3
Axe's Fall: Insurgents Motorcycle Club Book 4
Banger's Ride: Insurgents Motorcycle Club Book 5
Jerry's Passion: Insurgents Motorcycle Club Book 6

I love hearing from my readers. You can email me at: chiahwilder@gmail.com.

Sign up for my newsletter to receive updates on new books, special sales, free short stories, and ARC opportunities at: http://eepurl.com/bACCL1.

Visit me on facebook at: www.facebook.com/Chiah-Wilder-1625397261063989

Made in the USA
San Bernardino, CA
29 August 2016